TALES
OF
FIRE
AND
FROST

A MYSTIC OWL
ANTHOLOGY

TALES OF FIRE AND FROST

TALES OF FIRE AND FROST
A Mystic Owl Anthology

MYSTIC OWL
A City Owl Press Imprint
www.cityowlpress.com

Cover Design by MiblArt. All stock photos licensed appropriately.

Edited by Heather McCorkle.

For information on subsidiary rights, please contact the publisher at info@cityowlpress.com.

Print Edition ISBN: 979-8-3632-3319-7

Printed in the United States of America

FROM THE DESK OF THE EDITOR

Mystic Owl is excited to present this not-for-profit anthology of spicy tales filled with mystical elements for your reading pleasure. All net proceeds will go to Girls Write Now, and organization with a powerful mission that we stand behind one-hundred percent:

Girls Write Now breaks down barriers of gender, race, age and poverty to mentor and train the next generation of writers and leaders for life. Together, our community channels the power of our voices and stories to shape culture, impact industries and inspire change.

CONTRIBUTING STORIES

Up on the Rooftop by Leslie O'Sullivan

Frost & Fever by A.N. Payton

Heart Shaped Box by Erin Fulmer

In Search of Starlight by Lilla Glass

The Light in His Darkness by Mabry Blackburn

A Christmas Flame by Joanna Morgan

Fit For a Goddess by S.C. Grayson

Long Lost by Lily Riley

A Charley Dalton Christmas by R. Lee

UP ON THE ROOFTOP

BY LESLIE O'SULLIVAN

A Rockin' Fairy Tale Story

UP ON THE ROOFTOP

BENEDICT BOYD HERDED EMPTY PEANUT SHELLS INTO A TIDY PILE with the toe of his checkerboard-patterned sneaker. Reaching across his bandmate and brobud, Claude, he scooped up the debris and dumped it into the repurposed umbrella stand that served as a trash can in their makeshift hangout on the roof of Hotel Caliwood. This was their haven to escape from contract negotiations, unfinished albums, and a lead female vocal who'd bailed on the band two weeks before their tour to be a judge on the reality talent show *You've Got a Gift*.

Claude's face shone holiday red in the glow of the giant neon Hotel Caliwood sign that loomed as a headpiece to their Hollywood Boulevard perch. "Afraid Santy Clause will be struck down on Christmas Eve by a peanut allergy, Ben?"

"Only an evil elf like you would ignore such risks to the big man."

Claude jabbed a thumb toward the Christmas Eve crowds on the boulevard below. "How does the jolly old soul even track it's the big night here in La Land? With all the dudes in shorts down there, it'll seem like the date on his Naughty and Nice app is on the fritz."

Benedict rubbed his hands on nubby couch cushions. "Why do

you think they stick a Santa hat on the Hollywood Sign?" He jerked his chin at the giant white letters on the L.A. hillside. "And the big ass tree on the roof of the Rampion Records Tower."

Truth was, Benedict's thin Christmas spirit hovered several levels below the holiday affront of shorts-wearing dudes in December. Here in the city of perpetual summer, there was no cool snap in the air or crush of shoppers hitting last-minute sales in Union Square like his holidays back at home in San Francisco. When Benedict passed a lone tree with leaves turning a vibrant red orange on his morning run, he practically wept. What he'd give to be skipping up the steps of his parent's Victorian on postcard row in the Bay Area with an armful of Christmas presents. They were both gone, and the former Boyd homestead was now an Airbnb. Selling that house had been the most soul-sucking decision he'd ever made, but he'd needed cash to bankroll the early days of his band. Benedict hoped wherever his folks were now, they knew his decision was the right one. That grub stake had allowed his band to do what it took to get noticed. After a respectable period of struggle, they'd hit the bigs when they signed with the Caliwood, Inc. record company.

Claude bumped his knee into Benedict's. "Your turn to name the boulevard stars, hokey dip biscuit. I need to win my fifty bucks back and grab Hero a Christmas prezzie before the ladies start showing for tonight's audition."

"Into buying her love?" Benedict twisted to avoid Claude's bro punch.

"I'm into her."

Benedict thumped his chest with a fist. "This money tree's not putting out. You can't beat me, amateur." Benedict peered over the roof rail to the line of pink concrete stars along the Hollywood Walk of Fame on the sidewalk below. "Only one person ever bested me at naming the stars, and she wasn't a callous, over-buttered mongrel like you."

His mind hiccupped back to a different winter night last year.

Leonato Andante, owner of Hotel Caliwood and C.E.O. of the Caliwood, Inc. record label always threw a holiday blowout the week before Christmas. The wily oldster booked a handful of up-and-coming local bands for the gig to peruse potential talent. He rarely signed a full band. Ben and the Boulevard Bunch was one of the few groups that had survived an Andante audition intact. Instead, Leonato was famous for harvesting single musicians and repurposing them into bands he personally crafted.

Benedict navigated the packed crowd at Hotel Caliwood's legendary Ghost Lounge as guests wandered throughout the space hoping to walk through a cold spot and hang with a spirit for a second or two. The ratio of people who actually experienced a presence and those who claimed to connect with the other side was seriously lopsided.

Feminine squeals near the end of the long bar topped with a sheet of thick red glass caught Benedict's attention. A supermodel wannabe in a shiny wrap dress with lines of pearls dripping down the skirt faced off with what he clocked as a walking garage sale advertisement. The second babe, a good eight inches shorter than the model, wore a patchwork, floor-length skirt topped off with a flouncy, hunter green blouse that Benedict assumed was supposed to say Christmas. He caught a glimpse of neon yellow high tops peeking out from under the dress.

The supermodel wannabe stamped her stiletto onto the black marble floor. "You bogarted my ghost spot."

"That's assuming ghost spots are bogartable." Garage Sale adjusted the single tall feather on her threadbare slouch hat and stood her ground. "Whose game is it really? Do we seek them, or do they seek us?" She closed her eyes and swayed. "I'm not getting a cold spot here." Garage Sale gazed up at Supermodel. "Honey, maybe you just need a jacket?"

Supermodel stomped off in a huff to search out an unbogartable ghost experience. Garage Sale took advantage of the shift in the human puzzle to slide into the new open spot at the crowded bar. Benedict grinned in admiration of her strategy to gain liquor access.

"Heya," she called to the bartender, slapping a rhythm on the bar top. "Free drinks tonight, right?" She yanked off her hat and ruffled her head of short, messy hair. "I want a whiskey sour with more sour than whiskey. Don't get me wrong, I do want to taste the whiskey. I do not want to rock an alcohol-wince face."

Benedict's grin widened at the unfiltered incredulity on the bartender's face. As a drink dispensing pro, the dude recovered quickly. "Anything else I should be aware of in the preparation of your beverage, Madame?"

Benedict drifted closer to the interchange, drawn by the babe's saltiness and overall irreverent vibe.

She rested one elbow on the red glass and stared the bartender down. "Five cherries, and if you screw up my order, I'll make you redo it." When Benedict laughed, she whipped around. "Did I invite you into my business, Blondie?"

He shoved his way between Garage Sale and an actor in a tight-fitting, on-trend blue suit. Benedict opted for a casual move and leaned on the bar. "Correct first letter placement, and you nailed the N, D, and I. Wrong order though. Give my name another shot."

"How magnani-mouse of you." She ran an assessing gaze from his own messy blond mop to the black leather slip-on sneakers he wore for the soiree.

Benedict scratched a claw through the air. "It would be a cat-tastrophe if you didn't at least try."

The bartender set her drink down a nick too hard. One of the cherries escaped over the rim and rolled across the bar. She glared and then tossed the drink back like a boss.

"You wince-faced," said Benedict.

"Dude disrespected the alcohol balance of my order," she said and popped cherries into her mouth one at a time. "Thankfully, not the fruit."

"Your dinner?"

"Just the first course." She slid her hand down his arm until her fingers twined with his. "Dance with me Bene-dick."

He startled. Damn, she knew him. Was she a fan? Cool. Groupie, not so much. "Benedict," he corrected. "You know my band?"

"Bene-dick and the Boulevard Bunch. I heard you play this soiree last year."

"The last time you bogarted ghost spots and free drinks?"

"It's my annual buzz. Holiday traditions are important."

The lack of blushing or gushing nixed her out of the groupie column. What was this salty babe's story? "It's Ben and the Boulevard Bunch."

"Yep, sounds better without the dick." She laughed. "There's your wince face." Garage Sale dragged him into the throng of sweaty holiday dancing. "Thanks for asking, Bene-dick. Oh, that's right, you didn't. I'm Beatrice."

For the rest of the evening, they sparred in attempts to outdrink, outdance, and outsnark each other until the party wound down. Benedict craved a guaranteed victory over her, so he brought Beatrice to the roof of the Caliwood for an ultimate duel to the death in his game of list the Hollywood Walk of Fame stars in the correct order.

Beatrice's brash confidence distracted Benedict. He lost to her in the game where he usually ruled supreme, a spectacular fail. He didn't care. She matched his insane competitiveness, and it was the biggest turn-on he'd ever known. Their holiday hook-up on the old, ratty couch still singed his memory. As they recovered in each other's embrace, the damn woman named every planet and constellation that hovered in the L.A. sky. Beatrice was as infuriating and unforgettable as the ghosts that perpetuated mischief at the Caliwood.

The band left the next morning for months of touring, and Benedict, in his arrogant glory, assumed Beatrice would look up his high-profile ass to pursue their sexy combustion. He was, after all, the lead singer of a band on the verge of their next top-of-the-charts hit.

He'd never seen her again.

"I'm a callous over-buttered mongrel? Damn, Ben. We'd be done with the album if you could write lyrics as snappy as your insults."

Benedict bristled. Claude was right. He was brilliant at tunes and shit at lyrics. "Okay," he cracked knuckles while his pal held the cell screen at the ready to confirm his recitation of the boulevard stars. "Starting between Gower and Argyle, here goes. Lucille Ball, Gregory Peck, Montgomery Clift, Rock Hudson, Gene Kelly..." He named stars past Vine Street and almost made it to Cahuenga Blvd. before mixing up the order of Lassie and Ronald Reagan.

Claude busted out one of his slick dance moves. "And a dog takes down the dawg."

"You still lost. I'm keeping my fifty. You'll have to steal mints from the bar to give Hero for Christmas."

A flurry of car horns on the street in front of the hotel drove them both to the rail. A clutch of five women in matching green-and-red sequined mini dresses linked arms and headed into the hotel.

"Damn it," said Benedict. "I told Leonato no girl bands. We need one female singer. One."

Claude's glazed stare was exactly the reason for the girl band ban. "The hook-up/breakup danger from a girl band infiltration could mess with the group both musically and morale-wise. I don't want to screw with our sound or dynamic."

"Be real, Ben. It only takes one babe to rock damage."

"Not the right one." Benedict checked his watch and studied the stream of females flowing into the Caliwood.

Claude hummed. "Bigger turnout than I expected for a Christmas Eve audition."

Benedict scratched his head and stared at the moon framed by one of the neon red Os in the Hotel Caliwood sign. "Showing up tonight signals the level of dedication I'm looking for. No more flight risks like freakin' Cassie." He was determined not to settle this time for someone using his band as a steppingstone. He had a long list of requirements on his interview checklist this go-round. A kickass voice would not be enough. They needed a bandmate, a contributor, not a user.

A bright flash drew his attention back to the boulevard.

Claude white-knuckle-gripped the rail. "Ben..." His brobud's eyes stretched wide.

Benedict followed his stare and had to grab the rail himself to stay upright. Below them, a woman who loomed tall despite their bird-of-prey POV froze all movement around her on the sidewalk. She was dressed in tiers of white chiffon ruffles that appeared to be giving off their own light. In fact, an aura like the afterimage of a flash pulsed around her.

"Is she...glowing?" asked Claude.

"Got to be the dress. It's picking up the hotel's overenthusiastic twinkle lights."

At that moment, the woman glanced up. Thirteen floors between them telescoped into nothing. Benedict met her icy blue gaze that mirrored the exact color of his own eyes. Ice crystals danced in his blood stream, a contrast to the unseasonal evening heat. He shivered. She shot a dazzling smile their way.

"God, I hope she can sing," breathed Claude. "Let's get to it."

Benedict shared Claude's pull to inhabit the same space as the woman in white. He recovered enough to give Claude a shake. "Hero. Focus, Dude. You're into Hero."

Claude teetered and blinked a few times. "Hero. Yeah, Hero."

Good, Claude needed to stay focused on Hero. Benedict exhaled. He wanted no competition making an in with the glowing singer below.

Benedict was halfway to the stairwell door when his friend ripped off a string of curses.

"Ben." He pointed down to the sidewalk. "Isn't that..."

A different figure lingered on the sidewalk, fixated on the entrance to the Caliwood. It was as if the photographic negative of the enchanting vision in white had appeared. This shadowed woman with a guitar slung over her shoulder was as out of focus as the bright babe had been clear. Benedict opened the top drawer on the imitation Chippendale dresser they'd appropriated from a hotel suite to give their rooftop hangout a touch of class. He snatched the pair of binoculars and trained them on the woman.

The feather in her top hat collided with his fresh memory from moments before.

Beatrice.

"...your Christmas party hook-up from last year?"

Benedict lowered the binocs. It was true. Beatrice had only been a hook-up, but the term sounded wrong, sour coming out of Claude. Hook-ups weren't supposed to make you feel like you'd met your match. By definition, they were hot and immediate, a single evening's satisfaction. They weren't memory makers that still stuck a year later.

At the Caliwood's annual holiday fete last week, Benedict had roved the crowd, searching for Beatrice. She'd never shown. He closed the place down until only the clean-up crew and his pathetic longing were left amid half-drained glasses and sticky tabletops.

Benedict's adrenaline spiked. Beatrice was here now on Christmas Eve at the audition for his band. The element of surprise was all hers.

Claude and Benedict hit the Ghost Lounge to join Leonato and their bandmates, Alfie and their drummer, D.G. short for Dead Guy, since he'd been voted most likely to become a future resident ghost at the Caliwood. Benedict took the end seat behind a banquet table facing the stage and pretended to scribble on a yellow legal pad. He snuck glimpses at the auditioners that milled outside the doors, hoping to spot Beatrice. Did he want to catch her eye? Should he? Hero flitted around, slapping name tag stickers with numbers on the women and directing them to line up outside the lounge. She was as organized as Claude was scattered. Together, they made a tidy picture. If only Claude would step up and embrace their inevitability instead of his half-assed wooing.

Leonato rapped on the table in front of Benedict. "Go time. Alfie, D.G. and I will screen them first in the ballroom. If they don't offend our eardrums and there aren't any red flag answers on your ridiculous questionnaire, Ben, we'll pass them in here to you and Claude." He adjusted the red velvet skinny tie trailing down the front of his shiny green button-down. "This insta-audition better pay off, Benedict. You're screwing with the timing of my Christmas Eve goose dinner."

Benedict swallowed his frustration. These may be auditions for his band, but after they'd all been blindsided by Cassie's epic bail, Leonato insisted on sticking his C.E.O. of Caliwood, Inc. hands in the audition pie. The boss's message was clear: Wildcards not welcome.

"Apologies to the goose, Leo."

Benedict was on his tenth game of explicit content hangman with Claude and second beer. Leonato hadn't sent anyone their way. He debated on a third beer to douse his disappointment when the brightness in the room intensified tenfold. He looked up to see the singer in white glide into the room. Her dress had a train with twinkle lights embedded in the fabric. This close, he saw her white chiffon layers were infused with what seemed to be chips of glass. No wonder she glowed. Her poufy hair was as white as the dress and looked like the frosted top of a wedding cake.

Benedict had to touch her. He came around the table to take

her hand. When his fingers closed around hers, his skin dotted with reflections of the glass chips in her long sleeves.

"It's delightful to meet you, Benedict." When her grip tightened, his two-beer buzz upgraded to a five-beer haze. Ice blue eyes commanded his attention.

Claude sidled up to them. "I'm Claude. Rhythm guitar and vocals."

When the woman in white shifted her focus to his bandbro, Benedict swore her eyes morphed into a hazel color that perfectly matched Claude's. "Tressa Divine."

Freakin' Claude actually bowed and kissed her free hand.

An urge to pull Tressa away from Claude roared through Benedict. He dropped her hand and took a step back before he gave into it. She flashed him a smile that left him with little doubt she sensed the effect she'd had on him.

Benedict backed up until he bumped the table. "Whatcha got for us?"

"An answer to your wishes," Tressa cooed.

He managed a nod to the mic on stage. "Please."

Tressa floated up the two steps and swiveled so her train spread out before her, adding to her wedding vibe. Benedict allowed himself to melt into the pull of her luminous presence. He heard nothing else, not his own breathing, not Claude beside him. When the woman in white sang, pinpoints of light dotted the room in a mirror ball effect, reflecting the intense blue at the core of a fire. Her voice caressed the notes of the song like a fingertip sliding down his bare chest. As Tressa built to her finish, delicate snowflakes fell from the ceiling but disappeared before touching the floor.

"Shi–fu–damn," groaned Claude.

His friend's voice snapped Benedict out of his hallucination. He was back in the Ghost Lounge with its dark wood and red décor. There was no snowfall, no disco ball, only an otherworldly beauty curtsying on stage. He pinched the bridge of his nose. Benedict lived in a haunted hotel for heck's sake. Every flavor of bizarre had gone down within these thirteen floors. Reports of ghosts, altered realities, fountains running backward, and once, even the water in the swimming pool turning to blood were part of Caliwood lore. Two beers and sinking into his imagination during Tressa's performance could easily conjure disco dots and imaginary snow in his right brain. He jumped to his feet and held out a hand to help Tressa down the steps.

"That was..." Benedict's grasp on language dissolved.

"Enchanting," said Tressa with a wink.

"Totally," gasped Claude as he gawked at the singer.

Benedict studied Claude's dreamy face. He'd quiz him later about their potential shared vision of dots and snow. Without releasing her hand, Benedict escorted Tressa to the doors of the lounge where Hero tapped her foot in percussive annoyance and glared at Claude.

"You're cool to stick around for a bit?" asked Benedict. "We just have a few more people to see before we make our decision."

Hero swooped in and ushered Tressa to the greenroom next to the lounge where the musical acts hung out between sets.

Benedict did the drunk shuffle back to the banquet table. They'd found their singer. Hell, they'd scored a muse. He wanted to tell the rest of the women to pack it in. No one could outdo the transportive experience of listening to Tressa sing.

"She's it, right?" asked Claude. "Tell me she's it."

The hunger in Claude's eyes confirmed his own ache to fold Tressa into the band.

"Where do you want me?"

Benedict's gaze whipped to the woman marching across the lounge toward the stage.

"Up there, I assume."

Claude hissed in Benedict's ear. "It's your Stevie Nicks impersonator."

Beatrice stopped in front of Benedict, one hand on a hip, the other resting on a guitar strap. Her burnt crème brûlée hair stuck out from under a purple top hat with the same feather from her slouch hat the year before. Under a bedazzled denim vest, the black lace shirt did nothing to hide her neon pink bra. A red leather pencil skirt clashed with aqua cowboy boots where every bit of stitching had been gone over with bright colored marker.

Time folded. It had been less than a moment since he'd danced with this woman and traded barbs that left marks, at least for him. Benedict's face flamed. "Beatrice."

She raised her eyebrows. "Bene-dick."

Before he could return her verbal volley, Claude rose next to him. "Hey, Beatrice, is it?"

"Beatrice Sharpe."

Benedict swallowed a laugh. It was the perfect name for her. Sharp tongued. Sharp witted. Sharp and sexy in her latest garage sale ensemble.

Claude switched to serious auditioner voice. "Thanks for coming, Beatrice. The position has been filled."

She clicked her tongue. "What is this, a temp agency?"

Beatrice's directness drove Claude back into his seat. Benedict set a hand on his shoulder. "Dude, let her sing."

His bandbro lowered his volume. "Ben, there's eclectic and then there's pathetic."

"I can read a room, Bene-dick." Beatrice spun and power-walked toward Hero and the exit.

Benedict shot from behind the table to cut her off. "All Claude means is that we have a front-runner, but I haven't cast my vote." The words spilled from his mouth like a faucet turned to full. Hadn't he just agreed with Claude that Tressa was a freakin' gift from the gods? "I want to hear you sing."

Their gazes locked. "Don't humor me because of"—she whispered—"history."

"It would be a cat-astrophe if you didn't sing."

She cocked her head to the side, the hint of a smile at the corner of her mouth. "How magnana-mouse of you, Bene—"

He laid a finger on her lips. "Dict. Benedict." It took her pulling his hand down to break the contact. Benedict turned when Claude huffed behind him and gave him a shove. "Claude, go tell Hero that Beatrice is our last listen."

What the hell was he doing? Tressa was a find beyond their wildest dreams, but Benedict couldn't bear to watch Beatrice walk away—again. Did guilt slap him in the face? He never tried to go after her. Shit, all he had was a first name. She was the one who had a better chance to track him down, and there'd been nothing but crickets from her.

"I didn't know you were a singer," said Benedict.

"You didn't ask." Her mouth twitched into a sly smile. "Maybe I'm not, and you're going to have to paste a neutral mask on that rockstar face of yours for five whole minutes." With a chuckle, Beatrice took the stage and waited for Benedict and Claude to settle in. "Do you want me to cover Cassie's part in something or is original your thing?"

Claude breathed, "Who the fuck cares?" low enough for Benedict's ears only.

"Your call, Beatrice," said Benedict. He nearly said her name aloud again. *Beatrice.* It was a lovely name. *Beatrice and Benedict.* He bit the inside of his cheek and embraced the now instead of memories of the night Beatrice's lips found a dozen creative ways to fit against his.

She fiddled with her guitar. The pause gave Benedict space to be present. Then she began to sing one of their hits, and present was the only place he wanted to be.

"*If you fill my glass with sin,*
I will take you for a spin.
If you fill my glass with wine,
I will press your lips to mine.
If you fill my glass with gold,

Stories surely will be told.
If you fill my glass with sighs,
We will dance across the sky."

Benedict forgot to inhale. Cassie had never inhabited "Fill my Glass" this way. Their absentee singer zipped through the song as a fun-filled romantic romp. The band often opened with it as a light-hearted invitation for their audience to sit back and enjoy the show. Beatrice's version teased, hoped, and promised new depth. Fluff shifted into fodder for a new, unforgettable finale to their set.

"Huh," said Claude. "Not bad."

Benedict stared at the table and whispered. "Not bad *let her keep going*, or not bad *thanks but there's the door*?"

Claude pursed his lips and nodded at the stage. "Okay, Beatrice..."

Benedict didn't miss the strain in his friend's voice, but he couldn't tell if it was because Claude was more drawn to Beatrice's voice than he wanted to be, or if he was on his last drop of patience since Benedict hadn't given her the boot yet.

"Hit us with a few bars of your original stuff," said Claude in a flat tone.

Her opening riff pulled Benedict in hard and fast. The vocals undid him as she told the story of them, of a crowded bar, verbal jabs, bodies learning how to dance together. It was about that night, that party, this woman and him.

"Up on the rooftop,
Two hearts paused
You dared me to name stars
First below and then above
Together, we felt the sky
And lost a night
Up on the rooftop."

. . .

Emotions sprayed through him. Benedict burned to banter, to compete with Beatrice, to make music and love with this compilation of garage sale fashion that surrounded a sizzling core he'd sampled for a single night.

Claude dragged him to the far end of the room. "What's going on, Ben?"

"Beatrice is good. Really good."

"Good for you or good for the band?"

Benedict's band-leader brain kicked in. "Shit, I don't know Claude. Tressa and Beatrice both rocked it hard. It's a question of the best fit."

"Then let me get the guys, and we'll jam it out. See who sweetens the Cassie gap best."

Benedict looked over his shoulder to where Beatrice sat on the edge of the stage. This didn't feel like a gap-fill scenario to him anymore. Tonight, was a game changer. From what he'd heard in their audition, either woman would redefine his band. It was a question of which one nudged their art in a direction he could wrap his head around.

While Claude gathered the band, Benedict joined Beatrice on the edge of the stage. It took him longer to collect himself than was comfortable for either. "The story you told in your song is the same one I've relived this whole year." Benedict gave an ironic chuckle. "Not nearly as beautifully as you narrated it, of course."

"I wanted to get over you."

"Why?"

Beatrice snorted. "You were supposed to be a Christmas present that I returned for the cash."

"What if I'd rather be one you kept?"

The Boulevard Bunch chose that moment to blow into the lounge. Right behind them, Hero lead Tressa into the room.

Leonato took the wheel. "Here's how this is going to go down. First the boys will jam on hits from their catalog with Tressa and then swap out for Beatrice. Let's compare the synergy, people."

Beatrice gave Benedict a joyless smile and retreated to the end of the banquet table farthest from the stage to watch Tressa and the band.

Benedict could describe their set with Tressa as the delicious, whipped cream topping on an iced vanilla latte. When he shared a mic with her, it was smooth, sweet, and easy. The woman in white blended and wove her voice through every riff, verse, and chorus. Her improv meshed perfectly with the band. Zero resistance. Zero friction. All silk. Leonato fired up the stage lights to build a performance vibe, but Tressa outshone them, her sparkle reflecting off the chrome of D.G.'s drum set and the bridge pins of every guitar. He and his bandmates floated in a musical trance of blurred vision and sugary notes.

Leonato and Hero gave a standing ovation. Beatrice stared straight at Benedict and gave her head a subtle shake.

"Take five, and then we'll bust the next jam," said Benedict and made his way to the end of the banquet table where Beatrice sat, agitation coating her expression. "Say it."

Beatrice slapped a palm to the table. It reminded Benedict of the way she'd slapped the red glass of the bar on the night he met her. "Tressa's got the fluffy, showy vibe down cold."

"Is that a good or a bad thing?"

"It's not a Ben and the Boulevard Bunch thing. You're selling out your edge for a shiny diamond that I suspect is fake. But, hey, maybe you're up to diluting your sound."

"Sniping won't earn you an advantage."

"Oh, right. I'm supposed to play nice and go kiss my competition smack on the lips." Beatrice's gaze dropped to Benedict's lips for a beat and then lifted. "And then kiss your ass."

Benedict felt a flash of heat in his crotch, remembering the pleasure of Beatrice literally nipping his ass.

Beatrice lowered her voice. "I believe in your damn band, Benedict. Forgive me for giving a shit about the beauty of the original sound that put your group up here." She slashed the air above her head. "Instead of replicating the music of a hundred other vanilla-flavored jacklick bands at this level." She lowered her hand a few inches above the black marble floor.

"If that was supposed to be a compliment, you might want to try sanding off the splinters first next time."

Beatrice jutted her chin. "And here I thought you enjoyed my splinters." She grabbed her guitar and strode to the stage.

Benedict took a moment. It was so easy to fall right back into the joust with Beatrice. A joust he very much wanted to continue. He was last to hop onto the stage. D.G. rapped his drumsticks together and they were off.

Beatrice was razor wire to Tressa's tinkle of Christmas bells. Benedict's body thrummed, his energy reaching across the scant space between them to collide with the electricity surging off Beatrice. Fuck sweet, he wanted this combustibility. He closed the space between them and gently laid his hand on Beatrice's throat to feel notes rumble before they spilled from her lips. To his surprise, she reached up to do the same to him. They closed their eyes and sang, two entities fused into one by fire.

The set ended. They dropped their hands while both panted and sweated. It took all Benedict's reserve not to grab the front of Beatrice's stupid bedazzled vest, yank her against his chest, and devour her mouth.

The floor beneath them stuttered. Benedict's gaze swept the room looking for cover the way it always did when a quake hit. He swore he saw a ripple suck back under the chair where Tressa sat, the picture of fury. As he clocked her anger, a frigid rush of air swept past Benedict, blowing hair into his face. A breath later, Benedict swore the curtains framing the double doors to the lounge fluttered slightly. Any ethereal company hanging with them here in the Ghost Lounge just made tracks to the exit door. He'd only felt such an obvious presence once before in the ancient library on the top floor of the Caliwood when the wavy form of a little girl with ringlets and a pinafore had appeared and asked him to read a story.

No one who spent any amount of time in the Hotel Caliwood held on to their skepticism about spirits for long. Leonato swore when you bumped into or through a ghost, you experienced its emotions. This icy blow that nudged him had a frightened vibe. What spooked ghosts? When Benedict looked back at Tressa, concerned the invisible visitor might freak her out, the singer's angel face had returned with no hint she'd felt the fleeing spirit.

"Thank you, ladies," said Leonato. "Excellent work. Please allow us to impose on your holiday evening for a bit longer." The band and Hero followed him to the end of the bar away from the stage. Leo lined up shot glasses, filled each with golden Christmas cheer, and set one in front of each band member, Hero, and himself.

Benedict summoned his take-charge voice. "Before we vote. Thoughts? Comments? Concerns?" He stared at Claude.

"Not an easy call," said D.G. He spun a finger around the rim of his glass and shot a rapid-fire and retreat glance at Benedict.

Claude glanced over his shoulder to Tressa. "Different vibes, both hot. Here's the big Q. Who would you rather spend months on tour with? The purr or the growl?"

"Not cool, Claude," said Benedict, heat rushing up the back of his neck.

Claude flicked his wrist at Beatrice. "It's as cool as your hook-up throwing shade after Tressa's set."

"Hook-up?" said Alfie and Leonato at the same time.

Benedict got in Claude's face. "Our history has zip to do with my decision."

"Maybe you don't need a babe in the band at all," said Hero and gave Claude side-eye.

"Not negotiable," said Leonato. "The feminine texture is key to the group's sound."

Hero shrugged. "Fine."

Benedict felt water closing over his head. He wanted Beatrice in the group so badly it gave him chest pains, but this band was every-thing to him—his joy, his brothers—hell, they were all the family he had left. What right did he have to slash a hot knife through their bond over Beatrice? Tressa was the smart choice. The woman in white had her own brand of magic. He felt it during their set. He couldn't deny that. Tressa's vibe was refreshing while Beatrice offered friction.

His band wanted fresh. He craved friction.

Benedict had to side with his people.

Leonato reached across the bar to grab his wrist. "Ben?"

Benedict pressed his lips together and gave a curt nod. "Drink to Beatrice." To his surprise, Hero joined him in tossing back their shots. They shared the sad smile of defeat. "Drink to Tressa." Leonato, Claude, Alfie, and D.G. downed their Jameson.

Benedict's throat burned with whiskey and regret. He thumped the glass on the bar top for another shot to chase the regret. This decision made sense. As hot as his internal flame burned for Beatrice, the woman, and Beatrice, the performer, being thrown together on the road for months could boil passion down to a reduction of *Get the Fuck Away from Me*. There'd be zero support from a band who didn't want her in the first place.

The group stilled and watched Benedict throw back the second shot. He gave Leonato a single, sharp nod.

"Let's Christmas, people," said Leonato and snatched the glass out of Benedict's hand. Benedict's boss grimaced as he crooked a thumb into the darkened room. "Who's the messenger? You or me, Ben?"

"My band, my call," sighed Benedict. He'd be kind and complimentary, and if Beatrice wasn't too pissed off, ask her out. They were adults, musicians, professionals. She'd understand the choice was about rebuilding the band, nothing personal. The hell of it was that Beatrice added an element that worked, and that was personal to him. Whiskey flared hot in his empty stomach. He always strived for his band to bring the level of heat they'd raised in the set with Beatrice. Ben and the Boulevard Bunch singed psyches with chorus and verse. Yes, Tressa's presence cut with a seductive edge, but it went no deeper than a scratch. Beatrice revved their music into a wildfire.

The band shifted to where Tressa perched near the stage while Benedict was left to ruin Beatrice's Christmas. He pushed off the bar and turned toward the seat at the end of the banquet table she'd claimed.

It was empty.

Beatrice didn't wait for the *atta girl, better luck next time*. Benedict's brain cross-wired. Clearly, she'd gotten the picture and wanted to leave with dignity. He should give her the grace to do just that, but Benedict couldn't bear to let her disappear from his life again.

He bolted through the doors of the Ghost Lounge and sprinted down the stairs instead of taking the pokey elevator. He caught Beatrice by the arm just as the doorman swung the door open for her.

"Let go, Benedict."

Her correct pronunciation of his name was a sucker punch. "You can't leave," he stopped short of adding *me*.

"Ben, the lady was on her way out," said the doorman with bouncer body language and a warning in his voice.

"Beatrice, give me two minutes?"

She nodded to the doorman and dragged Benedict past the indoor fountain in the foyer and tucked in behind a ten-foot-high palm. "I saw your bro drink vote. What's left to say?"

Benedict would have given a kidney for Claude to stand next to him and support what he was about to do, but that was a no-go. He was the leader of the band. This was his call and his risk to take.

"Beatrice, truth—you're a live wire, and I'm a wet hand."

She was as rigid as the ochre, stucco wall behind her. "Yet, I'm the one who just got electrocuted."

Benedict stepped closer and cupped her face. "We're always going to be flint and a spark to each other. That can cause a serious rift in a band."

He felt Beatrice resist and then soften at his touch. Her hot breath slid across his face to give him the strength he needed for his next words. The line he shouldn't cross blazed as bright as a neon tube at the tip of his toes.

"Do I have your promise if any shit between you and me threatens the band, you'll walk away?"

Her hands covered his. "What are you saying, Benedict?"

"Yes, Ben, what are you saying?" Leonato's voice cut through the sound of the fountain.

Benedict locked gazes with Beatrice until she mouthed, "Yes." He slowly turned to face his band, Hero, his boss, Leonato, and Tressa, the enchanting singer in white. They stood in a half circle, caging Benedict and Beatrice against the wall. Everyone had coats thrown over arms since it was still too hot to put them on. He caught Hero's toxic glare at Tressa's white vinyl coat draped over Claude's arm. They all stared, waiting for Benedict's answer to Leonato's question.

Benedict forced down a swallow as he shored up the nerve to negate the wishes of the folks who'd put him on the map. They'd chosen Tressa. Shit, would Leonato back him now? The boss had veto power over Benedict, but he'd never overturned a decision before.

He hoped this wasn't the night that changed. Oddly enough, he felt no guilt when it came to Tressa. This babe was going to make it big, and he'd own being the fool who let her slip through his grasp. Beatrice was the one he couldn't let go. Ever since he'd lost her a year ago, Benedict knew he'd dinged his future with a cavalier rocker attitude. Arrogance had cost him something precious and important. He should have asked for Beatrice's number before they went to the roof that night. It was idiocy not to quiz every person on Leonato's guest list to track her down. Benedict refused to screw up this second chance with her.

Every jab they'd thrown at one another between then and now screamed to Benedict that Beatrice was his match. She wasn't abrasive to be abrasive, there was truth in her intention. That same raw truth was the fire behind her music. Benedict felt his soul shift when he sang with Beatrice. His music was on the verge of taking on a new edge, a new purpose, a new energy, and she was the one to walk with him hand in hand into that new reality.

Beatrice Sharpe was his new reality.

"I was welcoming Beatrice to Ben and the Boulevard Bunch."

The collective jaw drop was so in sync it looked rehearsed.

"Ben?" asked Claude. "Are you saying..."

Benedict nodded at Beatrice and then met Tressa's gaze. "I'm saying it was a hard call." He gave a nervous laugh. "A nearly impossible call, but I believe Beatrice is the best fit for the band. I'm truly sorry, Tressa, if there was any misunderstanding. You're extraordinary." Benedict searched for a convincing explanation. "We'd be holding you back."

A flush rose from Leonato's chin to his cheeks. Before his boss could unleash a word of protest, Benedict caught the flash of fury he'd seen before on Tressa's face after he'd sung with Beatrice. It was aimed straight at him.

The cold blast followed a heartbeat later. A sheer barrier like the first hint of winter ice on a pond rose like a wavering bubble around them. Benedict heard Beatrice gasp beside him at the same moment images of figures who appeared to be trapped beneath the bizarre ice wall flashed and then vanished. Benedict recognized a flicker of the little girl he'd encountered in the library. Off to his right, a couple dressed in finery suited for an award show of the 1920s blinked in and out. The blond movie bombshell whose presence was indelibly stamped on the Hotel Caliwood blew him a kiss.

Ghostly encounters at the hotel were part of its truth, but this was beyond anything he'd personally experienced or heard tell of. A violent shudder ran through Benedict as this freaky reality began to make sense. The icy sphere that held them captive was made from the ghosts of the Caliwood.

Beatrice reached out to touch the undulating wall. The moment her finger made contact, the presences inside began to shriek. Each time one materialized it appeared to claw at the thin bluish wall. Benedict grabbed for Beatrice and she for him as a deafening version of the bells he'd heard in Tressa's audition pierced their ears. The temperature plummeted to near freezing as writhing ghosts continued to test their thin blue prison. Outside the ghost boundary, Leonato, the band, Hero, the doorman, and guests who only moments before had been milling in the lobby stood as motionless as the water that had ceased to fall from the grand fountain.

Tressa stepped through the boundary with a predatory glare locked onto Beatrice and Benedict. Light pulsed beneath the chiffon layers of her dress. As she lifted her hand to point at them, her voice grew as deep as a strike from D.G.'s kick drum.

"This dream you grasp with rising joy,
The pair of you will soon destroy.
What once shone bright as future charm,
Will sever bonds and spirits harm.
A curse I summon soon will rise,
When shattered hearts swear to despise.
May pain surround you fated pair,
For slights delivered, souls despair.
While one shall travel forth alone,
The other shackled tooth and bone.
Do not deny that chance does dwell,
Despite sweet torment hope hides well.
Until the day when words reveal,
Broken oaths with truth may heal."

With a sweep of Tressa's arm, the hotel trembled, and the enchanted woman in white faded away. The shimmery wall of ghosts melted into the ground without leaving a trace.

Leonato and the band all wore smiles that hadn't been there

before. The boss held out a hand to Beatrice. "Welcome to Cali-wood, Inc."

Claude nudged her shoulder. "Serious heat between you and my man, Ben."

"Really, Claude," said Hero, her lips in a twist.

Claude raised his hands in surrender. "I'm talking onstage heat."

Benedict's heart thudded when he noticed Claude no longer held Tressa's white coat. The woman had vanished as thoroughly as her freaky words and the wall of icy spirits. Not one member of the band spoke a word about her.

Beatrice stared at them as if everyone were completely off their nut. Benedict shared her opinion but had no explanation about the vanished singer and the ice bubble. When Beatrice locked hands to her hips, clearly prepared to unleash the WTF question, Benedict grabbed her arm and headed for the elevator at a run. He heard his name being called by Leonato but kept going. They needed to unpack the weird together before the bombardment of questions kept them from escaping, and everyone decided they'd lost their minds.

As soon as the gilded elevator door closed, Benedict grasped Beatrice's shoulders. "Are you alright?" He started to pat her arms, ribs, and hips as if he was afraid she wasn't in one piece.

"Stop, Benedict." She pushed him away. "What the fuck was that? Did the ice queen just slap a curse on our heads? That's some serious sour grapes. Where the hell did she go?"

"I don't believe in curses."

"Clearly Tressa does."

Was Tressa's curse all that Beatrice heard or saw? Benedict started to question his own sanity. "Any thoughts on ghosts? Or say, an ice wall?"

Beatrice gripped the brass handrail lining the walls of the eleva-tor. "Thank, God, you saw all that too. Does shit like that go down here all the time? No, don't tell me."

Benedict inhaled deeply, calmed by Beatrice's spice. "Is this your version of 'we're not going to talk specifics'?"

"Now you're getting it."

"Beatrice, whatever you think you saw, I did too. I live in a frickin' haunted hotel, and it knocked me sideways. I've had experiences, but no, I've never seen shit like that go down here before."

"Dude," she delivered an open-palm smack to his chest. "Can we land on tabling the weird until I wake up tomorrow and haven't grown horns and a tail? I'm mega freaked."

They used the rest of the ride to catch their breath. When the doors opened on the dark, neglected, top floor library, Beatrice hung back.

"Stay here. Something's not right in that room. I've had my fill of *out there* tonight."

Benedict took her hand. "It's okay. The library always rocks intense vibes. The hotel is full of shall we say, *charged* spaces."

Beatrice still refused to leave the elevator. "Why didn't I clock this shadow pull in here last year?"

He smiled. "If you recall, we were buzzed on a few jolly cocktails and in a totally different head space." Benedict's expression tightened. "Not running from a WTF moment."

She dared a step into the room and pulled Benedict with her. "I'll ignore the creep factor for now, but if books start talking and dancing on the table, I'm out of here."

Benedict squeezed her fingers. "Deal." He led them past high shelves, the rolling ladder, and a long mahogany table. He decided to risk a move and pressed his hand against the small of her back to guide her through the door to the roof stairwell.

She turned to him then. "I prefer to go back to last year's head space instead of losing it over whatever just happened in the lobby." His skin heated with the same intensity he'd felt when they sang together. Benedict's gaze fell to her lips.

Kiss me so I can kiss you back.

Beatrice smiled and moved onto the first step. He raised his chin and started to lean in. The door to the library banged shut behind them. Beatrice climbed up another few steps, out of reach, and blew a gust of breath. "Last year, I was ready to wipe the floor with your smug ass when you challenged me to that ridiculous Walk of Fame game." She held out a hand to stop him. "You don't get a rematch tonight. We're up here to process the weird."

Benedict passed her and threw open the door at the top of the stairs. The Hollywood night was dark and clear. Stars clung above the hills, twinkling as if they knew it was Christmas Eve. The red neon from the Hotel Caliwood sign cast a warm glow over the rooftop. He held the door while Beatrice stepped onto the roof. She wandered to the rail to take in the view.

Benedict approached with caution, leaving multiple escape routes open to her. He longed to press up behind her, kiss her neck, and confess his stupidity in ever letting her go. Benedict needed Beatrice to know every bone in his body caught fire when he sang with her. They should wrap their heads around Tressa's onslaught while it was still fresh, but all he cared about in the moment was Beatrice here with him. "I missed you."

She spun to face him, expression hard, tongue sharp. "Whose fault is that?"

Her tone dumped water on his fire, and he steamed. "You left."

"You never called."

"How could I? No number. No last name."

Fury and the glow of the sign made Beatrice's expression more terrifying than the look on Tressa's face when she'd hit them with that ice bubble curse. Fire and ice. Neither forgave when they came for you.

"Bullshit, Bene-dick."

He yanked the phone from his pocket and brandished his screen at her. "No Beatrice in here."

She stole the phone from his hand and threw it on the couch. "You didn't have your phone that night, Jacklick." Beatrice pulled the bottom drawer of the Chippendale knock-off so hard it flew out of the dresser and landed with a thump on the rug also pilfered from a hotel suite. She launched the bedspread they kept in there for chilly nights through the air onto the couch. The next thing that flew at Benedict was one of the yellow legal pads he used for writing crappy lyrics. There on the top page was the name Beatrice Sharpe, a phone number, email, and a list of social media.

"When you never called, all I thought about were these lyrics we wrote about the road." She flipped past the top page of the legal pad to one filled with words.

As Benedict read, his legs wobbled, and he sat down hard on the couch. Here it was, a love song to being on tour, meeting strangers, getting lost in the buzz of the music. "This is frickin' genius, Beatrice. We wrote this?"

Beatrice snorted.

Benedict stared at her. "You wrote this." Of course, she did. He was shit at lyrics.

"I knew as I was writing these words, I could never compete with that high, that level of love you feel for the road." She plopped down next to him. "I wasn't surprised you didn't call." Her fingers grabbed the front of his shirt. "But I wanted you to." Their gazes locked as breath heated the air between them. Beatrice pushed him away and stared at the sky. "God, I wanted you to."

Benedict carefully slid the legal pad into the top drawer of the dresser. He couldn't lose this first song they'd made together. He couldn't lose Beatrice. Pointing first toward the southwest horizon, Benedict began. "Jupiter and Mars are easy to find. There and there." He raised Beatrice's arm. "It's so clear tonight, Saturn's making an appearance, here." Benedict felt her gaze on him. "To the north, both dippers, Polaris, Perseus—"

"You learned the sky."

"It's all I had left of you." He cleared his throat. "Back to the south—"

Beatrice's mouth crashed into his, and her fingers slid through his hair. He fell back onto the ratty, old cushions with her covering him. The top hat flew off her head. The fake jewels of her vest pressed through his shirt and jabbed his skin. Without releasing her mouth, he rid her of the vest.

Her kisses were attacks, and his, counterattacks. Teeth and tongues collided and clashed in a competition Benedict didn't care if he lost. There would be no gentle explorations, only explosions. A year of pent-up dreams of Beatrice launched his erection straight into the go zone.

Beatrice's leather pencil skirt bunched up. He grabbed her ass, and not waiting to shed his jeans, slid her up and down over his cock. When she picked up the rhythm on her own, he slipped his hands under her black lace top and pink neon bra until his thumbs found her nipples puckered and waiting.

Beatrice didn't like to wait. "Sit up," she ordered and settled herself on his lap, so they were face-to-face.

Benedict obeyed his muse. She whipped off everything she wore above the waist. He replaced his thumbs with lips, sucking hard on one of her breasts and then the other. Her skin was warm and slightly salty from sweat as he swapped lips for tongue and teeth. Beatrice groaned and ran her hands under his shirt to flip it over his head. She stroked and tugged at the hair on his chest until the answering hiss of her name on his lips satisfied her.

"Beatrice," he said again and kissed her deeply. "I want more than one night. Tell me you believe we have a shot this could work."

She ripped open the buttons of his fly, snaked a hand down his boxers, and gripped him hard. "It's working just fine.'"

Benedict eased her hand out of his pants. "You know what I mean. The band. Us. Can it work?"

Beatrice bit his bottom lip. "We'll make it work, Benedict." After taking his tongue deep in her mouth, she leaned back to search the dresser drawers until she raised a foil-wrapped packet in victory. "Do you come here often?" she asked with a wonderfully naughty smile.

Benedict ran fingers through her feathery hair. "Not since you."

He tried to access the waves of heat that called to him beneath her wadded-up skirt and growled when it wouldn't give way. "Please take that damn thing off."

Beatrice stood and wiggled out of the skirt until she wore only cowboy boots with the marker-colored stitching. "You know what goes great with cowboy boots?" She lifted a boot to rest on the edge of the couch to invite him in.

Benedict lost no time diving in to taste the sizzle between her legs. When he sampled her in earnest, Beatrice threw her head back and cried out, "Jeans." Shakily, she grabbed the waist of his pants and boxers at the same time and pulled until they dropped onto the rug. Beatrice ripped open the condom. "Come on, Benedick. Let's give Santa a show that will knock him out of his sleigh."

Benedict playfully threw her down on the couch, closed his hands around the ankles of her boots, and spread her legs. He went on the offensive with a growl only bested by Beatrice's drawn-out moan as they raced to see who would crash over the edge first. It was a tie.

After they fell, the two stretched out on the couch. Beatrice rubbed her nose against the stubble on Benedict's jaw. "When did you know you'd choose me?"

"The minute you walked into the room."

She swatted his shoulder. "Liar."

He bit her fingers. "I don't have the courage to lie to you, Beatrice. The repercussions would be terrifying." Benedict freed a strand of hair caught on her lashes.

"More terrifying than that bogus curse from Ms. Tressa Divine?"

He held her tighter. "So, we've landed on bogus?"

"I'm not fond of the alternative."

"Bogus curse or not. You're joining the band and me. You and me, Beatrice, you and me?" Benedict collected the slow burn of the passion he'd been storing in his heart for a year and kissed it into Beatrice.

Her answer was the song she sang to him at the audition with one minor revision.

"Up on the rooftop,
Two hearts paused
You dared me to name stars
First below and then above
Together, we felt the sky
And ~~lost~~ found a night
Up on the rooftop."

ALSO BY LESLIE O'SULLIVAN

The Rockin' Fairy Tales Series:

Pink Guitars and Falling Stars

Gilded Butterfly

Wild Azure Waves (coming January 2023)

Behind the Scenes Series:

Hot Set

Press Release (coming May 2023)

ABOUT THE AUTHOR

LESLIE O'SULLIVAN is the author of *Rockin' Fairy Tales*, an adult romance series of Shakespeare/fairy tale mash ups set against the backdrop of the Hollywood music scene, available from Mystic Owl, an imprint of the awesomeness that is City Owl Press and the Behind the Scenes contemporary romcom series of the romantic entanglements behind the camera on a wildly popular TV show. UCLA Bruin for life with a BA and MFA in Theater Arts and Theatrical Design as well as years on the faculty of their amazing Department of Theater. Fairy tales, Shakespeare, Star Wars, Broadway, and Outlander are a few of her favorite fandoms. Beach-loving California girl.

FROST & FEVER

BY A.N. PAYTON

1

THE SEVERED HEAD STARED AT ME WHEN I OPENED THE DOOR. Perched on the corner of the table, thick blood dribbled across the polished surface and gathered onto the stone floor. The sightless eyes seemed to stare into my soul, as though he could see into the twisting depths and found me lacking.

I'd expected Zavier's stern form sitting at the end of the long wooden meeting table, but the head surprised me.

I paused in the doorway. The knob suddenly felt heavy in my hands.

I hadn't seen a dead body since the demon battle ended, and I'd planned to keep it that way for the rest of my life.

For a moment, I considered leaving. Zavier had requested me for a meeting, but he hadn't mentioned violence would be involved. With my commitment to Queen Sal's court temporarily on hold, Zavier didn't have more influence over me than any other civilian.

But I had fought with the old man in the midst of battle. His gray hair served as a guidon in the night, reminding the rest of us that age didn't matter in the face of fear and death. A thick swell of panic swarmed through me, the way it always did when I remembered that night, but I owed Zavier more than a single meeting. I owed him my life.

I closed the door slowly, turning the knob until it shut soundlessly in the frame, and sucked in a deep breath. The strong scent of ink and paper almost hid the metallic scent of blood. Almost. I held my breath anyway, until my pounding heart slowed and anxiety ebbed from my mind.

"Zavier," I forced a smile and tried not to look at the body part bleeding on the table, but that proved too difficult. Glossy brown eyes stared through me beneath a head of ginger hair. I didn't recognize the man. Relief at that small comfort calmed me further. "Why did you summon me? You know I requested a break from court. Are you revoking my respite?"

Zavier shook his head. It had been a year since the demon battle ended in our victory—barely. I watched him kill countless enemies that wore the faces of our loved ones but were irredeemably possessed by demons. I hadn't been able to look at anyone the same way since that battle.

"Of course not, Saffa. The Queen would be displeased if I did that, and she's already trying to push me into retirement." A weight dragged down his tone. The First Seneschal would fight Queen Sal on retiring until one of them breathed their last. "But I would rather wait to explain until you are both here."

Both? I hesitated beside one of the sturdy chairs tucked into the table and wondered who else the old witch invited.

Zavier raised a brow, and a thick blanket of dread dropped over me. He didn't have to say the name. I knew.

Footsteps echoed outside the door. My heart increased with each step. I recognized the steady rhythm and timed pace. I'd been beside those steps as they fought hand-to-hand with black-eyed beasts, cutting blades through enemy necks, wondering if they really were the monsters, or if we were.

Other feelings wrapped among the memories—a soft touch of a tender caress, hasty promises whispered in the dead of night, a longing so deep, I thought it would cut me into pieces too small to recognize.

The door opened and *he* stepped inside. Remi's gaze flicked across the severed head, Zavier reclining in his chair, and then brushed over me.

My heart stopped. My throat closed.

Remi's eyes widened, but he smothered the surprise. He entered the room and closed the door as carefully as I had.

The vampire pulled out the chair across the table from me and sank into it. His presence washed over me like a fresh rain. It had been months since I'd last seen him, but his gaze across my skin felt like the first time.

"How can I help you, Zavier?" Remi's voice—the same one he used to whisper promises in my ear—sent chills down my spine.

Promises I couldn't keep.

"Thank you both for coming," Zavier's tone remained professional. I hadn't been to court in several months, but the flatness told me something bad had happened. "You're probably curious about the head."

I pressed my lips and nodded, matching Remi's blank expression. I refused to be the first to show emotion.

"This man was one of Rueben Emerson's rebels," Zavier said. I flinched at the name. Sal had killed the traitor Emerson in battle, but the impacts of his reach stretched deep into the kingdom. A rather vicious band of rebels continued to attempt assassinations on the queen, and undercurrents spoke of their grander plans, though nobody knew what they were yet. "Before this man met his end, he revealed the rebels are planning an attack at the Winter Gala tomorrow night."

A coil of emotions rippled through me. After the demon war, the vampire kingdom of Vari Kolum had been destroyed. The vampires celebrated winter in a way we did not, and without their home, morale sank quickly. Queen Sal decided to blend the witches' annual art gala with the vampire winter festivities, creating the Winter Gala.

Remi sucked in a breath. "And we believe his confession?"

"I do," Zavier said. "He traded the information to save his life. Had he not then attempted a rather rash escape, he would have kept it. However, he injured two of my guards. His death was almost guaranteed."

"What do you want with us?" Remi asked.

Zavier's calm gaze crossed over me and then the vampire. "You both have intimate knowledge of how the rebels work." He lowered his voice. "Probably much more than you wish to have."

The words sat between us as loud as an angry beast. Remi had been kidnapped by the same rebel organization, forced to drink magic blood, and mind controlled in an attempt to kill the queen.

"Doesn't Queen Sal have anyone else?" he asked. I pretended not to hear the sliver of fear in his voice.

"Remi, I know the pain this request must place upon you," Zavier reached his hand out as though he might clasp the vampire's palm from across the table. "Trust me, I would not ask if there was anyone else. And Saffa," he turned to me, "you know the state of the country. Our supplies are dwindling even as our numbers grow. New Henosia must support the witches, vampires, and humans that call it home, but we need more food and resources. I won't ask Queen Sal to look into this matter. She's already stressed enough with the dipping supplies, but I won't place my trust in anyone less competent either."

Knowing Zavier held me in such high esteem should have been a compliment, but I'd rather he hadn't summoned me at all. Walking the familiar castle halls brought back enough memories of the past. Now, he asked me to return to the violent roots I'd vowed to avoid after the war.

"This threatens more than the Gala," Zavier continued. Maybe he'd read the doubt across my face. "The rebels have something terrible planned, and we need to know what it is so we can stop them. It's our friends and families at stake."

He directed those words at me. Remi had lost his family long ago, and suffering from trauma at the rebels' hands left him untrusting of "friends." But my family lived inside the kingdom's walls and would suffer whatever chaos the rebels had planned.

I opened my mouth, not sure what I was going to say.

"I'll do it," I heard my own voice as though listening outside my body. "I'll help you stop the rebels at the Gala, but then my debt to the kingdom is through. I'll be asking Sal to leave her court, permanently."

The old witch grimaced but ducked his head in acknowledgement.

"And you'll need my experience as their captive to help Saffa discover their plot," Remi said.

I'd tried to avoid looking at the man, despite the chills rippling down my arms, but the exasperation in his tone drew my gaze up. I expected him to be studying the severed head or glaring at Zavier, but his eyes caught mine in a sudden wash of bitterness and anticipation—the first bite of a spring berry that wasn't quite ripe yet.

"Yes," Zavier said, but neither of us really heard him.

Remi's eyes on mine brought back all those memories I'd been running from. I shoved away the echoes of his touch. I'd had happiness and joy once, only to have watched it be submerged in demons and darkness. I had no intentions of trusting the world again.

"I'll help Saffa," Remi said.

Zavier dipped his head. "Thank you, both. This man was captured and killed in a storage silo near the outskirts of town. We believe the rebels used it as a makeshift headquarters. It may be a good place to begin unraveling their plot."

He stood and grabbed a handful of the dead man's hair. Blood and thicker fluids sloshed to the floor in a series of wet noises.

"I'll see you both at the Gala. I trust this will be over by then."

Zavier circled behind Remi. The door opened and shut, leaving Remi and I alone.

I needed to say something, but my mouth felt dry as cotton. I rolled my tongue over my teeth. My mind spun in circles, searching for the words. Nothing.

Remi appeared as tense as me. He leaned forward as though he might stand, then dropped his shoulders in defeat.

The moment stretched between us as cold as the icicles caught in infinite suspense across the edge of the castle. I could almost see the transparent crystals dancing in his gaze. The heat of passion that once burned between us had faded into a cold, careful distance.

My soul mourned the loss.

"Saffa," Remi broke the silence. I sucked in a breath at my name on his lips. I had known I wouldn't go my entire life without seeing him again, but I hadn't expected it to hurt so much. "It's been a long time."

Ten months and eleven days.

"It has," I tried to keep my voice level and hoped he didn't hear the tremble. "I trust you've been well?"

A dagger of pain flashed through his eyes, gone in a moment. He didn't want to give away any emotion, and I understood that. I hadn't earned that trust. Not since I'd left him almost a year ago.

"I have..." he hesitated, fumbling for the right word, "survived. You?"

"The same," I said. The words sounded sadder than I'd intended. "Survived" exactly described the statis I'd lingered in the past year.

"What do you want to do first?" Remi asked.

I froze. There were so many things I wanted to do that I'd forced out of my mind. I longed to reach for his face and feel that soft skin touching mine. I knew he'd smell like rain and sunshine and something sweet—honeysuckle?—and I wanted to wrap that scent around me. I knew I shouldn't. Nothing lasted forever.

"For the case?" He raised a brow.

"Oh, yes." Of course, he was talking about the assignment Zavier had just passed to us. I wanted to shake my head, but I knew it wouldn't clear the cobwebs. "We should visit the silo, where Zavier said the man was captured."

"That sounds good," Remi said.

I tried not to look at him as we crossed the room. His steps echoed beside mine, the way they had in the hall of Vari Kolum as we'd both walked into battle a year ago. We had been a team then. What would we be now?

I reached for the knob, and my fingers met warm flesh instead.

A spark dashed beneath my skin at the place our hands met. My heartbeat filled my ears, sudden and erratic.

I should move my hand and let him open the door.

There were a lot of things I should do.

Instead, I pushed my fingers harder into his skin and took the touch I craved. I sucked in his smell and held my breath until my head swam.

"Saffa," Remi caught my fingers in his. He pulled my hand to his chest, and his heart beat for me as well. "I don't know..."

"Shh." We both knew the history between us. I didn't need to hear it.

Pain flooded his gaze. Those perfect lips parted, and a flick of his tongue behind his teeth rolled a fresh wave of longing deep into me.

Remi stroked my fingers. He studied my face, and whatever he saw made him draw closer to me. My eyelids became heavy. I leaned into him. Anticipation buzzed through my lips, and he shifted his gaze to them, as though he felt the current too.

He was going to kiss me.

Please.

The door snapped open. I jerked back and Remi fumbled his hand toward his belt, revealing the hilt of a short sword.

"My Liege and Lady," a dainty little maid dipped into a bow, sloshing a bucket of water dangerously at her feet. "I'm sorry to interrupt. Zavier sent me to clean the room. He didn't mention it would be occupied."

Remi glanced at me.

"It's not," he said and started down the hall, abandoning me in the doorway. The sudden chill left me colder than before.

2

THE SNOW DID ITS BEST TO CREEP INTO MY BOOTS, BUT THE FUR lining and tight laces kept it out. Remi didn't seem to mind the frost. He moved through the layers of downy ice as though it were a brisk summer day, despite the white tufts of our breath preserved in the air. I knew he moved in battle just as easily.

The stone silo thrust from the frozen ground in defiance of gravity. A wooden roof perched atop the rounded shape and slanted enough to prevent snow from building. It wasn't a huge silo, likely ten paces from side to side on the interior. The ground around the outside had been packed down from Zavier's battle. Blood puddled and froze into rivulets that would remain until thaw.

I tried not to look at the blood. It represented so much of the trauma I'd fought to overcome.

"Zavier said there was only one person killed here," Remi gestured to the scattered stains on the white snow. "What's the rest of this?"

"He said the silo had been a headquarters building. I'm sure they fought a larger force and several rebels managed to escape."

"Maybe," Remi knelt beside the pooled blood, pulled off his gloves, and gently touched the surface. Frozen solid. It had been here for a few hours, at least.

Memories slipped from my mind of Remi covered in magic symbols and wielding a power able to destroy a stone building like this silo. The image faded, leaving behind the vampire staring at me.

I shook my head. "Sorry."

He continued to watch me. What did his memories reflect over me? I shuffled my weight on my feet and covered my discomfort with pretend cold.

"Don't be." He stood and gestured to the silo door. "Ladies first."

The rough wooden door jerked open at my touch. The round room harbored a solid table, a pair of chairs, and a few unopened crates. Whisps of grain dust coated the floor as reminders of what the room used to be. Large spreads of parchment covered the walls, and torn pieces still clung to nails where someone had ripped them off.

"Zavier and his men already searched the place." I pushed my gloves into my coat and ran my finger along the edge of a shredded page where one of our soldiers must have confiscated the parchment. "I'm not sure there's anything left here for us to find."

"Zavier would have told us if they'd found something useful," Remi said. "We'd better double check what they missed."

He ducked through the low doorway. Shadows spilled across his face in the dim room and settled in the hollows of his cheeks and jaw. He'd lost weight since I'd seen him last. The change sharpened his body, offering peeks of lean muscles beneath the winter clothes. A rush of sadness swept through me. He was different now than when we'd last been together.

Remi stalked the perimeter of the room and squinted at the pages remaining on the wall. Simple maps outlined our kingdom. Inventory notes listed rebel supplies, but the dates were weeks old.

These pages didn't bear any importance for our mission, nor did they mention the Winter Gala at all.

I let Remi examine the walls while I shifted through the mess on the table. Trash and old food clustered on dirty plates. Tiny teeth marks revealed rats had already had a grand feast we'd likely interrupted.

My hand bumped against something hard beneath the trash. I pushed plates and folded papers out of the way until the sunshine streaming through the open door illuminated two thin, stone tablets.

I lifted one tablet from the table. It stretched about two hands high and one and a half across. Thick marks had been inscribed into the stone and then painted with dark black ink. I traced along one of the symbols, but it didn't hold any magical qualities. I turned it, bringing the tablet more into the light.

Remi was there. I froze as my left arm caught his chest. Trapped between him and the table, I teetered off balance. He grabbed my arms and steadied me.

"Thank you," I said, sinking weight back into my heels.

He didn't release me. His grip turned soft. New callouses along his palms caught at my dress as he brushed his hands down my arms. I held my breath, trying to savor the feelings.

"You never need to thank me, Saffa," he said, scanning my face. He took in every detail of my expression, and I had no idea what he found inside it. His brows bunched, and he parted his lips in a warm breath.

"The war hurt you, didn't it?" he asked.

The question stung. I tried to avoid thinking of the wars, both the centuries-long war against the vampires that ended with Queen Sal and King Kadence's partnership and eventual marriage, and the demon battle after that raged for one night and changed my life forever.

"You don't have to answer." Remi flicked his gaze down to the stone in my hand. "It hurt us all."

He held his hands out and I set one tablet in them. Remi turned toward the light and stepped nearer the door. I let out the breath I'd been holding, and some of the ache in my chest faded.

I hadn't talked about the war or the battle to anyone. Hearing my thoughts and fears on Remi's lips drew out a comradery I hadn't expected. I didn't think anyone could understand the pain and suffering I'd gone through that night.

Had I been wrong? The darkness in his tone sounded so familiar. The same one from my thoughts.

"These symbols are ancient Awriban. The Awriba Dynasty ate up most of the Southern region in the third millennium." He went quiet. "It's where the rebels discovered the spellwork for the mind control they used on us."

I set my hand on his arm and hoped it brought a small comfort. Remi still carried the guilt that he hadn't been able to rescue the others that had been kidnapped. The rebels had been smart with their targets and had only taken people without family or connections. In fact, we suspected they had a vampire ally feeding them information. We'd never found the others that were taken, or any signs of their bodies.

"Do you know what it says?"

His eyes turned glossy as he studied the words. "Some kind of spell, I think. It mentions death, but also something else. I'm not sure of the translation."

"Why did Zavier and his people leave them here?" I asked.

Remi shrugged. "They probably didn't understand what they were looking at. They haven't spent months studying these symbols and ancient magic history the way I have."

Surprise sparked in my chest. I didn't know he'd decided to study the magic that had once controlled him. It shouldn't have been startling. One way to take control of the past was to make sure it could never happen again.

Which was why I'd left Queen Sal's court and intended to never return.

"They'll come back for these." Remi scooped the second tablet into his hand and balanced the heavy stones with his superior vampire strength. He turned to me, and a deceptive sparkle danced in his eyes. "Feel like casting a spell?"

I couldn't stop the smile from spreading across my lips.

3

My soul sang with contentment after using my magic. The spell sank through the silo, ready for any intruders to spring the trap. Using magic felt second nature only to breathing.

"I miss it sometimes." Remi scooted beside me where we hid deep in the tree line. My power had dashed away our tracks and covered any hint of our scents.

"What?" I asked, pretending the warmth of his body blending into the icy cold snow didn't affect me. "Having to watch your back knowing someone is trying to kill you all the time?"

"The magic. The feeling of power sitting in the bottom of my chest and knowing what I could do with it." Remi looked at his palms as though the power may return. It wouldn't. The spell required detailed symbol work and blood from an exceptionally powerful witch. Once the symbols had faded from his skin after the battle, the magic had fled too.

"I can't imagine not having magic," I said and shuddered at the thought.

Remi laughed and threw his arm over my shoulders to nestle me into his side.

I froze. The laughter slipped away. The action seemed so natural it took Remi a moment to realize what he'd done.

He drew the arm away. "I'm sorry."

"Don't." I caught his wrist. "It feels..." *So many things...* "good."

He kept his arm in place, but tension tightened the muscles.

"I don't want to overstep my boundaries," he said through clenched teeth. "I know there's a reason you left and didn't want to see me again."

There were a thousand reasons I'd left. None of them were because I didn't want to see him again.

"I left because I couldn't handle everything that happened." I tried to pick around the memories that burned like acid in my mind. "The demons, killing creatures wearing the faces of people I knew and then walking away from them like their lives never mattered. You were beside me that whole night. Looking at you... made me remember them."

"That's not what you said when you left."

I bit my lip. The past year felt like I'd lived in a perpetual fog. "What did I say?"

The wind rustled through the trees and dropped tuffs of soft powder snow across our backs. The ice burned into my stomach despite layers of furs and leather between them. My socks had become a solid ring around my ankles. With Remi pressed beside me, I didn't want to move. All the discomfort was worth it.

"You said I brought out the worst in you," he whispered.

Daggers shot through my heart, swift and sharp. A rush of bile threatened to climb up my throat.

Those words. So harsh.

"I'm sorry," I said and knew it wasn't enough. "I was lost, Remi. I didn't know myself anymore."

He turned to me. His lips pulled into a frown, and a new hardness stiffened his jaw. "I didn't understand it then, Saffa, but I do now." His gaze turned distant, and I knew he wasn't beside me in the snow anymore. His memories drew him somewhere far away. "I looked at myself and the experiences I'd lived through, and I thought life was over for me." He gave an awkward half shrug. "Turns out it's a lot harder to kill a vampire than I thought, even if he wants to die."

His words shot more pain through me, etched with spasms of fear. I tried to imagine Remi ending his own life, but the images proved too painful.

Beneath the sorrow sat a layer of rage.

"You wouldn't dare do something so outrageous," I hissed.

He half smiled. "No. It turned out I was even too cowardly to try. Instead, I funneled the anger into learning more about the spells they cast over me. I've studied so many texts, myths, rumors, you name it. But I didn't realize I was missing something until I was in that conference room this morning."

My pulse picked up. "What was it?"

"You." He refocused on my face. "I realized that running away from everyone has only made me crave you more. I miss you, Saffa."

Tears filled my eyes, and I wiped them away before they could freeze. Staying away from everyone was the only thing that let me cope with the memories and the fear. Maybe it had also been my downfall. I'd avoided those in my life that loved me. It was easier that way than to imagine their deaths over and over again.

"I miss you too," I said.

Remi turned to his side and brushed a strand of hair from my face. His leather gloves concealed the feel of his skin on mine that I so desperately wanted.

"We don't have to miss each other." He leaned in and the smell of a summer's day washed away the lingering traces of winter. Heat from his breath fell over my lips and woke the sensitive nerves beneath my skin. An ache low in my body pulsed with my heart-beat. I wanted more.

He hesitated, almost touching me but not quite.

He waited for me.

I closed the gap and consumed his lips with mine. He groaned and shifted, pulling me on top of him. There was a reason we were supposed to be quiet, to remain hidden in these woods, but logic fled my mind. I only felt Remi against me and the sense that I'd finally found the first step toward closure.

Friendship. Joy. Comradery.

I opened my mouth and deepened the kiss. He obliged, giving me all he had, and I soaked it in. He was a tempting, warm spring, begging me to sink into him, and I had nothing left to withhold.

I spread my legs and put his hardness between us. I broke the kiss to catch my breath and pressed more kisses into the side of his neck as I rocked against him. Waves of pleasure spilled over me. I suppressed my own groan and moved again, until Remi's breathing turned ragged.

"Saffa." My name on his lips turned my mind to ash. Nothing else mattered excepted the space separating us and how badly I wanted it gone.

I tossed my gloves to the side and pulled open the buttons of his coat, exposing the simple white shirt and black breeches. These had to go, or at least get out of my way. I tugged his shirt up, undoing buttons or ripping them—I wasn't sure—until his skin warmed my chilled palms.

The sight of his chest captivated me, and I slowed my progress. Hard bands of muscles lined the planes of his body that used to be softer. Bulky places said he'd been devoted to strength training, but the swells gave way to a leanness that only came from hand-to-hand sparring.

Studying the ancient script wasn't the only thing Remi had done to fight his own demons. He'd made sure he could physically fight them as well.

The vampire grabbed my hands. His blue eyes had faded to a bright silver that shone like the moon across my face.

"Don't stop," he said, an edge of panic in the words.

I let a small smile slink across my lips. I had no intention of stopping.

Beneath the longing and eagerness inside my chest, something else tugged at me, foreign and demanding. *Tug, tug.*

I ignored the feeling and bent to Remi's chest. I pressed kisses into his skin, starting high and slipping lower and lower. He wound his hand into my hair and arched his back, begging for more of my touch.

Tug, tug.

I froze, momentarily distracted.

"Do you feel that?" I asked.

Remi groaned. "I only want to feel you, Saffa, against me, forever."

Hunger rose inside me. I wanted to fulfill that wish for the both of us. I leaned back into him and let the flavor of sweet jasmine carry me away.

TUG. TUG.

I jerked my head up. Magic spilled around us and pulled through my reserves. The mystical web I'd weaved around the grain silo snapped shut into a tight trap, but whoever I caught fought against me. A wave of powerful magic bit into my spell, tugging even more power from me.

I staggered, falling onto Remi's chest in a much less appealing way.

"They've sprung the trap," I said through clenched teeth. I cast a new spell over the remnants of the old, trying to strengthen it.

Remi's eyes widened and focused, the silver bleeding back to blue. He helped me from him, and I mourned the loss of his heat, his heart beating beneath mine. He jumped to his feet, sprinted toward the silo, and disappeared into the trees.

Vines of hesitation pulled me back. Anxiety wrapped around my limbs, turning them heavy and stiff. I hadn't held my sword in months, much less faced an opponent. I chewed on my lip as my body and mind rebelled against each other.

Could I do it again? Could I start a fight that might end in someone's death?

Magic jerked on my spell again and stole the breath from my lungs. I gathered the power in my chest into a strong stream and drove it into the midst of my spell. It grew stronger, trapping the intruders inside its perimeter.

"Saffa!" Remi called.

He needed me.

The imaginary restraints around me loosened. I slipped from their grasp and fled into the forest, chasing Remi's snowbound footprints toward the silo. As I neared, the peaceful nature sounds shifted into the familiar grunts and groans of battles.

Flashbacks swelled across my vision. *A claw, attached to a pus-covered nightmare with black eyes, streaming toward my face. Pain biting into my skin as I dodged a strike too slowly.*

The icy tendrils of snow against my skin pushed the memories away. This wasn't the lost kingdom of Vari Kolum. This was New Henosia, where vampires, humans, and witches could live peacefully together. We'd fought, bled, and died for this to be our home.

And these rebels were trying to steal it from us.

Rage replaced the doubt and insecurity, swelling from the pit of my stomach until it encompassed me in a fever warm enough to drown out the winter's cold.

With my sword raised, I ran toward the battle.

4

TWO OPPONENTS SHOULD HAVE BEEN EASY. ONE FOR EACH OF US. BUT my sword felt heavy and unfamiliar in my hands. Each swing took longer than it should have and made my gait awkward. It had been too long since I'd practiced, and my enemy's watchful eye tracked every mistake.

The woman I fought had long black hair and wore a bored expression. Thick bands of muscle lined her arms, suggesting she regularly practiced some type of combat training. It didn't surprise me. Many of the rebels had served in our armies during the vampire war. She fought with two short knives, driving her close into my strike range but also making her much faster than me. The pressure of her magic charged the air as she fought against my spell that trapped both rebels within the perimeter.

My breath hissed out as her blade grazed across my wrist. I pulled my strike and stepped back, putting space between us while I caught my breath. My chest burned. We'd been engaged for less than a few minutes, and doubt began to creep into my mind.

Maybe this would be my last battle.

I shook my head. I couldn't let those words poison my thoughts. I'd survived much worse than fighting against one lone witch.

She tipped her head, and a wave of ebony hair slid over one shoulder. "Aw, have I frightened you, little witch?" Her words sounded soft and slippery, a snake meandering through the forest floor.

I spun my sword, letting my wrist stretch and warm up. I refused to answer her taunts and ignored the little stings they delivered.

Her sharp gaze crossed over me again. "You are afraid. I see it now."

She struck without warning, stepping into my reach and crossing her blade over my heart. I forced my sword up, and her knife clashed away from my body by barely a breath. I aimed a punch toward her face as she stepped back, but she slipped her forearm between us and blocked the blow.

I staggered away, breathing hard.

"Were the demons the last things you fought, girl?" We circled each other, feet crunching in the icy snow. I wished she'd find a hidden berm to sink into. "Tell me, do they still haunt your dreams? Do the stolen voices of your dead loved ones sing lullabies in your ears?"

I tried to keep my expression flat, but the twist of her ruby lips spoke of my failure.

"What are your plans at the Gala tonight?" I demanded, changing the topic.

A brush of emotion flashed across her face. Surprise, perhaps, that I knew about the Gala.

She charged at me, swinging one blade high and the other low. I heaved my sword up, trying to block both strikes, but the heavy blade moved too slow.

Sparks flew as I bounced her strike away from my gut, but her second knife dipped across my cheek. Hot blood poured down my face.

I pushed her from me and aimed a kick to her chest. My foot made contact, sending her away, but the rebel maintained her balance despite the blow.

She studied the blood on my face with a smug smile. "Can't go to the Gala looking like that. Maybe I've just saved your life."

I resisted the urge to touch the wound. "You admit you have plans for the Gala then?"

We met again, blades clashing against each other, the sounds of metal on metal screaming into the trees. I tried to break apart, but she grabbed my wrist and held me close.

"The Gala will be a night to remember," her gaze faded as though she was no longer on this field, in this fight. "There will be blood and death and redemption. And at the end, rebirth as we have never known."

I pushed her from me, driving my sword at her again. She backed up, but her focus had faded. My sword cut into her side, and blood blossomed through her clothes. Satisfaction ate through me. This woman wanted to hurt my people, the ones I'd killed to protect, and I wouldn't let her. If tonight had to end in death, it wouldn't be my body in the snow.

The woman prodded at the wound and grimaced. A red hue danced across her face, and anger tightened the thin lines around her eyes.

"You will pay," she ground out.

Her knives turned to silver streaks as she ran toward me across the field. Over her shoulder, I caught a glimpse of Remi, engaged with his opponent, then only dark hair and silver blades consumed my vision.

My body groaned as I blocked each strike. I tried to keep up with her punishing pace, but the rebel had more recent practice than me, and it showed in her skills. I ground my teeth. Regret at the past year leaked through me. I should have known my place was beside Sal, keeping our people safe. I never should have left or let my training slack. The loss, the trauma, I'd needed to work through it, not run away.

Her knives cut into my skin. I managed to keep half a step

ahead of her, preventing the tips from sinking all the way into my body. Blood peppered the snow at our feet until the white turned crimson.

She would bleed me out one slice at a time.

Remi's grunt echoed across the field and drew me from my trance. I risked a glance over my opponent's shoulder—taking a sharp stab to my forearm in return—as Remi's foe pushed his short sword into his gut. The vampire looked up with fire in his eyes and blood leaking down his chin.

Pain stabbed my chest, not sharp like cuts from the knives but equally as damaging. Remi had just come back into my life. I couldn't let him leave me again.

The woman recognized my distraction and smiled for a moment. She thought she had me wide open and waiting for her strike. If she had looked into my eyes, she would have seen her own death in their depths.

Instead, she moved in.

I planted my feet and raised my sword. The discomfort wore away, replaced with determination. The weapon I'd struggled with suddenly felt as light as air. I pulled it between us, a lifeline of steel and leather, and her blades bounced from the metal.

The impact forced her back, and her mouth shaped into a surprised circle.

I felt a smile creep across mine.

I took another step and sank my sword into her chest. It split through the other side, drawing her close to me. I snatched one wrist and twisted until she dropped the dagger. Her other knife fell from shaking fingers as her body cataloged the fatal blow.

I grabbed her hair and forced her to look at me.

"The Gala," I said. I ached to help Remi, but this was our only shot to fulfill the mission Zavier had given us. I had to trust Remi could survive a few more minutes. "Tell me everything."

Her lids fluttered as hot blood streamed down my sword hilt.

Each frantic pump of her heart pushed her closer to death's door, and yet, no fear spread across her face.

"It will be glorious," she whispered, and blood painted her lips. It seemed to transform her from something more than a dying witch, something eternal and immortal. "From the death of thousands, one shall be reborn. She who is death, come to reclaim her realm."

The witch blinked hard, as though waking from a dream and realizing where she was. She looked between us, and a flash of magic danced through her soul.

"No!" I yelled, but it was too late. I pulled my sword from her gut before the death spell could taint her blood and spread to me. The magic pulsed through her, and she collapsed at my feet.

"Is she dead?"

I turned as Remi neared. His opponent lay bleeding out near the silo, turning the ground black with stained blood as the woman did.

"Yes. Don't touch the blood." I pushed my sword into the blackness and a hint of smoke escaped. "It shouldn't be toxic once the fluid leaves the body, but it's better not to take risks."

"I thought suicide spells were illegal." Remi toed away from the spreading stain, and I followed.

"They are. All black magic is illegal in New Henosia, as it was in Ededen." Black magic was dangerous, addictive, and bloody. It turned witches into mindless creature craving their next taste. But it was very, very powerful.

Silence settled for a moment.

"Did you get any information from her?" Remi asked.

"That they are planning a massacre at the Gala to have someone be...reborn?" I ran the word through my mind, but it didn't conjure anything. "You?"

Remi nodded. "The same thing. 'From the death of many comes the second life of one,' or something like that. A moment later, he was dead."

I chewed my lip. We hadn't gotten any closer to what Zavier had tasked us with. The Gala was still in danger, and we didn't know the larger threat.

"What should we tell Zavier?" I asked, turning from the body to find Remi's eyes already on me. A deep hunger consumed the irises, shifting his blue eyes to a solid silver, like a handful of coins in the moonlight.

"Remi..." His name pressed against my lips like a woven blanket, a fire in the midst of a winter storm, a delicious beverage I'd only dreamed about and never tasted.

The vampire moved in a blur, wrapped his hand around the back of my head, and buried it into the tangled locks of my hair. He leaned in, hesitating for a moment while his nostrils flared to check whether his approach was invited or not, and I knew he scented the hormones seeping from my body.

It was. It very much was.

Remi pressed his lips to mine.

"Let me get this straight," Remi said as we dragged the two bodies of the rebels we'd killed through the snow. We doubled up the fabric on our hands to avoid touching even a hint of contaminated blood. "We killed the rebels instead of interrogating them. And we don't know anything more about the attack on the Gala. What are we supposed to tell Zavier?"

"We tell him that we know their intentions for the Gala and will have a plan in place to deflect them."

"So we lie?"

"No," I huffed as though the accusation was ridiculous. "We simply rephrase the truth."

"The rebels are planning a massacre. If we mess up, people will die."

I chewed my lip. Remi was right, but I knew we were stronger now that we were together. We could handle whatever the rebels threw at us.

"We'll round up some more soldiers to help us," I said. "Zavier doesn't even have to know."

Remi paused and maneuvered one body around a fallen log. "That'll probably work."

I smiled, even as we both knew such a trick would never work on the old witch. But he trusted us, and we would prove that trust.

5

"It is a joy to see you back in court, Saffa," Zavier said as I entered the Gala. I'd avoided any heeled shoes in preparation for the upcoming fight, and the train of my black gown—which could be ripped away at a moment's notice—trailed the marble floor.

"Thank you." It felt right to be back. Something about the organized chaos of court life reminded me of good times, before demon faces haunted my dreams.

Last night, a different face had made an appearance. One that drew me close into his body and made sweet love to me and washed the doubts away.

People milled through the Grand Hall. White silk spilled down the walls to turn the traditional stone into a rich winter's wonderland. Last year's Gala had separate booths to showcase the artwork. This year, everything displayed in the open and combined into a single room of splendor. Even the guests seemed to compliment the theme. White crystals sparkled like fresh snow down layers of swaddled fabric. Hints of crimson highlighted carefully tailored gowns and an array of winter flowers, such as the soft purple of a lenton rose, decorated many noblewomen's hair. Soft plucks of stringed instruments floated around us.

Zavier leaned close to me. "I need to thank you for investigating the rebel threat. I expect everything is taken care of for tonight?"

I forced a smile. "Of course."

"And the surplus guards Remi requested be armed and prepared outside are simply for...reassurance?"

I glanced at the man's cloudy eyes, which shone with a bit of humor. He knew exactly what we were up to.

"Yes," I looked anywhere except at him. "Reassurance."

A waiter passed carrying a platter filled with glasses. Tiny bubbles flickered through gleaming liquor, as though gold had been melted and poured into the cup, topped with a flick of champagne.

Zavier snatched a glass and passed it to me.

"Perhaps you'll need one of these for tonight." He winked and bowed before meandering into the crowd.

I pressed the glass to my lips and downed the contents in one gulp. The delicious flavor of vanilla and butterscotch couldn't wash the tightening anxiety from my throat.

A single violinist stepped onto a raised dais where two thrones waited for their occupants. Chatter hushed as the musician pulled the bow across the strings, and an eerie, somber note spread out. He rocked his body with the melody, twisting one haunting tone into another until they blended into a single rhythm. A little sad, but high, hopeful notes rang between each softer sound.

Faces fell as the music revived memories preferably forgotten— those of broken bodies on the ground, of stolen vampires painted with tainted magic and killed for sins not their own, of death and demons and darkness. Tears burned my eyes. Others gathered their friends into tight embraces, more sought comfort among the golden cocktails.

The notes shifted. The darkness fell away in a blaze of rhythmic glory. It spoke of our victory over the demons without uttering a single word. It sang about the fall of Vari Kolum and the end of Ededen, together, revived into New Henosia, named after the long-forgotten history of our kind when we lived in harmony. Before war, bloodshed, and hatred.

The final notes rang through the hall, promises of a better tomorrow, awe at the progress we'd already made.

A hand fell on my shoulder as the heavy curtains parted. Queen Sal and King Kadence stepped into the dim light to the sound of hushed applause.

"The rebels have been sighted." Remi's scent brushed over me before my mind registered his words. "We're needed outside."

I squeezed his fingers and turned to follow him. Sal glanced my way, and one dainty brow rose. She opened her mouth and stepped toward the side of the dais as though to come to me, but Kadence leaned toward her with a question. She teetered on the edge for a moment, and I escaped the Great Hall before she turned back.

I expected a heavy weight in my chest, but it didn't appear. I'd see Queen Sal—one of my best friends and the queen who led her people into battle against the demons—again soon. I didn't have to miss her right now.

"We have groups of soldiers securing each quadrant of the perimeter, and a floating group of five more per quadrant. The watchers on the walls reported unauthorized personnel moments ago. They seemed to be carrying moving baskets," Remi said as we slipped through the staff passages into the winter air.

"The baskets were moving?" I asked. The train of my dress wound beneath my feet. I reached around my back and pulled at the delicate bow drawn low at my waist. The fabric freed, and the skirt fell to the ground, leaving me in a black silk top and thick cotton breeches that the skirt previously concealed.

Remi scanned me. "I preferred the skirt."

I rolled my eyes. "It's easier to stab people in breeches."

He shrugged, but I knew he pictured peeling the dress from my body and holding me close like we did yesterday. I forced the image from my mind before it made me crave the same.

Shouts erupted through the night. I pulled the sword from my waist sheath, and Remi already had his blade up. He smiled a fierce cut of teeth in the darkness.

"Let's do this."

All my doubts and insecurities about battle and war fell away. I'd been raised to fight. Taking a break gave me clarity about my life and told me this was where I needed to be.

I smiled too. "After you."

Guards engaged a large group of rebel fighters, but more spilled over the walls, despite arrows raining from the watch towers above. Grunts and moans seeped across the grassy lawn but remained muted. We didn't want to draw attention from the Gala inside, and the rebels certainly didn't want their presence more announced.

I cut down one man as his feet landed on the ground. He abandoned the basket he'd gripped over the wall and leveraged a small knife from a back sheath.

A little red chicken popped its head from the twine basket. I froze, catching the creature's gaze for a split second.

The chicken squawked and leaped from the container. It sprinted into the night.

A silver knife blurred at my face, and I sidestepped, sprinkling a hint of magic through the space. The blade slowed as though striking through water. The rebel grimaced, and his own magic pushed at mine in an attempt to break the spell.

I cut my sword into the side of his neck. His magic slipped away with the blood leaking down his chest.

A shadow covered the dim lantern light, and I tensed in anticipation for the slice of a blade into my body. Instead, Remi appeared at my side.

"There's so many of them," he studied the fight. Our guards engaged several rebels, but more dropped from the walls. Human shapes carrying armfuls of wicker baskets sprinted past our lines, engaging the second defense before the hall doors. We held them off, but sheer numbers would soon push us back.

One rebel halted between the defenses. He pulled a chicken from his basket and severed the head in a clean strike. I couldn't hear him from this distance, but his lips moved in a chant. Some kind of spellwork. The rebel covered his hands in chicken blood and painted a symbol in the grass.

Magic, thick and heavy, snapped into the air—the beginning of a very dark spell.

I gripped my sword, prepared to step toward the man, but another solider appeared. He cut the rebel's head off, and it rolled my way, settling with blank eyes looking at me.

"They're preparing a spell," I said. More of the rebels began freeing their chickens and ending their lives with a quick jab. Guards slaughtered the spellcasters, but enough of them painted symbols into the grass first, and the magic thickened. "They don't have to reach the Gala, they just have to finish the spell."

"What does the spell do?"

"I don't know, but it would be bad." Animal sacrifice was only legal under very specific healing spells, and only by approved spell-casters. It was more often found in black magic.

Remi had said the tablets we'd found in the silo had mentioned spells and death. The words of the woman I'd killed came back to my mind. *From the death of thousands, one shall be reborn.*

"It's a resurrection spell." Horror seeped into my voice and bile boiled in my gut. "They're casting a circle with the intention to kill everyone inside it and raise something else. Once they finish the animal sacrifices, there will be a human sacrifice, and anyone caught in the perimeter will die."

Remi's eyes flashed silver as he estimated the size of the circle. "Not just the Gala then."

"The whole castle," I whispered.

"There're probably more rebels outside the other walls. What are they raising?"

I chewed my lip. I'd studied enough ancient history with Elaine to know more than the average person, but I wasn't an expert. I tried to remember some of the symbols on the tablets from the silo.

"A goddess, I think." What had the witch said? "Of death? I'm not sure, but the human sacrifice won't be random. It will be someone specially prepared for the ceremony. They'd be wearing white robes and anointed with herbs and oil."

"A volunteer?"

I shook my head. "Not necessarily."

Remi pressed his lips. I knew he remembered his own kidnapping and being forced to submit to the rebels' will, against his own.

"It would have taken them weeks to prepare the sacrifice. If we can find them, we can stop the spell."

Magic flung over us as a heavy blanket. We didn't have much time before the rebels completed the circle.

"We have to get to the other side of the wall. They wouldn't send the sacrifice into the middle of battle," I said.

Remi and I sprinted past the engaged soldiers and streaks of chicken-carting rebels. The main gates were closed, but a side door stood propped open. The gate guards watched with wide eyes as we streaked by them.

People filled the grassy field outside the castle walls. More baskets, likely filled with chickens, huddled in their tight grips. Nobody paused to pursue us, too focused on the mission, on their thirst for death.

Alone in the moonlight, nestled in the tree line of the path toward the gate, sat an unobtrusive wooden wagon. It stretched tall, able to fit probably two or three shorter men and wide enough to require at least two horses to pull. I wouldn't have thought twice about its presence, as merchants often spent the night parked along the edge of the roads, and many merchants attended the Gala tonight. Except this wagon emitted a powerful magic I'd only felt once before—when I'd touched Remi while he was under the rebels' spell.

He froze beside me as the power brushed over him as well. His lips tightened with the familiar feel.

"The sacrifice is in there," he said. "And it's not a willing volunteer. I can feel the mind control magic."

I nodded.

The shouts and yells behind us suddenly amped up into triumphant cheers. The weighty magic snapped taunt.

"They've finished the circle spell." We turned our gaze to the wagon. "The human sacrifice is next."

A single lantern lit inside the wagon and spilled light between the wooden planks.

We ran.

Remi jerked the iron lock from the wagon's gate. The doors slipped open, displaying two men and one woman huddled around a makeshift table balancing on four square stones.

A young man lay across the table dressed in thick white robes. His blank eyes stared at the ceiling, but his chest rose and fell in soft waves. Mind controlled, but not sacrificed. Not yet.

Remi drew his sword and thrust it into the closest rebel spellcaster before the others realized they'd been caught. The man tried to speak, but blood trailed from his lips instead of words.

The second man jumped from the wagon. I thrust my sword toward his gut, but he sidestepped in a swift motion and raised a short dagger. He turned back to me, and fury burned in his gaze. I watched his body, waiting for the subtle hints of his next attack, but I didn't catch the tell in time.

I ground my teeth as his blade cut through my wrist. His dagger buried into the cluster of nerves near the surface of my skin, and acidic pain chewed up my arm and spread into my back. My sword fell from my hands, resting in my own blood on the grass.

The rebel smiled at me, his blade already bearing my blood.

"I've got it." Remi appeared beside me and eyed the man. "Go rescue the sacrifice."

Remi engaged him in a flurry of sparks and red droplets, and the two moved away.

I turned toward the wagon and caught the woman's eyes. She shifted her gaze from me to the man on the wooden platform.

"No!" I yelled and launched myself into the wagon.

A knife flashed in her hands. Even as the man remained immobile, oil and herbs scattered across his ashen face, dread filled his expression as he watched the weapon descend.

I lunged forward, calculating my odds. She would complete the sacrifice before I could engage her in a fight. My sword still rested in the grass beyond my reach. Aiming a punch or kick would take longer than the swift flick of her blade into the man's chest, and my magic would need time to gather before I could use a spell—time I didn't have.

One option remained.

I fell between the victim and her approaching blade. The woman's face pinched into a sea of red, but her strike had been too sure. Where the sacrifice's chest had been moments ago, my body now covered.

The knife sank into my gut. I groaned as white-hot pain ate into my skin. Agony spread as the spell tried to take hold of my life and pull it away. Except, I wasn't the right sacrifice. I didn't bear the correct preparations that would complete the final spell.

The magic slipped from me like hot oil in a pan. The circle broke, unable to hold its shape without the final ingredient.

Relief swept through me. We'd saved the Gala and the castle.

The witch screamed. She pulled the knife from my back with a sucking sound and plunged it back into me. Air tried to gurgle through my pierced lungs, but only warm fluid filled its place. Again, she pulled the weapon out and stabbed me again and again, sinking hatred into every strike. I raised my hands to block her blade out of instinct, but they did nothing to halt her aim.

"Do you know what you have done?" She punctuated each word with a thrust of her knife. "Years of preparation, wasted in a moment. And for nothing! You have only delayed the inevitable. The Goddess will rise and reclaim her realm, and your life will end he—"

Her words cut. A silver sword poked through the side of her throat. Remi dragged the blade through her neck, and the witch's head tumbled to the side.

"Saffa," his soft voice filtered through the static claiming my mind. Gentle hands rolled me from the table, but I didn't feel any pain. The warm blood soaking into my back felt good in the winter air.

"You did it," Remi pulled me to his chest. He tried to smother the turmoil in his words, but I could hear it. He knew he was losing me. "You saved Sal, Kadence, everyone."

I gasped for air, but a floating calmness claimed my body. Death, like all changes, was scary, but it wasn't bad. My fear of dying and loss had found solace these past few days, while Remi reassured me that I was more than my history.

I closed my eyes, letting the fuzzy sound of a familiar heartbeat lull me to sleep.

"What is this?" Sal's voice seeped through the cracks in my mind. "Is she dead?"

"Your Majesty," Remi's voice sounded distant and thick, as though speaking through tears. "We learned of a rebel attack on the Gala, and Saffa managed to thwart their plans. She's been gravely injured."

All I heard was silence.

"Kadence, please fix this." I could almost see Sal's hand flick toward us in my imagination. "Then I want to see all of you in my chambers tomorrow. If you're going to be doing missions for the court, I need to know about it. Let me guess, Zavier was involved? That man needs to retire, for his own good..."

Sal's lecture continued into the night, but something pressed against my lips. I'd heard rumors the king's blood could heal even death wounds, though Sal had never verified such abilities. Sweetness funneled into my mouth, and I gulped it down until sleep finally settled my mind.

EPILOGUE

REMI PUSHED THE RING ONTO MY FINGER. THE SILVER BAND SLIPPED around my knuckle and settled as though it had been there forever.

I smiled as I put a matching band around his finger in return. Whisps of snow twisted around us to rest on the icy surface of the frozen lake at our heels. Cushioned imprints of animal tracks and brown strands of hibernating lake grass peeking between snowbanks were the only witnesses to our little ceremony. We didn't have vows or promises to pledge in the soft winter's light. We'd already said everything that needed saying.

Remi set his fingers along my cheek. Another reason to have a wedding without any guests. We didn't have to be embarrassed when the love turned to desire. He bent down and let his lips caress mine, tainted with that sweet floral flavor and reminders of what love should be.

"Is it right to get married after discovering a rebel organization is trying to awaken an ancient goddess and unleash her into our world?" I asked. Bands of pain flicked down my back as though I could still feel the witch's knife in my flesh. Kadence had healed me, but the scars went deeper than skin.

"I think that's the best time to get married." Remi laughed, and the sound was everything I'd longed for.

He smiled at me. Joy filled his face, but darkness still clung to the depths. I knew mine looked the same. War had created a brokenness that would never heal. But we didn't need it to. We just needed someone to sit beside on those darkest days, to press close to in the middle of the night, to wash away the shadows when they grew too thick.

We weren't emotionally healed or perfect, and we never would be.

I smiled, because I was okay with that. I had Remi and he had me. It would be enough.

"I love you," I whispered.

The grip around my waist turned hard, hungry for something more.

"I love you too," he said.

HOLIDAY RECIPE

Molten Gold Cocktail

INGREDIENTS

- 1 shot Vanilla or Peach flavored Vodka
- Half a shot of Crème de Cacao
- Half a shot of Butterscotch Schnapps
- Champagne as desired
- Edible gold powder as desired for visual effect
- Hard sugar crystals (optional)

INSTRUCTIONS

If desired, prime the glass rim with a little water and dip into the sugar crystals until they cling. Fill glass with ice. Add vodka, crème de cacao, and butterscotch schnapps to a shaker with ice. Shake and strain the liquid into the prepared glass. Add small amount of gold powder, lightly stir, and top to desired point with champagne.

Enjoy and always drink responsibly!

ALSO BY A.N. PAYTON

Eternal Alliances Series:

Hellfire and Honey

ABOUT THE AUTHOR

A.N. PAYTON is a fantasy romance author who is also navigating the tides of motherhood. She has a degree in biology and is passionate about the intersection of fantasy and science. When not writing or chasing a toddler, she can be found working on one of her many side projects, playing video games with her husband, or sleeping.

HEART SHAPED BOX

BY ERIN FULMER

HEART SHAPED BOX

SEBASTIAN RITTER HAD A PROBLEM, AND THAT PROBLEM WENT BY THE name of Lily Knight. Beautiful, half-succubus, and wholly dangerous, she could drain his life force with a single touch.

He prided himself in skillfully and efficiently solving problems. As the founder of Ritter Security, tech industry golden boy, and a senator's prodigal son, he had plenty of power and privilege at his disposal with which to solve them.

And solve them he had. By age thirty-five, he had his entire life figured out, his bachelor status confirmed and settled. He would work hard, play hard, and never let one get in the way of the other.

Relationships were a liability—or rather, he was a liability in relationships. An intimate partnership was just a system like any other, requiring care and maintenance to last. Ignore the little glitches, and eventually, they'd generate a blue screen of death.

He'd learned that years ago when his last relationship fell apart. By the time he figured out that he'd bricked the whole thing, it was irretrievable. Helena, his ex-wife, had explained the problem numerous times, both explicitly and implicitly. He was too aloof, too serious, always buried in work, and didn't know how to let go of control over anything.

She was right about all of it, but he didn't know how to be anyone else. He'd put himself back together as best he could and made a new plan that didn't require skills he didn't have. No strings and no entanglements meant no one would get hurt. Problem solved.

Then in the space of twenty-four hours, all his best-laid plans dissolved before his eyes, and his theory unraveled in an instant. That night, he met a problem he didn't know how to resolve. Even more concerning, he didn't want to.

More concerning still, he had fallen completely and irredeemably in love with her.

"Mr. Ritter, sir?" Around the conference table with its tasteful seasonal centerpieces—potted poinsettias adorned with red silk ribbons—seven Ritter Security team leaders stared at Sebastian with expectant expressions.

"What?" Sebastian snapped. His focus had drifted, and his focus never drifted.

"We're waiting on your decision on the winter holiday marketing strategy, sir."

He had no idea what the holiday marketing strategy entailed. This meeting had gone on far too long. "I'm in agreement," he said at random. "Let's take five."

The department heads exchanged glances, but they gathered up their folders and tablets before filing out. They probably wondered what was wrong with the big boss, but they were too polite—or intimidated—to say so.

He sighed and scrubbed a hand across his face. His head wasn't in the game. What *was* wrong with him?

But he already knew the answer. Lily occupied a significant percentage of his waking thoughts these days. It was to her that his mind had wandered during the second half of an interminable quarterly earnings report.

He was already lost the night he met her, though he didn't know it yet. He was done for even before he woke up in a blood-soaked hotel room to witness a woman's life draining away in front of him, as everything he had worked for and built for himself slipped through his fingers.

In the wake of Penelope's death, it had all seemed so hollow. He'd erected a firewall around his heart, a life in solitary, and for what? Would the four walls of a prison cell really be so different? The fact that he was innocent of the crime with which they charged him didn't mean a thing in the bleak face of that empty truth.

When Lily walked into that dingy interrogation room after it all fell apart, she didn't fear him. She didn't automatically respect his status, either. She didn't care that he had more money than he could ever need or a father in the halls of power. Staring him down without flinching, with the cool strength of steel in her eyes, she told him exactly what she thought of him.

That wasn't much, because she thought he was a murderer, right up until he reached out and touched her. That fleeting moment transfixed him. It was as though she looked into his soul and *saw* him, all of him, and even then, she didn't look away.

That was the only explanation he could come up with for why he couldn't get her out of his head.

It wasn't her succubus powers that captured his attention. He hadn't felt that way with Penelope. She was a succubus too, and they'd fed each other's needs with no question of anything more. It was simple. He preferred to keep things simple—or, he *had*.

But then Lily came along, prickly, resistant, sarcastic, and unsolvable. Nothing came simply with her. She eluded him, deflecting all his probing questions, while behind the barriers, her aching, vulnerable heart showed itself in tantalizing flashes. Somehow, he couldn't get enough.

She irritated him at times, no doubt of that. But she also offered the one attribute he couldn't resist. In her stubborn loneliness, her guarded heart, she presented a *challenge*.

More than that, though, she reminded him of himself.

His phone, forgotten on the conference table, buzzed insistently. He flipped it over and frowned at the lock screen before he picked it up.

"Hey, Sebastian. It's Danny." She didn't have to introduce herself. Lily's best friend spoke with a rich, brassy drawl he recognized instantly, even if her name didn't flash on his caller ID.

"Hello, Danny." Sebastian switched his phone to his other ear, his jaw twitching with sudden tension. "To what do I owe the pleasure? I hope everything's all right."

One of the lesser-known hazards of dating a supernatural being was how much he worried for her safety. Then again, maybe that was just a hazard of dating Lily Knight. She'd assured him repeatedly that the danger that stalked her when they first met, the murderer who'd tried to ruin his life, was gone for good, though she wouldn't tell him exactly how or why. On the other hand, she had an impulsive streak a mile wide and a knack for doing things the hard way.

"Yep, everything's fab," Danny said. "Hey, I wanted to ask you, do you have any holiday plans this weekend?"

"No, I—"

"Great! You'll make it to our HannuMasFriendsWarming then."

"Hannu-what?"

"It's a combined Hannukah, Christmas, Friendsgiving, and housewarming party. We're poly-celebratory in this household, and we like to mix it up."

"It's kind of you to include me in your holiday polycule." He couldn't help but crack a smile at her relentless, ridiculous portmanteaus. Moreover, no one had ever invited him to a Friendsgiving before. When Helena left him, he'd lost most of their mutual friends and hadn't bothered to acquire more. He enjoyed his own company well enough, but Danny's invitation sparked a warmth in his chest he didn't know he'd missed.

Danny laughed. "Like I could leave you out of it? No, I'm not letting you off the hook for the holidays. Lily would love to see you."

Lily's name brought him up short because she hadn't mentioned anything about this party on their last date. They saw each other weekly, and she seemed to want to keep things at that level, though he had made bids for more time with gentle persistence. "That's news to me."

"Well, it shouldn't be. Of course, she wants to see you. She's just too proud to ask you herself. I'm surprised you haven't figured that out by now."

And there it was, the data he'd failed to notice, the bug in the system. "I didn't want to assume she and I were at the stage of spending holidays together."

"Oh, please." Danny sighed dramatically. "In that case, I'm doing you a favor. I'm not usually a fan of idiots to lovers, but she happens to be one of my favorites. Idiots, that is."

"I'll choose to ignore that you just called me an idiot by association." He aimed for his most severe tone, though Danny's delivery was more disarming than insulting.

"Don't bother, it was very pointed. Look, Sebastian, I'll be blunt. Lily has no family to see on the holidays. She usually spends December at the district attorney's office, taking on everyone else's extra work, except—"

Ah. Now he understood. "Except she's not working this year."

A pang of regret echoed behind his words because Lily had lost her job as a prosecutor after she stuck her neck out for him and refused to press charges. In the brief touch they'd shared, she'd somehow come to believe in his innocence, and for that belief and her dedication to finding the truth, she'd lost everything she'd worked so hard for.

"Good, you're keeping up. You'll be there then? Saturday night, six o'clock. Berry's making her famous latkes. You won't want to miss them."

"I'll be there," Sebastian conceded. The conversation had gotten away from him. Apparently, his attendance at this event was a foregone conclusion. "She knows you're inviting me, I hope."

"Oop, gotta go." Danny didn't seem to have heard his last statement. "Bring your favorite holiday dish. And don't be late."

"Of course not," he said, indignant, but Danny had already hung up. He frowned down at the phone.

Now he had a new problem. What kind of gift could a man with too much money to spare get away with presenting to his proud and prickly not-quite girlfriend on the occasion of HannuMasFriendsWarming?

A gift guide for this situation didn't exist. He would have to go to the source.

But he had to be strategic about it. This situation required subtlety, a delicate touch. He didn't want to spook her.

He needed a plan.

Later that evening, Lily slid into the passenger seat of his Corvette and immediately torpedoed The Plan.

"We need to talk about holiday gifts." Her eyes flashed brilliant green, their direct gaze hypnotic. She wore a light purple button-up blouse with one of the slim black A-line skirts she favored, the kind that would almost certainly ride up her thighs during their planned activities. She had, however, heeded his instructions and chosen reasonable footwear with no significant heel, even if they were knee-high black boots with a faux suede finish. "You're not planning on getting me anything, are you?"

He tore his focus away from her long enough to shift the car into gear, pulling out into traffic by way of giving himself time to formulate a response. "It sounds like you don't want me to."

"You *are* planning on it. I knew it." Her triumphant tone implied she'd tricked him into confessing a capital crime instead of a reasonable, thoughtful, normal gesture.

"I generally like to get gifts for people I'm dating, yes." Feeling hurt by her defiant, misplaced pride didn't serve any purpose. "Even more so when I care about that person."

Damn. Had he said too much? Probably, because Lily crossed her arms and scowled. "I wish you wouldn't. Seb, you know I can't afford to get you anything nice."

Oh. Of course. If he had thought about things from her perspective for even a moment, he might have figured out that was the root of her stubbornness. "It's not an obligation."

"Maybe not. But I'd still feel bad about it."

"Well." He cleared his throat. "That's more or less the opposite of the desired effect. No gifts. Got it."

"You're upset," she said with a soft intake of breath. "I didn't mean it like that."

Double damn. He still forgot sometimes how effectively she could read his feelings. He should have controlled his reaction better. "It's fine. Don't worry about it."

"No, it's not. I mean—it's not about you. This is my issue. I'm the one who got herself fired."

"You got yourself fired because you were helping me."

"Not...entirely." She stared down at her hands, folded neatly in her lap, but her knuckles were white. "I screwed up a lot of things, and it wasn't all for your sake. No. I have no one to blame but myself."

"I said it's all right." He looked back at the road ahead with an effort, taking the onramp east toward Treasure Island. "There's no need to beat yourself up so much about it."

Her faint laugh carried a tremor. "I can't seem to help myself."

"Then perhaps I should order you to stop."

He said it softly, his voice pitched deliberately low, and this at least had the desired effect. Her head came up sharply and she turned to stare at him. "Sebastian..."

"Yes, Lily?"

"Are you trying to distract me from my shame spiral?"

"I thought that was obvious." Something had shifted in the small cabin of the Corvette, stirring his body in response. At least he had something to offer her that she would accept.

"I thought you were teaching me how to drive stick tonight, not..." She stopped and laughed, this time more full-throated, less shaky. "I walked right into that one, didn't I? The other kind of stick."

"I don't see why we can't do both. After all, you only need training with the car. You're already admirably skilled at the rest."

She flushed a little at that, and he allowed himself a slight smile. Making a succubus blush: now, that was an accolade he wished he could put in those profiles journalists loved to publish about him.

Even if she was, as she so frequently liked to remind him, only half-succubus.

"Do you want to come up?" she asked, later still, when he dropped her back at the house she now shared with Danny and Berry.

The driving lesson had gone well. She'd only ground the Corvette's gears a little and burned the clutch once after stalling. All and all, a productive session, even if they both practically had to sit on their hands to avoid touching. Lily insisted they not make skin-to-skin contact, worried that an energy drain would leave him incapable of driving them back over the bridge. She overestimated the danger, but then again, that assumed they would manage to stop touching each other once they started.

Still, her question took him by surprise. They didn't spend much time in her space, and he hadn't even seen her new room in

Danny's house. She preferred his bachelor pad for the privacy. Frankly, he did too, for the comfort of his own well-ordered home, with a place for everything and everything in its place. Lily's living conditions tended a bit too much toward chaos for his taste.

Maybe that was why he answered cautiously after taking a breath. "If you'd like me to."

"I would." Her eyes gleamed, catching the amber glow of the streetlamp.

He didn't love leaving the Corvette on the street in this neighborhood, but Lily Knight had invited him into her inner sanctum, and that meant something. What else was insurance for, anyway, if not to enable carefully considered risks when justified by the potential rewards?

He held the passenger door open for her, and she gave him the look of flustered surprise she did every time. It seemed odd that a woman with her powers had never gotten used to dates treating her well. Maybe she still didn't expect it from a man like him. He allowed himself a wry smile at the thought. San Francisco tech executives didn't exactly have a reputation for good manners.

Lily let them in through the side door leading into the garage and turned to press a finger to her lips. Her eyes were alight with mischief, as though they were teenagers sneaking in late. Sebastian raised a brow at her, but the teasing question died on his lips when she took him by the hand and pulled him toward the stairs.

Her fingers twined with his, leaving him lightheaded, his body tingling with the connection that snapped into place between them. When they reached the landing at the top of the steps, he couldn't wait another moment. He pulled her back toward him, turned her around, and kissed her.

The sound she made in her throat went straight to his cock. It strained toward her, instantly rock hard. He deepened the kiss, seeking more sounds like the first, but after a moment, she pulled away. Her face glowed in the dim light from the stairwell, but the shadows in her eyes spoke volumes.

She was holding back again, worried about taking too much energy—or kether, as she called it—from him when all he wanted was to give her everything he had. His breath caught and he put a palm flat against the wall to steady himself.

"You're in your head again," he said, when he could speak. "Lily, it's all right."

"Not here." She pushed the door and stood aside, gesturing him in. "Come on. I won't have you falling down the stairs."

She had a point there. He stepped inside, ducking his head to avoid brushing the sharply sloping ceiling of the little garret room, and paused to take it in. So, this was Lily's inner sanctum.

"It's very…cozy." How she lived like this, he couldn't fathom.

Then again, circumstances had forced her to fit the contents of her old apartment into this single room. Boxes littered the floor, with more against the near wall in stacks of dubious structural integrity. The closet looked in danger of popping open but for the overflowing laundry basket set in front of it as a doorstop. Under the high point of the roof, Lily's cat Delilah sat primly in the center of the double bed atop its crocheted coverlet, blinking sleepily at him.

"I made the bed for you," Lily said, laughter in her voice, and shut the door behind them.

"I see that." He took the few steps needed to cross the room and extended a hand to the cat. Delilah deigned to sniff his fingers, then pushed her head against his hand, demanding that he stroke her. If only her human had so few qualms about asking for what she wanted.

"Not exactly the type of accommodations you're used to, are they?" Her tone had a note of challenge in it once again. She stood by the door, arms folded, as if still undecided whether she wanted to let him stay.

"Perhaps. But the company is excellent." He scratched the cat's silken head, his attention captured by a shoebox half-shoved under the bed. "Lily, please tell me that's not what I think it is."

"What?"

"This." He bent to retrieve the box, handling its weight gingerly. As expected, it contained the uselessly ornate custom pistol she'd confiscated from a deranged gunman. That had been during the wild week after they'd met, right after she'd kissed him with unrestrained hunger for the first time, kissed him until his knees buckled and he saw stars.

His cock hardened at the memory, but he had to address this travesty before he let himself get too preoccupied. "Whoever taught you gun safety should be ashamed of himself."

A smirk tugged at her lips. "That was you."

"Yes, and I'm duly ashamed." Options for wiping that smirk away crowded his mind, and he tore his gaze from the temptations of her mouth. "You can't keep a loaded weapon like this. It's not safe. You need a lockbox for it."

"I know." She came to his side and took the box from him. Fitting the lid back on firmly, she pushed it further under the bed, out of sight. "But it hasn't exactly been on the top of my priority list."

He steeled himself from the invitation in her tone. "Well, it should be."

"So, sue me. I have other priorities." She straightened and pressed against him until he had to sit on the bed or lose his balance. When he did, she straddled his knees, running deft fingers through his hair lightly, careful not to brush his scalp.

The sensation sent a shiver from the back of his neck to the base of his spine and further tightened the fit of his slacks. "You're trying to distract me."

"I thought that was obvious." Her lips curved, her gaze holding his with a magnetic force strong enough to short out an entire server bank. "Is it working?"

The woman was incorrigible. That gun had silver rounds in it, too. It was the one thing in the world that could kill her outright, and she kept it unsecured under her bed. "No. Yes. Promise me you'll do something about it. Or I'll have to do it myself."

"Do what?" She dipped her head, her mouth hovering a bare inch above his own.

"You'll see." With a growl, he grabbed her by the waist and flipped her onto her back on the mattress. Delilah chirped in protest and jumped down, but Sebastian paid her no mind. Lily's eyes flashed, her lips parted, and she bucked her hips toward his. Her skirt had ridden up, as he'd predicted.

"Oh no, you don't." He knew an advantage when he saw one, but he held himself in check—barely. "Remember, you have to tell me what you want."

"You," she whispered. "Sebastian, I want you."

The hitch in her breath as she said it almost undid him then and there. Capturing her wrists, he drew them gently above her head and held them with one hand, her long sleeves a thin layer between his hand and her hungry skin. She had more than enough strength to break free, but instead, her lids lowered, and she whimpered, back arching, breasts threatening to burst open the buttons on her blouse.

"Wait for it," he told her, just to hear her whimper of desire turn into a whine of protest. Still, she let him hold her down.

She chose to obey him in these moments. His head swam with arousal at the thought, and his fingers fumbled on her top button before he wrestled himself back under a fast-eroding control.

"Why?" Her voice thrummed with an echo of the power she wouldn't use. "Are you going to make me beg for it?"

He smiled at that. "Don't I always?"

"Every time," she said. "It's almost like you enjoy it."

"Are you saying I'm some kind of pervert, Ms. Knight?"

Her eyes popped open, and she fixed him with a mock-glare, though he would bet the frustration was real enough. "That's exactly what I'm saying, *Mister Ritter.*"

"Guilty as charged." The last button came undone, and he

spread the shirt out to either side of her with careful precision, a deliberate unwrapping. She wore a thin white camisole beneath it. This he lifted to reveal her slender waist and heaving ribcage before he pressed a long kiss over her hipbone.

She gasped at the contact. He felt the pull of her under his lips and tongue, magnetic and heady, an intoxication that clouded his mind with deepening need. Turning his attention to the skirt now barely covering her upper thighs, he pushed it up further, his free hand rougher now and no longer precise.

Beneath it, she wore—nothing. Not even one of the lacy black, scrap-of-thin-fabric thongs she liked to sport for their dates these days.

Her legs fell open, her pussy gleaming and wet with the slick of her arousal. There was no barrier between them, nothing to stop him sinking into her and taking her.

He raised his head and found her watching him with a lazy smile of triumph.

"Well? Did you still want me to beg?" But her body had already started begging for her, her pelvis tilting up to offer all the access he could want and then some.

He dipped a single finger into her, strummed her once with a delicate touch, like a particularly fine instrument. The gentle pull of her energy drain tingled along his skin, and her smile broke. She shook beneath him, moaned for him, the sweetest sound he'd ever heard.

"Now more than ever." He'd always had an ear for music.

She sighed, and it wasn't frustration anymore. It was her capitulation.

"You know you can have your way with me," she said, low and throaty, barely more than just a moan. "Any way you want me, I'm yours."

He covered her with his hand, and she ground up against it, her juices coating his palm as he held it still and steady. "I'm going to need you to be a little more specific."

"Please." Her voice was halting now, one good stroke from incoherence, and now he had her right where he liked her. "Please fuck me, Sebastian."

Her surrender was the only gift he wanted from her, so he took it slow and savored it.

With the lightest pressure, he circled her clit, taking her just to the edge of orgasm and no farther. She had better control over her kether pull than she gave herself credit for, but she lost it when she came. That intense pull would feel amazing, right up until he passed out, and he wanted this to last. He wanted to watch her fall for him.

The thin barrier of a condom helped mitigate the pull. She pouted when he snapped one on, though it couldn't prevent the contact where their bodies met. All the same, it took every ounce of control he possessed not to drive into her hard and fast when she begged like that. Instead, he entered her on a long, leisurely stroke, buried himself in her, and held her pinned for a long moment as she writhed on the knife's edge of pleasure, impaled on his cock and pleading for release.

Only then did he begin to move, deliberate at first, then with steadily increasing force. She bit her lip to hold back her rising cries, shuddering with each thrust. Her eyes met his, her irises brilliant green around blown pupils, and she said his name, halting as a prayer.

He answered it with his mouth over hers, and they fell together over the edge of her climax as her power drew him into the soft, dark oblivion he craved as much as her submission.

On Saturday night, Sebastian arrived at the house at six p.m. sharp. The outside of the restored Victorian blazed with multicolored string lights, including a full set of rainbow LED icicles ringing the eaves that made him smile. They hadn't gone up yet when he'd visited earlier in the week, so someone had been busy. He'd put money on Danny.

He set his portable food warmer on the step and rang the doorbell with the hand that wasn't occupied with carrying several heavy gift bags. After a minute or so, the door swung open. "You're early," Danny said sternly. "I thought you were the tamales."

"You said six p.m.."

"Is it six already? Well, you're the only one not on gay standard time. No, it's all right. Come in, come in." Her gaze fell on the warmer. "What's in there? Looks fancy."

"Not tamales," he said. "I hope you like beef Wellington."

"Holy... That *is* fancy. I knew I liked you for a reason."

"And this is for the house." He handed her one of the gift bags. "Happy... HannuMasFriendsWarming. I hope I got that right."

Danny laughed. "You do credit to your gender, sir."

Behind her, the kitchen door banged open. "We have a problem," Lily announced. She wore an apron that said *Kiss the Cook* over a knee-length, long-sleeved sweater dress the color of a good merlot. "This pie crust is a— *Sebastian!* What are you doing here?"

"He brought beef Wellington." Danny shot him a comically wide-eyed look. "I'll leave you to it." She mouthed "sorry" at him, grinned, and vanished into the depths of the house, leaving Lily and Sebastian to stare at each other, speechless.

"I take it Danny didn't tell you I was coming," Sebastian ventured finally.

"She did not." Lily had flour dabbed across her nose and a hectic flush in her cheeks. "Also, we told everyone else to be here at six-thirty."

"Ah. It would seem I was misinformed." He took in her stocking feet, which were also somehow smudged with flour, and her rolled-up sleeves. "You're really making a pie?"

"Allegedly. An attempted pie." She nodded at the bag in his hand. "What's that?"

"This is for you." With a modicum of trepidation, he held it out.

"Seb!" She took it, scowling no more than he expected. So far, so good. "You promised no holiday gifts."

"Hush. It's not a holiday gift. It's a housewarming present, which is non-reciprocal. Also," he added, "a safety precaution."

"A safety... *Oh.*" She pulled the paper aside, realization dawning. "I said I'd take care of that."

"No, you didn't."

"Well, I meant to!"

"And have you taken care of it?"

"No." She set the bag down on the hall table and pulled out the small lockbox. It was a little bigger than the shoebox, but still small enough to store under the bed.

"It's biometric," Sebastian said. "You can set it to your fingerprint or a PIN code. That way, no one else will be able to get to your weapon and use it against you."

"I see." She looked up at him, her flush deepening. "That's very... I don't know what to say."

"The generally accepted response is to say thank you." He thought this over. "In the alternative, I would allow a kiss."

"It *is* following the letter, but not the spirit of the law," she pointed out. "You're getting off on a technicality."

He bit back the innuendo that would probably push his luck. "Then I suppose I'll have to throw myself upon the mercy of the court."

"Hm," she said, but she stood on her tiptoes to kiss him, a quick, electric brush of her lips over his that brought back fresh memories of their last night together. "Thank you, Sebastian."

"You're welcome." Memories weren't the only thing on the rise. He leaned in for a second kiss, but she pushed him away.

"I've gotten flour all over you." She brushed at the lapels of his coat, which only compounded the issue. "And I need some kind of Christmas miracle to make this pie crust come together or we won't have dessert."

"Maybe I can help," he said, shedding the now-floured coat. "Show me this alleged pie."

She did a double take. "You *bake*?"

"Pastry is just science. And a little bit of engineering." He had to grin at her expression. "Please tell me you didn't think I used store-bought pastry for this Wellington."

"You made that *from scratch?* No, never mind. I need all the help I can get."

In the kitchen, he assessed the pastry situation while she dropped the gift bag at the bottom of her stairs. Lily's work area suggested an explosion in a flour factory, but the crust itself seemed sound enough, if a bit crumbly. He cuffed his sleeves at the elbow and busied himself with the rolling pin. After a moment, he looked up to find her watching him from the doorway.

"You know," she said softly, "you never told me what you wanted."

The question caught him off guard in the midst of the delicate process of transferring the crust to the tin. He nearly dropped it, which would have meant starting all over. As it was, it only landed a touch off-center. "I have everything I could possibly ask for."

Lily's gaze didn't waver. "That's not the same thing."

"It's enough." He slid the parchment paper out from under the flaky, barely cohesive pie shell with a sigh of relief. "There. Your crust is fine, Lily."

"Is it?" she whispered, and by her tone, she didn't mean the pastry.

"Yes." He couldn't ask for her heart, not when it had so recently been broken. All he could do was help her hold it safe.

His own feelings would keep, at least for now.

ALSO BY ERIN FULMER

Cambion Series:

Cambion's Law

Cambion's Blood

ABOUT THE AUTHOR

ERIN FULMER (she/her) is a public benefits attorney by day, author of urban fantasy and science fiction by night. A 2020 Pitch Wars alumna, she lives in sunny Northern California with her husband and two spoiled cats. When she's not writing or working, she enjoys hatha yoga, taking pictures of the sky, playing board games with friends, and napping like it's an Olympic sport.

IN SEARCH OF STARLIGHT

BY LILLA GLASS

"When warmth and sunlit pastures are all you've been blessed to know,
the grass somehow seems greener buried 'neath the stark, white snow."

1

PRINCE ARYN HAD NEVER KNOWN ANYTHING BUT SUMMER. HAVING spent each of his twenty-three lives presiding over the Seelie capital of Talunasa, where the sun was fixed high in a cloudless, cerulean sky and the leaves never withered, his existence was one of endless daylight, warmth, and comfort. He would not have changed a single detail for anyone.

Well, maybe for *one* person…

"Would you take a look at that?" Kyllean elbowed Aryn in the side, nearly knocking the atlas from his hands. "I call bagsies on the Sylph."

Aryn begrudgingly tore his eyes from a map of the Winter Wastes to spare the pair of women across the street a fleeting glance. Both were stunning in their own way—the Sylph, a pretty, pastel maiden with flowing white hair to match her robes; the Maithe, a sun-kissed beauty who'd used glamour to augment her glossy, bronze ringlets and bustline.

"You may have them both, if they're so inclined," he said, returning his attention to his tome. "I'm a little busy."

Kyllean's grimace was practically audible. "What's the point of going to the market if you're going to spend the whole day buried in a book?" he huffed. "You've got libraries aplenty back at Samhria. Give those girls another gander and tell me honestly—what's wrong with them?"

Aryn didn't need to look to give an honest answer. "They aren't *her*."

The brigadier's silence carried all the judgement of an hour-long lecture. They'd had this conversation a dozen times, and Aryn was beginning to doubt Kyllean would ever understand. Though all fae lived multiple lives, only the eternal monarchs shared those lives with the same person each time around. It didn't matter that Tearan had yet to reveal herself in this lifetime; Aryn would rather pine for her than kiss anyone else.

"You're not being fair to yourself." Kyllean's voice dripped pity as he grabbed hold of the almanac, gently tugging it from Aryn's grasp. "We've all heard the stories, Aryn. Yes, you and Tearan were literally made for each other, but not a single lifetime has passed in which she hasn't broken your heart. This is the first time you've reached adulthood without her by your side; would it kill you to have a little fun before the cycle repeats?"

A hollow yawned open in Aryn's chest. Having read the accounts of his history ad nauseum, he knew the tales better than anyone. Tearan was fickle where he was loyal, capricious where he was calm, and impulsive where he was unyielding; it was in her nature to eventually pull away, no matter how tightly he clung to her. Perhaps, as he aged, those memories would return to him in all their dolorous detail. For now, he recalled only how his heart fluttered at the sound of her laughter, how her eyes shone like burnished copper when she smirked, how she brought more light and warmth into his world than Talunasa's blinding sun.

Surely, those joys were worth whatever heartache they heralded.

"I am not passing judgment, friend," Aryn said, placing a hand on Kyllean's armor-clad shoulder. "Nor do I doubt that you mean anything but the best, but it is my burden, my honor, and my *choice* to walk the path the Creator has paved for me." He offered the soldier a gentle smile. "Now, why don't you hand the book over and go talk to those girls? As much as I appreciate your company, you shouldn't waste your off hours watching over me. I am not half as fragile as the King Regent suspects, and I'm confident I can parse through these wares without getting myself abducted or assassinated."

Kyllean pursed his lips but returned the atlas to Aryn. Scoundrel though he was, a more devoted guard or caring friend had never existed. And Aryn would know.

"Ten minutes," the soldier commanded as though he had authority. "That's far longer than it should take to buy a few Shadow-damned books."

Aryn nodded, making no promises, and Kyllean marched toward the girls. From the way their eyes roved his gilded uniform, they shared both his interest and intentions. The station of royal sentry was neither auspicious nor exciting, but, as Kyllean was so fond of saying, it had its perks.

Finally alone with the tables of books—not accounting for the impatient hobgoblin who glared at him from the sales counter—Aryn tucked the atlas beneath his arm and resumed his search for all things Unseelie. He'd have been content researching at the palace, Samhria, but his people's vanity had trickled into the libraries, so most every tome detailed Maithe history or lore. After twenty-three lifetimes spent ruling the Maithe, Aryn had learned more than enough about them.

The Korrid Sidhe were another story.

As the Highest House of the Unseelie, they contrasted the Maithe in nearly every way imaginable. Where Aryn's people were considered the pinnacle of the creation—sculptors of light who'd been steeping in summer since the dawn of time—the Korrids were sallow, wretched beings who lived in a land of endless cold and darkness and could bend both to their will. If the rumors held weight, their queen had recently set her glassy gaze on long-held

Seelie territories. Aryn cared little for gossip but saw no harm in preparing for the worst.

After a moment more of searching, he'd scrounged up three more promising titles—*A Brief History of Unseelie Politics, The Pilgrim's Guide to the Shadow Realms,* and *Rites and Rituals of the Winter Court.* He was eyeing a collection of Deepwinter Solstice recipes, wondering whether that particular stone was too small to bother overturning, when the shopkeeper's shout shattered his focus.

"Thief!" The hobgoblin pointed at a Glaistig girl—all green-draped curves and tangled red curls—who'd slipped from the tent with a book beneath her arm. "Someone, stop her!"

The Glaistig winked over her shoulder, giggling brightly, and the sound of her laughter set Aryn's heart aflutter. When she broke into a sprint, he tossed his tomes aside and barreled after her, propelled by an urgency he hadn't felt in ages.

The market was a bewildering maze of tents and wagons, but Aryn gained ground with every twist and turn, his eyes locked on his target despite the patterned fabrics and bushels of gemstones that glittered in his periphery. Now that the daylight hit her straight on, he could see the glamour wafting around her—a subtle shimmer of magic only an illusionist could spot, let alone sculpt. Between her laughter and the chase, his heart was already racing, but that confirmation goaded it to a gallop, and his feet followed suit.

He finally caught up when she dashed into a tailor's yurt and met a dead end between two racks of gossamer gowns.

"Tearan?" he asked, breathless. "Is it really you?"

She turned slowly to face him, the stolen tome still tucked into the crook of her arm. Though the pale mask she'd crafted looked nothing like the stunning, sun-kissed face from his memories, he'd have recognized that mischievous smirk anywhere.

"You really do know me, don't you?" she asked, arching an

eyebrow. Though she'd colored her irises a convincing crimson, all Aryn could see was candlelit bronze.

"Prince Aryn?" Kyllean called from somewhere in the streets, interrupting the reunion. "Have you found her?" His were not the only gilded footsteps racing about. In fact, it sounded as though a whole contingent of guards were on the prowl, eager to earn a royal accolade.

"Well, Aryn?" Tearan perched her hand on her hip. "Have you found me?"

Aryn had a hundred questions of his own, but they seemed to have lodged in his throat. As the guards drew closer, he realized there were more urgent matters at hand. "There's...there's no Glaistig in here!" he managed, edging as close to a lie as he could.

Most of the boots began marching away.

Tearan smiled, and the sight stunned Aryn from stag-spike circlet to sole. She planted a summer-warm kiss on his cheek, lingering long enough to make his heart ache, and placed the pilfered book in his hands. "Mind returning this for me, dearest?" she asked.

Before Aryn could answer, she'd slipped through the dresses to freedom. He remained frozen—his mind reeling and his cheeks fever-bright—until Kyllean's voice freed him from his trance.

"There you are!" The soldier strolled up behind him. "*Creator*, Aryn, you had me worried!"

"I'm... I'm sorry for darting off." Aryn turned, blinking his bewilderment away. "I thought I saw her head this way."

"Happens to the best of us." Kyllean patted Aryn's shoulder. "She'll show up again, eventually. We should head back to Samhria, for now, assuming you've found what you were looking for." He peered at the book in Aryn's hands, then burst out laughing. "No wonder you wanted to shop alone! Are you sure you don't need to call on one of those girls?"

Aryn glanced down and nearly dropped the tome. The cover illustration featured a couple twined in an extremely intimate pose, and the title was similarly salacious. His cheeks flushed even warmer than they had at Tearan's kiss—the exact reaction she'd doubtless been hoping for—but, embarrassed though he was, he couldn't help smiling.

Twenty-three lifetimes, and she hadn't changed a bit.

2

A FULL DAY HAD PASSED, AND ARYN'S CHEEK STILL TINGLED WHERE Tearan had kissed him. He tried to study in his chambers, but in the silence and stillness, he could think of only her. Eventually, he disguised himself and ventured into town again—this time, unaccompanied.

The Lodestone wasn't an ideal reading environment, but it was easily the quietest pub in Talunasa, especially midday. It had been literal ages since Aryn's last visit, so he didn't recognize the barkeep. Thankfully, the man showed the same disinterest as his predecessor when Aryn dropped his glamour, ordering a pint of amber and a specific booth toward the back. Aryn slipped him an extra silver to keep it that way. He did not want to lose his secret haunt, should word of his outing reach the King Regent.

Only once he'd settled onto the bench, stacking his tomes on the table, did he begin to doubt the wisdom of his trek. A lifetime back, when he and Tearan were young and love-drunk, they would sneak away from their respective chaperones and meet at that very booth to share a drink, some chips, and more kisses than were appropriate for a public setting. Warm though the memories were, they nearly drowned Aryn in want and worry. If Tearan missed him the same, she would surely have claimed her crown already.

Resolved to finish his pint before sulking away, Aryn grabbed the topmost of his tomes and flipped through its pages until he landed on an illustration of the Korrid palace, Gemhread. Colorless and grim, the ever-ice fortress sat upon a plane of snow that dipped and crested like beachside dunes, its gleaming spires and jagged battlements stretching toward an ink-dark night spackled with silver. Aryn shivered at the sight. If the Korrids were half as cold and cruel as their castle, they would prove formidable foes.

"Do you remember starlight?"

Aryn's heart leapt at the sound of Tearan's voice, and it nearly burst free when he turned to see her standing beside the table, undisguised. A soft smile graced her honeyed lips, her eyes shimmered with familiar mischief, and her smooth, chocolate tresses pooled at her feet, the light from a distant window limning them in a halo of purest gold.

Tearan giggled at Aryn's obvious awe, tossing a glossy lock over her shoulder, and he forgot her question—along with nearly every thought he'd ever had.

"Do I..."

"Remember starlight." She slid into the booth beside him, and heat sparked through his skin where her arm brushed his. "Before the worlds were made, before sides were drawn, before the Creator cast us from the sky, we would dance among them, suspended in the void. The darkness didn't frighten us back then, and we certainly didn't think it evil. How could it be, with all the brilliance it harbored?" She looked at Aryn, a restless longing burning in her eyes. "Do you remember?"

Aryn did remember. He remembered the constellations, arranged like notes on invisible staves, and the music they'd make when he strummed them from a distance. He remembered their polished silver gleam, their burnt-cedar scent, the way it felt to drift past them—like cracking the curtains of a chilly room to let in a sliver of sunlight.

When he next glanced at the illustration, the ink looked that much bleaker. "This doesn't do them justice."

"No, it most certainly does not."

They sat in silence for a moment, staring at the lackluster starscape, their forearms barely touching. Aryn longed to grab Tearan's hand, but the thought thoroughly flustered him, so he spoke instead. "I have no one to talk to about the time before the fall." He smiled sadly. "The others don't remember it—not in any detail, at least. They only listen and nod, as they do when I speak of anything. It's nice to have an actual conversation on the matter, even if it's made mostly of pauses."

The fire in Tearan's eyes flared all the brighter. "So, you understand, then?"

"About the stars?"

Tearan shook her head, a dark lock falling across her cheek. "About our lives." She grabbed his ale and took a deep drink. "It's clockwork, Aryn, and not only the conversations. Each day, we waste the bulk of our hours in the throne room, passing judgement on matters we couldn't possibly understand. Occasionally, if we're very lucky, we move to the Grand Hall to do the same before an audience."

"That's not all there is to it," Aryn said, though he'd never minded the work. "We've attended our share of festivals and fetes."

"And, were we commoners, we might even have enjoyed them. But we're burdened with *these*." She flicked Aryn's circlet askew, smirking when he reflexively straightened it. "There are always so many traditions to adhere to, so many hands to shake, so many speeches to give. *Shadows*, even our dances were choreographed ages back, the same steps and spins and sweeps for every song, every ball, every lifetime." She stole a second sip of ale, as though punctuating her point. "Can you honestly tell me, after twenty-two cycles, you're not raring to try something new?"

Tearan's comments unnerved Aryn for more than one reason. Though beautiful, her burgundy dress had been made from homespun fabric, accessorized with simple chord jewelry. She wasn't merely guessing that she'd enjoy time as a commoner; she'd tried it. Breathtaking as she was, she couldn't have possibly spent all that time alone.

"Something new?" Aryn asked, throat tight. "Or *someone*?"

Tearan laughed—a hollow sound so unlike her usual candlelit giggle—and waved him off. "Oh, like you haven't used your freedom to its fullest, pretty as you are."

Aryn's heart plunged. The texts had never specified Tearan's weapon of choice for piercing his heart, but he'd long feared unfaithfulness played a part.

Perhaps sensing his sorrow, Tearan darkened. "I...courted a boy from the outskirts for a while," she said, her voice dripping guilt. "It never went beyond chaperoned strolls. Once, I attended a play with a poet from the bay—a comedy, or it tried to be. A week back, I kissed a pretty barmaid down at Caryl's Tavern. It merited me a free side of butterbread."

"And?" Aryn held his breath, fearing the answer as much as he needed it.

"And..." Tearan grabbed his hand, "they weren't *you*."

Relief washed through Aryn, potent enough to make his head swim. He wasn't sure whether to kiss Tearan or simply keep staring into her beautiful, brazen eyes.

Before long, her attention shifted back to the tome. "The Winter Wastes, The Shifting Wilds, The Blight Bogs..." she read aloud as she flipped backward through the pages. "Unseelie territories, correct? What were you doing here, other than hoping I'd appear?"

Aryn blushed to know his motives were so transparent. "My hopes weren't in vain," he said, smiling meekly.

"They seldom are." Tearan tucked a golden lock behind his ear. Her fingers brushed his cheek on their way back, trailing heat. "But you didn't answer my question."

Aryn shifted uncomfortably, uncertain how much he could share. As his partner and peer, Tearan should have been privy to palace matters, only she hadn't accepted her crown yet. "It's only gossip."

"You abhor gossip." Tearan quirked an eyebrow. "If you're giving a rumor weight, it must be supremely unsettling."

Aryn inhaled deeply, glancing to the tome and back. If he could discuss his concerns with anyone, surely it was Tearan. "Some Solitary allies recently returned from the Winter Wastes," he said, squeezing her hand. "They claim Neachta intends to expand her kingdom into the Light Realms."

Tearan looked shocked for all of a second before bursting into irreverent laughter. "Is that all?" She finished off the last of Aryn's ale. "The Unseelie have long nipped at our borders; what's one more squabble?"

Aryn blinked, equally disturbed and fascinated by her flippancy. "I'm not talking about a battle, Tearan; I'm talking about *war*. The Korrids are the vilest of Unseelie—cold and calloused to their cores. If they are truly bereft of honor while we are bound to it, how can we possibly hope to defeat them?"

"Now, we haven't really gotten to know the Korrids, have we?" Tearan shrugged, her tone too playful. "Surely, they can't be all that bad."

Again, her logic perplexed him. "It's how the Creator arranged things. If we Maithe are closest to Heaven of all fae, then surely the Korrids are closest to Hell."

Tearan smirked as she stood, sliding her fingers from his. "If He truly loathes them so," she said, sauntering away, "why did He give them the stars?"

3

DESPERATE FOR SLEEP, ARYN HAD DRAWN HIS HEAVY BROCADE curtains and snuffed out all but the feeblest of candles, but thoughts of Tearan kept him lucid. How in the worlds could he hope to slumber with her honeysuckle perfume haunting him and the sweet song of her laughter ringing in his ears?

It wasn't fair. She should have been lying beside him, stealing a smidge more of the covers with her every toss and turn. He should have been able to roll over and brush the hair from her face, kiss the candlelit curve of her jaw, and yank the blanket back only for her to mumble a curse and swaddle herself that much tighter.

He supposed he could understand her reasoning. She'd never been fond of routines and responsibilities, and palace life was nothing but. Her fickle passion was the thing he'd always loved most about her, dangerous though it could be. Surely, there was a way he could both feed her fire and keep it contained...

A sharp rap on the window startled Aryn upright. Samhria had been crafted along the massive branches of Talune, the First Tree, and his quarters were near the crown. Either his visitor was a woodpecker, or they were a startling combination of fearless and foolish. Curious, Aryn shrugged off his covers and stretched to his feet, leaving his rapier on its stand. If an assassin had the decency to knock after climbing all that way, they deserved a brief but genial greeting before falling to Talune's roots.

He threw open the curtains, then startled back at the sight beyond the sill. The thing clinging to the window ledge had crackling brown skin to match Talune's bark and billowing leaves for hair. Before Aryn could run for his rapier, Tearan dismissed her disguise in favor of a trickster's grin.

"Are you just going to leave me hanging?" she asked, her breath fogging the windowpane.

Relief and panic flooded Aryn all at once. Realizing the danger Tearan was in, he rushed to toss the window open. She slid easily over the sill, having traded her flowing gown for tight trousers and a lace camisole that left little to memory.

The moment her toes hit the rug, Aryn's arms were around her, squeezing tight. "You could have gotten yourself killed," he breathed.

"Relax, dearest." Her laughter tickled his collarbone. "I connived my way through most of the palace, and those last couple stories were hardly a dangerous climb."

A single chuckle escaped Aryn's lips. They'd always had very different definitions of danger. Once his pulse reverted to its natural rhythm, Tearan pulled away just enough to smile up at him.

"Happy to see me?" she asked.

He was, despite the compounded frights she'd given him. Her presence in that room was both an answered prayer and a dream come true.

It was also a breach of etiquette.

"I'm thrilled." He released her, shying back a step. "But...this is my bedchamber."

"I'm well aware." Tearan took a bold step forward.

"And I don't keep servants." Another step back.

"Old habits die hard." Another step forward.

"So, we don't have a chaperone." Back.

"That's kind of the point." Forward.

Aryn bumped into the bed and nearly tumbled backward. Tearan sided with gravity, pushing him to the mattress. His nerves sparked like lightning as she climbed atop him and straddled his hips, her hair falling around him like a curtain. One second, her lips wore their usual smirk; the next, they met his with all the hunger of a wildfire. Her fingers fumbled with his hems, seeking skin, but he caught them before they undid the last of his laces.

"Wait," he managed in the breath between kisses. "We're not... We're not even courting, are we?"

"We've been married twenty-two times, Aryn." Tearan laughed. "It's not as though we haven't done this before."

"We have, and we haven't." Aryn's resolve startled him. With as much as he'd missed her, that scant excuse for a shirt should have been long gone. "I know you need spontaneity, but I need stability. I need to know we have a future."

Tearan smiled down at him, fluttering her lashes. "We've always had one before, haven't we?"

It wasn't really an answer, but it was close enough. This time, when their lips met, the hunger was mutual. Aryn had to fight to keep his hands gentle, his kisses soft. He pulled her further onto the bed and rolled her over, taking the lead. With every heartbeat, another detail came rushing back—he remembered how she liked to be kissed, how she liked to be touched, how she liked for him to move once she'd wrapped her legs around him.

For all the time Aryn had spent reminiscing about Tearan, there was so much he'd forgotten, like the way her body molded perfectly to his and the painful pleasure of her nails grazing his skin. He'd even forgotten the thrill he felt when she whispered his name, her back arching and her face flushing rose.

She whispered it twice before flipping him over and proving just how well she remembered *him*.

❄

Aryn held Tearan close, clothed only in her glossy hair. Her rhythmic breathing might have lulled him to sleep, were he not worried she'd vanish the moment his eyes closed. If it kept her there, he'd have stayed awake forever.

"I suppose it wasn't all so bad," she whispered, breaking the silence.

"Not so bad?" Aryn scoffed. "Surely, you misspoke. I believe the word you're looking for is '*phenomenal*,' but I would settle for '*exceptional*,' if you feel you must understate matters."

"I was referring to palace life." Tearan giggled, pushing him playfully. "But if, for all my stroking, I somehow missed your ego: yes, that was phenomenal."

Aryn grinned, brushing a chocolate lock from her face. With how she looked at him in that moment—her bronze eyes glittering and her smile soft as heather—he couldn't imagine feeling happier or more fulfilled. Nor could he imagine spending another night without her.

"Stay with me," he whispered, a prescient ache swelling in his chest. "Please, Tearan, you belong here."

Tearan's smile faded. "You know that's not an option. If I'm found here—"

"We'd be forced to wed." Aryn propped himself up on his elbow, his aurous hair falling over his shoulders to mingle with hers. "Would that really be so awful? As you said before, we've been married twenty-two times, and—"

"And that's twenty-two blessings amidst half a million curses." Tearan slid from the bed and began searching for her discarded clothing. "I'm not ready to return, Aryn."

Her words stung like an iron wound, leeching his warmth away. "Is there anything I can do differently?" he asked, rising to join her. "Anything at all that would change your mind?"

Tearan paused with her trousers half laced, looking up at him with mixed sorrow and adoration. Her silence lasted far too long— the space where a lie might have fallen, could the fae speak them.

"I'll be back before you know it." She kissed his cheek and started for the window, tucking her shirt into her beltline.

Aryn shook his head, bewildered by the shift in tone. "When?" he asked, catching up to her as she started over the sill.

"If I told you, it would spoil things." Tearan smirked over her shoulder. "As you said before, I need spontaneity."

"But *I* need stability," Aryn countered. "A future."

"Fair enough." Tearan's smirk softened and warmed all at once. "I'll stop by sometime in the next..." She hummed, mulling over her options. "...three nights. Scheduled spontaneity: how's that for compromise?"

Before Aryn could answer, Tearan hopped from the window ledge. He leaned over the sill to find only a tangle of branches below, then threw his curtains closed, determined to get some sleep while he still could. Tearan would return sometime in the next three nights. By then, he'd find a way to make her stay.

4

"WHY ARE WE DOING THIS, EXACTLY?" KYLLEAN ASKED, HELPING ARYN pull the curtains taught. "The seamstress is going to throw a fit."

Aryn grimaced, steadying an awl against the brocade fabric. He'd told his friend everything that had happened since their market trip—barring the more lascivious details—and he loathed repeating himself. "I've told you already." He punctured the curtain. "I'm trying to surprise Tearan."

"Ah, yes, Tearan, of course." Kyllean nodded tersely. "Again, I must ask: *why*?"

Aryn moved the awl, hoping he'd gauged the distance correctly. He remembered the patterns with vivid clarity, but that didn't mean he could recreate them. "Because she likes surprises," he said, piercing the curtain again, "and because she needs a reason to stay."

Kyllean watched Aryn work for nearly a minute—his eyebrow quirking higher with every hole punched—before asking the question Aryn feared most. "Shouldn't you be reason enough?"

Aryn stifled a sigh. It really didn't matter whether he *should* have been enough for Tearan. If he had been, she wouldn't have left him in every lifetime.

This time around, things were going to be different.

"Done." Aryn yanked the curtains from Kyllean's hands, and darkness filled the room as they fell closed. A sprinkling of sunlit specks stretched across the floor in front of the window, a little too hazy and much too yellow.

"It looks like moths attacked your drapes," Kyllean said. "As for the, um, 'stars'..."

"They're pathetic." Aryn glared down at the disappointing glimmers. "What about sprites?"

"Excuse me?"

"You know, *sprites*. They twinkle and hover and whatnot—the water variety even have a silvery glow. Perhaps, if I gathered a whole clique of them—"

"You want to release dozens of pests in your bedroom," Kyllean threw the curtains open, nearly blinding Aryn with a burst of sunlight, "to impress a girl?"

"Well, when you put it that way, it sounds silly." Aryn collapsed into the nearest chair, rubbing his temples. "What should I do, Kyllean? She's all I've been able to think about for years. Now that she's finally returned, I can't lose her."

"But you *will* lose her." Soft though Kyllean's voice was, it cut like a knife. "I'm not trying to be cruel, but you know how this ends."

"That's just it." Aryn buried his fingers in his hair, knocking his circlet loose. "I don't know. Not really. The books are maddeningly vague on the subject, and, while my memories are clearer than those of most, they manifest just like everyone else's. When I was a child, I could recall only my past childhoods, as a youth, I remembered my youths—so on, so forth. By the time I remember Tearan's reasons for leaving, it will..." His breath hitched, strangled by a sob. "It will be too late."

Aryn could sense Kyllean's pitying stare without looking. Eventually, the brigadier sighed softly. "I...may know someone who can help."

✳

The Red Realm of the Daoine Sidhe—closest allies of the Maithe —was located either directly above or below Talunasa, depending on who gave the directions. Aryn kept quiet as Kyllean led him down a stone staircase that connected the two kingdoms, even when gravity flipped and the red clay desert that had sprawled below—broken by crystal gardens and rivers of magma—suddenly loomed above them. Only once they'd reached the bottom—er, top?—step did Aryn ask one of his many, gnawing questions.

"You have a close friend in the Red Realm?" He tugged at his collar, feeling suffocated by the arid atmosphere. "Why haven't I ever met them?"

"'Close friend' might be an exaggeration." Kyllean's smile bordered on a guilty grimace. The ruby sun above colored his armor coral, lending him an impish air. "She's more of a...useful acquaintance."

"Why do I feel like I don't want to know more?"

"Because you don't." Kyllean shrugged. "But you *need* to know more—if you really want starlight."

Aryn swallowed his remaining concerns as they marched through a city of clay cliffside buildings, over fields of shimmering fluorite riddled with quartz clusters, and down a narrow canyon marred by briarback tracks and wagon trails. His suit was sweat-soaked by the time they reached their destination—a series of yawning caves in the side of a red shale mountain.

"The Melding Caverns?" Aryn gawked at the nearest entrance. The caverns weren't technically off-limits, but they were useless to Seelie and Unseelie both. Unaligned Solitary fae often used them to pass between realms, sans potion, and the occasional mortal stumbled through them unawares. "I've no doubt that darkness hides beasts and bandits both, but it is not the type to harbor stars."

"It's a meeting place." Kyllean produced a taper he'd clearly pilfered from Aryn's room and used a match to light it. "Follow me."

Together they wound through a dizzying series of tunnels, each an echo of the last. Soon, they found themselves in a spacious hollow, the walls coated in shimmering white crystals.

"She'll arrive in five minutes, give or take." Kyllean leaned against the wall, examining his nails in the candlelight. "You're lucky I already had something scheduled."

"Why did I need to come with, anyway?" Aryn imitated his friend's posture, and the crystals bit into shoulders, rousing the scratches Tearan had left. "Couldn't you have brought...*whatever* back to the palace?"

"Her costs vary by the buyer," Kyllean's gaze dropped to his toes, "and she only sells goods to those who intend to use them."

Every word of that sentence sparked a question in Aryn. Before he could ask them, a robed figure burst through the wall beside him, crystals rippling in her wake. Aryn startled, reflexively pressing his palm to the wall. Still solid and sharp.

"Who is thissssss?" The figure lowered her hood to reveal a withered face covered in amber scales. Her silver eyes were slitted like a serpent's, and two tiny fangs poked from her lipless mouth, a forked tongue flicking out between them. "I never approved a guessst."

"A hag?" Aryn growled at Kyllean. "Why didn't you tell me?"

"Because you're a bit biased." Kyllean crossed his arms, his gaze shifting to the hag. "And so are you. Now, before you start hexing and stabbing each other, allow me to make introductions. Aryn, meet Lusca—yes, she's a hag, but she's not going to curse you. Lusca, meet Aryn—yes, he's a royal, but he's not going to tattle."

Lusca maintained her glare, and Aryn returned it with his own. Though hags were not technically Unseelie, they were the closest a Solitary could get. At best, they were unreliable friends—at worst, nefarious fiends.

"Fine." Lusca hissed. "What do you ssseeek?"

"Oh, nothing much." Kyllean tossed her a small sack of coins.

"A few bulbs of shadowroot, maybe some essence—I'm thinking pollen sprite this time."

"*Kyllean!*" Aryn blinked at his friend, aghast. He'd known the soldier was fond of strong drink and lightleaf, but contraband was another matter entirely.

"So I dabble." Kyllean rolled his eyes. "I have my weaknesses; you have yours. Speaking of, why don't you tell Lusca here all about her?"

"It'sss about a girl?" The hag smiled in the eeriest manner possible, her tongue tasting the air. "I sshould have known from the sssorrowful ssscent of you."

Aryn logged his lecture away for later, returning his focus to the uncomfortable task at hand. Careful to conceal Tearan's identity, he recited an abridged version of his struggle, emphasizing her wistful love of starlight.

Lusca wrung her scaly hands all the while, her reptilian smile stretching. "I've got jussst the thing," she said, pulling a glass bottle from her robe. Its contents were darker than the blackest ink, swirling with silver constellations.

Aryn knew a travel potion when he saw one. The pastel varieties granted passage between the Light Realms and were sold by most common vendors. The earthier recipes, linked to the Mortal Realm, were well-regulated but obtainable.

Then there were the darker hues.

"I really hope that's bound to an obscure mortal territory," Aryn said, knowing better.

"Mortal ssskies are cloudy thisss ssseason." Lusca shook the bottle, and the constellations rearranged, winking brightly. "You wanted sssstarlight, yesss?"

Aryn stared at the potion for a long while. Ominous though it was, the glitter reminded him of how Tearan's eyes sparkled when she spoke of the stars. He could only imagine how she'd light up upon actually seeing them.

"How much for two bottles?"

5

Aryn stared out his open window, hoping Tearan would appear, and the gentle breeze that rustled his ruined curtains chilled him more than it should have. After some haggling, Lusca had traded him a pair of potions in exchange for a day's worth of sunlight. While Aryn hadn't fully understood the terms, he'd felt colder since agreeing to them.

A box, meticulously wrapped and tied with a silver ribbon, sat on the bed beside him. Inside it rested four potions—two black, two grass-green—and a golden rapier, all swaddled in an ermine cloak. Lusca couldn't—or perhaps *wouldn't*—tell him the exact location the potions were linked to, but if that atlas he'd found was accurate, the Winter Wastes were mostly uninhabited wilderness steeped in snow. Wherever they landed, the fur would keep Tearan warm, and the sword...

Well, hopefully, she wouldn't need the sword.

As far as Aryn knew, no Seelie fae had ever set foot in the Wastes, aside from attending the occasional summit along the border. Technically, there were no laws against such journeys, but only because no one was foolish enough to make them. In addition to the Korrids, the land was home to brutish Ice Trows and legions of headless Dullahan—not exactly the safest of daytrip destinations.

"Waiting for someone?"

Tearan's voice nearly startled Aryn from his skin. He glanced around to find her leaning against his bookshelf, laughing hysterically.

"How..."

"I had a tunnel installed last lifetime." She wiped a bemused tear away as she sauntered toward him. "I won't reveal its location, but it leads straight to the kitchen."

"You installed a secret snack tunnel, and you never told me?"

"There were only so many leftover pastries each evening; I didn't need the competition." Tearan crawled onto the bed. "Now, don't look so betrayed. I promise to make it up to you."

"With pastries, I hope."

"With something sweet." She brushed his hair aside and pressed her lips to the nape of his neck, sending sparks down his spine. His thoughts turned to a tumult as her kisses drifted and deepened, finding their way to the sensitive crook of his shoulder. By the time he shook his head clear, she'd freed him of his tunic and was working on his belt.

"Not yet," Aryn whispered, half-hating himself for it. "I have a gift for you."

"I know." Tearan smirked. "I'm *trying* to unwrap it."

Aryn chuckled as he grabbed the box from the bed beside him. Tearan snatched it eagerly away. Somehow, she undid fifteen minutes of wrapping in a quarter-second, then tossed the lid aside, her eyes widening on the ermine cloak.

"It's gorgeous, Aryn," she breathed, caressing the fur. "But...isn't it a bit warm for Talunasa?"

Aryn nodded. "There's more."

Tearan gingerly folded the corners of the cloak back, revealing the potions and blade nestled inside. "We're going on an adventure?" Her smile shone like sprite light. "Where to?"

"It's a surprise," Aryn said, knowing she'd prefer that answer to any other.

Within seconds, Tearan was dressed and armed and ready to go. Aryn took a bit longer to prepare, and she bounced on the balls of her feet all the while. He couldn't recall having surprised her this way before, but he resolved to try it again next lifetime and in every lifetime thereafter. In all his many memories, she'd never looked so happy.

Blade and coat donned, Aryn uncorked a bottle. "Are you ready?"

She kissed his cheek. "Always."

"Three...two..."

Tearan chugged her potion, and Aryn rushed to follow suit. The flavor surprised him pleasantly. Most such tinctures tasted of cheap gin and mulch; this was a strong, crisp mint with a smoky after-taste. Whatever the glimmers were, they tickled his throat on the way down.

Aryn's room smeared to a beige and burgundy eddy, and gravity spun with a similar zeal, lifting him from the floor. He reached out for Tearan but couldn't find her in the chaos, his fingers grazing only wind. Soon, streaks of black and white bled into the mix, and his feet landed on solid—and surprisingly slippery—ground.

The world stopped churning long before Aryn's stomach did, and he found himself not in a field of starlit snow, but in a long, vaulted hallway crafted entirely of quartz. Captive sprites fluttered inside the glass orbs which dangled from the ceiling, their silver glow sparkling against checker print tiles below, and a haunting melody wafted in from a distant doorway, beyond which lay a gleaming balcony backlit by effervescent light.

Tearan drifted down the corridor, drawn like a sailor to a Selkie's song, and Aryn scrambled after her, nearly slipping in his haste. He caught up right as she reached the doorway, and they pressed their backs to the wall before peering around the glassy frame. Aryn shivered, having never touched anything so cold.

Below lay a spacious ballroom, its peaked ceiling held aloft by glistening crystal pillars wrapped in spiraling evergreen garlands. Dancers twirled in pairs across the checkered floor, their bone-white skin contrasting with their inky suits and gowns. Above the crowd, an ocean of silver-blue sprites ebbed and flowed to the seemingly sourceless sway of violins, serving as the only light.

A crimson carpet cut a violent gash across the floor, then climbed the steps of an ivory alcove framed in silver fractals. There, a woman sat upon a jagged, glassy throne, her skeletal fingers laced beneath her chin. Her glittering, night-black hair was pinned up behind a crystalline crown, and her ebony gown pooled like tar at her feet, shadows wisping around the hem. Even from a distance, her eyes looked like clouded marbles. Malice seethed in their eerie depths.

Given Aryn's recent research, the pieces fell together easily enough. The walls were not hewn from quartz, but from ever-ice. The woman upon the throne was Queen Neachta. The reverie she surveyed was the Deepwinter Solstice celebration.

Aryn had whisked Tearan off, not to a starry paradise, but to the heart of the Korrid palace, Gemhread.

6

"We need to leave," Aryn whispered, fear skittering down his spine. He pulled the Talunasan travel potions from his pockets, but when he tried to hand one to Tearan, he was startled to find she'd vanished.

Panicked, he peered beyond the doorframe and saw Tearan descending a staircase to the ballroom, having darkened both her hair and cloak and blanched her skin to ivory. While she made a convincing Korrid, Aryn would have known her by her posture alone. Hopefully, the true Korrids were not so discerning.

When he donned a similar disguise, his temperature dropped by at least five degrees, and his thoughts grew hazy. Doubtless, the symptoms were linked to Lusca, but he had no time to ponder the particulars—not with Tearan sauntering straight into a viper's nest.

Weak though he was, he pushed off the wall and started down the steps, catching up as Tearan reached the second of four landings.

"What are you doing?' he hissed, resisting the urge to grab her arm. He was unfamiliar with Korrid customs and would not risk drawing scrutiny.

"I've long wanted to attend a ball as a commoner," Tearan's

frosted-glass gaze sent a shiver through him, "and you've been seeking information on the Korrids. It seems the Creator has blessed us with a perfect opportunity for both."

Aryn had about a hundred more objections, but he buried them as they descended the final flight of stairs. A pair of Dullahan flanked the bottom balusters, their armor so dark it swallowed the sprite-light that gleamed off the blades of their massive ever-ice axes. Though they lacked heads, Aryn somehow felt them staring as he and Tearan passed between them.

The moment Tearan's toes touched the tiles, she drifted swiftly and wordlessly across the frost-slicked floor. Aryn could not hope to catch her, lacking the grace and poise she'd been blessed with in abundance. Naturally, she accepted the hand of the first Korrid to proffer one, and Aryn's heart sank as they swept into a fluid dance. He hadn't been thrilled about attending the celebration, but he'd at least hoped they'd attend it *together*.

Utterly dejected, Aryn scanned the ballroom, seeking somewhere to sulk. There was much he hadn't noticed from the hallway: dozens of Dullahan standing sentry along the walls, a string orchestra huddled beneath the balcony, a feasting area cordoned off by evergreen garlands, almost entirely deserted. With few other options, Aryn started slowly toward the scarlet-draped tables, each overflowing with fruits and nuts and frosted cakes—gifts from the Mortal Realm, offered in honor of the Solstice. A dozen crystalline fountains rose from the bounty; surely, at least one boasted something strong enough to smother his sorrow.

He strode between the tables for some time before finding a fountain of mead. At least, he *thought* he detected a hint of honey amidst the cloying flavors of cinnamon and clove. The drink seared his throat in a pleasant way, restoring some of the heat he'd lost to his glamour. He was filling his flute a fourth time when fingers trailed across his back—summer-warm, even through his coat.

"I've heard Korrids have frigid skin," he muttered, eyes fixed on the fountain. "I'm surprised your dance partner didn't melt at your touch."

"You mean, like you do?" Tearan wrapped her arm around his, and the simple gesture threatened to thaw him. "You're not jealous, are you, dearest?"

"How could I not be?" Aryn forced himself to look at her. "Charming as you are, that man has probably already fallen for you."

Tearan tilted to her tiptoes, stopping just shy of a kiss. "Then he'll be disappointed to learn I'm spoken for." She winked, smirking. "Hopefully, the information I've gleaned can make up for any worry I've caused you."

While Aryn was relieved to learn she'd only been playing spy, her confession of devotion soothed him twice as much. Perhaps this impulsive venture had not been in vain after all.

"Shall we discuss your findings over a dance?" He smiled softly, tucking a glittering lock behind Tearan's ear.

"That would be lovely." She threaded her fingers through his, and, together, they drifted out onto the dance floor.

Aryn had never been the most agile dancer, and the frosted floor conspired with the mead to make him that much worse. Luckily, Tearan had always possessed skill enough for two. She led his steps with perfect poise, hardly lifting her feet as they twirled across the tiles, and every measure of music brought them closer. Soon, they'd melded into a tight embrace, their arms tangled and their hips brushing. The dance was unlike any of those practiced in Talunasa, and Aryn didn't mind one bit.

"Well, dearest," Tearan rested her chin on his shoulder, swaying in time with the violins "would you like to hear what I've learned?"

"Of course," Aryn said, though, honestly, he'd already forgotten about her subterfuge. With her body pressed flush against his, it was hard to focus on anything else.

"It seems the rumors held some truth," her breath tickled his ear, "but it is not so dire as you thought. From what Duke Ylin said—"

"That man was a duke?"

"Focus, dearest." Tearan giggled, nuzzling against him. "He was able to confirm that Neachta is crafting a battle plan, but only as a retaliatory measure. Apparently, she's convinced *we're* planning a strike against *her*. Unless something happens to confirm that suspicion, we've nothing to fear."

The words might have comforted Aryn, were it not for one unfortunate detail. "Our very presence here could serve as confirmation. We need to leave this place before—"

"There you are, M' lady."

The grim voice surprised Aryn and Tearan both, and they froze, angling to face the speaker. He was threateningly handsome for a milky eyed monster—clad in a dapper, black-and-raspberry suit, his alabaster hair frosted into perfect curls. A silver rapier gleamed from the scabbard on his belt, a perfect match for the buttons on his tailcoat and the delicate chain of his pocket watch.

"I understand you are new to Gemhread," he stated, his eerie gaze fixed on Tearan, "but it is common etiquette to share three dances before switching partners. The slight is forgivable, but I demand you join me for the remaining two."

Aryn felt Tearan bristle. She'd never been the type to tolerate demands. As amusing as it would have been to watch her knock the duke's teeth out, it would definitely have drawn unwanted attention.

"As it happens, we were about to leave." Aryn wrapped a possessive arm around Tearan's waist. "I'm sure you'll find another partner once you cease harassing mine."

It might have been impossible to notice the duke's dead eyes flitting to Aryn, were it not for the subtle flicker of his eyelids and the irritated curl of his lip. "And you are?"

"Hers," Aryn said, finally confident that she was his as well. "Now, if you'd kindly move aside..."

Before Aryn could take a step, the duke removed his velvet glove and slapped it across his face. Aryn's jaw flexed, but he held his breath, praying the gesture meant something different for the Korrids than the Maithe.

The duke's next words dashed that hope.

"I challenge you to a duel!"

7

DESPITE ARYN'S BEST EFFORTS, HE'D MANAGED TO DRAW THE SALLOW eyes of every Korrid in the ballroom—Neachta's included.

"It's about time something interesting happened." The Korrid Queen's words were more rasp than voice, but they carried through the room like a trumpet's bellow, bringing the music to a sudden stop. "Gather round, my children." She rose from her throne, and a shadowy haze followed her to the edge of the alcove. "The show is about to begin."

Tearan pressed close to Aryn as the dancers drifted toward them, forming an inky ring around a dueling ground as slick and frigid as a charlatan's smile. "You don't have to do this," she whispered to Aryn, worry threaded through the words. "There's no reason you should risk your life when I could skewer that cur myself."

"I don't doubt you could," Aryn said, warmed by her concern. "Unfortunately, he was wise enough not to challenge *you*."

Tearan's grip tightened around his waist, and teardrops glistened in the corners of her clouded eyes. Hours before, he'd have done anything to merit such affection; now, he wanted only to see her safely home.

"Don't you fret." He cupped her face, forcing a smile. "Just stand nearby. At first opportunity, I'll craft a distraction, and we'll make for an exit."

The tiniest of smiles tugged on Tearan's lips—not confident, by any means, but not dismissive either. "Be careful, dearest," she breathed, kissing him on the cheek.

The duke scoffed aloud. "I'll keep her company when you're gone, if that's what you're worried about." He wore the smug smirk of a man who dueled daily and hadn't been tagged once. "At least for a night."

Aryn caught Tearan by the shoulders right as she lurched forward, veering her toward the audience. Amazingly, she kept the course upon release, though she shot Aryn's rival her most withering glare.

"Shall we call it five paces?" The duke unsheathed his rapier with an unnecessary flourish. "Or would you prefer the extra bout of breath an additional five might buy you?"

"Five paces it is." Aryn produced his golden blade, cloaked in silver as part of his disguise. "The sooner I defeat you, the better."

"Not so fast," Neachta rasped from her alcove. Aryn glanced back to see a smile spread across her face, stretching her skin so thin he could see the contours of her skull. "It would be careless, leaving a body to rot in the Wastes, and far too merciful a fate." She nodded to the two nearest Dullahan, and they began marching toward the circle. "Let us up the stakes, shall we?"

Aryn was still puzzling over her words when a headless soldier knocked the rapier from his hands, replacing it with an ever-ice axe. Having never wielded such a weapon, Aryn nearly toppled sideways, thrown off by the unbalanced weight. His foe laughed from across the circle, though he wasn't handling his axe much better, and Aryn's throat went dry.

Neachta had upped the stakes, indeed. A natural death would have hurt Aryn's pride, but he'd have been reborn eventually. Those unfortunate enough to be decapitated by ever-ice enjoyed no such solace—their souls doomed to languish between lives while their body served as a Dullahan. Such enthrallment only ended when their master died or dismissed them. Neachta seemed intent on living forever, hording as many heads as she could.

A Dullahan made a chopping motion with its arm, and the duke marched forward with a sadistic grin plastered on his face. Aryn did the same, fighting to keep both his grip and gait strong. When he met his foe at the center of the circle, they stood back-to-back with Aryn facing Neachta. Hating the sinister gleam in the Korrid Queen's eyes, he let his own drift to Tearan. The troubled look on her glamour-masked face bolstered him by a startling degree.

When Neachta muttered the word, "Commence," Aryn started counting paces and priorities.

One...

Light's sake, this floor is slippery.

Two...

Surely, axes cut the same as swords.

Three...

Hopefully, there's no cutting whatsoever.

Four...

I cannot leave Tearan to rule alone for eternity.

Five.

Aryn whirled just in time to block a blow from his opponent, and a sliver of ever-ice cracked free on the shaft of his axe. The impact sent him sliding backward, but he managed to keep his footing, and the duke let out a triumphant laugh, lunging forward with a second attack. This time, Aryn dodged the axe easily. He might've landed a slash of his own, had he any intention of attacking.

As the duke stumbled past, flung forward by the strength of his strike, Aryn decided it was time to act. Surely, if an innocent bystander jumped from the crowd into the fray, it would cause enough confusion to allow for an escape. Subtly as he could manage, he moved to craft that very illusion. Glamour leeched from his body, gathered on his fingertips, whirled invisibly through the air, and...sputtered out.

By the time Aryn realized what was happening, the duke had regained his footing. His haughty grin had vanished, and his knuckles flexed red around the weapon. Apparently, the time for showmanship had passed.

Again, Aryn tried to summon his glamour, but the effort only left him frigid and dazed. He barely ducked his foe's next swing, and several sable locks fell to his feet, reverting to glossy gold. Aryn skated across the tiles, drawing attention away from the telltale tresses, then spun to shoot Tearan a wide-eyed glance. Creases formed across her perfect brow as understanding settled in.

When the duke next rushed at Aryn, Tearan did the same, wreathing herself in illusory fire with the flick of a slender finger. It wasn't the subtlest illusion, but it was certainly effective. Every Korrid in eyeshot scrambled back from the flames, gasping, Aryn's foe included.

Next thing Aryn knew, he was flying across the ballroom, Tearan's arms locked around his. False flames trailed alongside them as they ran, flickering and stretching and taking on strange hues. Soon, they morphed into exact reflections of Tearan and himself, complete with disguises and false flames of their own. Aryn gaped at Tearan in utter awe. She'd always been the stronger illusionist, but this bordered on miraculous.

"It's only glamour!" The duke's voice was the first to ring out over the startled din behind them. "They must be Maithe!"

"Seelie spies!" Neachta shouted. "After them!"

Aryn could practically feel the queen's skeletal finger pointing his way as her followers' footsteps swelled to a storm. Tearan scattered her illusions in a dozen directions, and the clamor grew all the more frantic. She pulled Aryn across the frosted floor, crossing paths with more than one pair of doubles, then sprinted into the nearest of a hundred dusk-dark corridors, letting her fire fade away.

ARYN BURIED HIS HANDS IN HIS POCKETS, CLASPING HIS TRAVEL
potions tight as he stared down at Gemhread from a distant, hillside perch. A small contingent of Neachta's forces circled the
palace, led astray by Tearan's false footprints, but the rest remained
within the ever-ice walls—probably still chasing after phantoms.

It must've taken an unfathomable amount of daylight to keep so
many illusions in motion at once, but Aryn was no longer
surprised. The sun itself could scarcely outshine Tearan.

"I've never seen anything so beautiful," she whispered, drawing
Aryn's eyes. She'd craned her neck to look up at the stars, and her
gorgeous face was bathed in their silver glow. The ethereal light
turned her hair to fierce mahogany and her eyes to gleaming gold,
but the awestruck smile that parted her lips was, by far, the most
stunning thing about her.

"Neither have I." Aryn wrapped his arm around her shoulders
and let his worries fade into the night. There was still much to fret
over—they might have just started a *war*, for light's sake—but it
could wait until morning. For now, he wanted only to enjoy a hard-
earned respite with the person he most ardently adored.

For the first time since their escape, he allowed his gaze to drift upwards, and he was lost at once to the luminous, glittering sea. Constellations sparkled bright among the milieu—stags and spriggans and warrior kings—and cloudy wisps of red-plum and navy roiled about the ink-dark depths, subtle as watercolors on obsidian. For a moment, Aryn's memories overtook him, and he was drifting between the glimmers, bathed in their silvery glow and burnt-cedar scent. Then Tearan nuzzled beneath his chin, her warmth bleeding into his skin and spirit both, and that past seemed dreadfully droll compared to the present.

A teardrop splashed on his collarbone, startling him. "I'm so sorry, dearest," Tearan muttered. "I truly tried."

"Whatever are you apologizing for?" Aryn shifted to look Tearan in the eyes, thoroughly confused.

Tearan took a deep, shaky breath. "Everything you've done tonight has reminded me of just how noble and selfless and wonderful you are, and of why"—her breath snagged, catching beneath her collarbone—"of why I could never deserve you."

"What in the worlds are you talking about?" Aryn cupped her face. "You are the most brilliant being in all creation; if anyone is unworthy, it's me."

Tearan shook her head, a fresh flood of tears welling along her lashes. "I've been terribly selfish. I know it's hard for you to understand, but I've had good reason to avoid you all these years."

"You were bored of palace life." Aryn forced a feeble smile. "I may not share your disdain for our station, but I understand it, Tearan, because I understand *you*. You are fire itself—passionate and unpredictable; it is only natural you should blaze a new trail every now and again."

"That's a portion of the truth," Tearan placed her hand atop his like she was afraid he'd pull it away, "but not all of it. I've read the stories, dearest, and I know how they end. While I honestly can't fathom ever breaking your heart, I know I've done it before, and I'm destined to do it again. I was trying to keep my distance because...because..."

"Because you don't want to hurt me." The sentiment soothed Aryn as much as it surprised him.

Tearan nodded, and another tear trickled free, catching on Aryn's thumb. "But I missed you desperately, and I'm weak. When I saw you in the market the other day, I couldn't resist reaching out, and now—"

"And now we're together," Aryn interrupted, caressing her cheek. "That is not a bad thing, Tearan. Do you have any idea how long I've been pining for you? How many nights I've spent wishing you were there to steal the covers? How many meals I've spent staring at the empty chair beside me, wanting nothing more than to grab your hand and chatter idly about whatever silly things we'd witnessed throughout the day?" He kissed her forehead, lingering, then returned his gaze to hers. "Let me be clear, my love: I would rather spend one wondrous week with you, knowing it will end in misery, than waste a full lifetime without you."

Tearan broke into a smile so brilliant Aryn couldn't help but kiss it, and they twined into an embrace warm enough to melt the snow around them. Though his pasts spoke of sorrow and storm clouds gathered in his future, Aryn allowed himself to drown in the present. In those stretched seconds, Tearan was his, and he was utterly, helplessly hers. There was much he did not yet remember of his history, but he was certain he'd never experienced a moment so breathtakingly beautiful.

It was worth whatever heartache it heralded.

ALSO BY LILLA GLASS

The Reel of Rhysia Series:

The Unseen (coming July 2023)

ABOUT THE AUTHOR

LILLA GLASS is an author from Olympia, WA. While fantasy is her first love, she dabbles in horror, sci-fi, and the occasional (gasp) non-speculative work. In 2021, she signed a four-book deal with City Owl Press for her darkly whimsical fantasy series, *the Reel of Rhysia*. The first installment (the Unseen) is set to be released in July 2023.

Lilla's short stories have been featured in several anthologies, including 13 by 11 and the *Bells of Christmas 2* (published by Papillon du Pere), *Enchanted Entrapments* (published by Madhouse books), and *Magic Beneath the Mistletoe* (published by Mystic Owl Press). Her fantasy comedy, "Best Spuds," received a Silver Honorable Mention from Writers of the Future in 2021.

In the rare event that she isn't writing, Lilla works one of those pesky day-job thingies, reads stories and poetry she wishes she wrote, hangs out with her husband and bunny, and tosses herself into the occasional mosh pit.

THE LIGHT IN HIS DARKNESS

BY MABRY BLACKBURN

AUTHOR'S NOTE

Father, forgive us – for this is fiction.
But in all seriousness, this installment is a prequel to the
shenanigans that take place in the upcoming novel *Graves Hollow:
Kill Devil MC Book 1,* which features the heretofore mentioned Dane
as the main character. We really hope that you accept our apologies
in advance for any feelings we may summarily eviscerate, but
please know that it's ALL in the name of the story and as strange as
it may be, everyone does get a happy ending.

All our love, Happy Holidays, and as always, enjoy the ride.
~ Mabry Blackburn

1

SOMEONE WAS GOING TO DIE.

As he pulled into the clearing that led to the clubhouse, Aim almost had to squint. Multi-colored twinkle lights draped over every single surface—the porch, around the windows, in the landscaping around the two-story, white farmhouse, on stakes lining the walkways...

On the bikes!

The pulsing lights, reflecting off several motorcycles, flooded out into the space between his car and the door, and it almost looked like a road accident had taken place with all the red and blue shining in the sky. Riding during the winter months wasn't something they typically did, but as they'd had to clear out the huge garage to accommodate the holiday festivities, the bikes had been moved out and lined up in front of the house that had been designated their clubhouse since the founding days of the Kill Devil Motorcycle Club. There was zero way in hell any of the others would have done this, and any person who'd spent any sort of time with the crew *knew* the bikes were off limits.

"Fuck." He grabbed the case of beer and his contribution to the stupid secret Santa exchange from the back seat. Mixing with the strobing Christmas lights was the sound of what had to have been the second run of the mandatory twenty-four hours of *A Christmas Story*. Aim glanced at the large window of the house's front room and grimaced. Sure as shit, even their own full-sized version of the *Major Award* was wrapped in lights.

"Nope. That's just a bridge too far," he spat out, slamming the car door.

He was already in sensory overload. He didn't celebrate holidays—not even birthdays—and there was no way he would normally have been up for whatever seasonal nightmare the guys might have come up with. He'd already been warned well in advance that tonight... Well, tonight there would be peopleing.

Fuck, he hated *peopleing*.

Ever since he'd been medically discharged from the service, the thought of spending hours with anyone other than himself made his skin crawl. Sure, he'd maintained a relationship here and there for the sake of sex, but nothing ever lasted more than a day or two. Afterwards, he rolled out and just *rode* until he felt the need to hit another town and give his ass a respite from the road.

Zero family, zero ties, and zero fucks to give.

He had no permanent address, and he liked it that way. When things got too heavy or too personal, he packed up what few belongings he had, straddled his softail Harley and lit out. It wasn't the greatest of coping mechanisms, but it was better than letting whatever demons lived in his head get the better of him.

And since he was a former sniper—yeah, there were demons.

A hell of a lot of them...no pun intended.

He would have been perfectly happy taking in every inch of the road for the next fifty years, but the damn carburetor on his baby had crapped out just as he'd hit a little back-water town in western North Carolina called Graves Hollow. The strange spiral of coincidences kicked off when he'd pulled into a garage and found his old USMC brother, Damian. Except now he was riding with a crew of guys that called him Deacon for some reason. An invite to hang out and crash at the club, some drinks and laughs and introductions, and somehow, three months later, Sgt. Andrew Fletcher had been redubbed Aim and absorbed into the fold.

He still wasn't sure why he'd stayed. Maybe it was the fact the camaraderie felt familiar to what he'd had in the military or the fact he didn't have to apologize for his gray morality. He kept saying it was temporary, insisting everyone in the club knew he would light out one day. But once again, there he was, shouldering a case of Yuengling and already mentally preparing himself to bury a body on Christmas Eve.

Fucking Christmas, man. And a party. He knew this wasn't a normal occurrence for them—the whole cover-everything-in-puke-inducing-tinsel-while-forcing-proximity-and-eggnog-just-to-celebrate-the-season—but why did it have to happen when he was still there?

With a soul-expelling sigh, he made his way through the nearly empty house toward the garage, first tearing into the case of beer and pulling out three bottles. He shoved two in the pockets of his leather jacket and twisted the cap off the third, drinking the damn thing halfway down before he pushed open the door. Once the metal door swung on its hinges, he got a full view of the absolute chaos inside and stopped dead in his tracks.

Sweet Mother of Christ. He wouldn't have been able to fathom it if he wasn't seeing it with his own eyes, but it was worse than whatever festive nightmare had been outside.

Inflatables. Inflatables *EVERYWHERE*. Giant, blow-up lawn ornaments that had zero to do with the season cluttered every corner of the room.

Puppies with Santa hats.

Penguins on fire trucks.

Holy shit is that a seven-foot-tall Grinch?!

Oversized Christmas tree lights hung from the ceiling and provided the only illumination, save for the movie on the flat screen over the makeshift bar. Not even the upright, rolling toolboxes had been spared. Each one was covered in... *Dear Lord, can colors be deemed loud?*

The sensory overload was entirely too much. Between the syrupy Christmas music blaring from each corner of the room and the bodies upon bodies of people he didn't even know, he was on the verge of turning on his heel and making his way out. He had just made up his mind and was beginning to flee when a loud voice from across the room stopped him.

"Aim!"

Shit.

Dane, the MC's leader, waved him over to the bar. Aim sighed resignedly and slowly edged around inflatable Rudolph. After draining the rest of the beer, he tossed it into a trash can before pulling another one out of his jacket, fingers brushing the little package in his pocket. He sidestepped over to a tinsel-covered Christmas tree, dropped the box beneath it, and focused in on the men, three of them now, waiting for him at the bar.

"Merry Christmas, Grumpy Ass," Dane said, raising to his full height. A strong hand clapped down onto Aim's shoulder, and the barstool next to him slid out. "I know this isn't your thing, bro, but honestly, it means a lot that you're here."

Dane sat back down on his own barstool and the fucking thing creaked. Aim expected it to give at any second and Dane's six-foot-four, 260-pound ass to crash to the epoxy coated concrete. Of course, it didn't happen. Aim chuckled darkly to himself. It couldn't happen because that would take away from Dane's air of...whatever it was he had. Legend? Mystery? His long, nearly pitch-black hair, gray eyes that shifted from silver to gunmetal depending on the light and his mood, and heavily tattooed arms tended to scare people before he opened his mouth. Already, even at the relatively young age of twenty-seven, his name was whispered for fear of waking the devil.

Caius, Dane's best friend and the club's VP, nodded in agreement, running his fingers through his mahogany hair. "Especially with all the effort the girls put into this."

"Was the effort supposed to induce hypertension, or were you already aware of the live seizure warning outside?" Aim responded with a bit of a snort. "I could see the clearing from a mile away. Thought shit was going down with all the red and blue lighting the night. I wouldn't have been overly shocked, considering your town has literally dialed the crazy to eleven lately, but damn. Oh, and by the way, there are lights on the bikes, so if we're going to bury bodies before it hits midnight, we may need to get on it. Pretty sure Jesus doesn't want to celebrate his birthday with murder."

Dane blanched and turned his head towards the inflatable Grinch. "*HANNAH!*" he bellowed.

Aim laughed and took another huge swallow of his beer. Less than a second later, he nearly choked on it, stopping dead in his tracks as a woman stepped out from behind the decoration.

She was dressed like an elf—a petite but surprisingly curvy blonde elf with the same gray eyes as Dane. A huge grin spread across her lips as she made her way through the crowd. She didn't say a word, just continued to beam at the large, dark man glowering at her. With two fingers, she tugged at the short, upturned hair at the nape of her neck.

"There's no need to yell, D. I'm right here. But your face is all sorts of lacking in the holly jolly right now. Is something...wrong?" she asked, her tone dripping with sarcasm about as subtle as an eighteen-wheeler. She had clearly been waiting for the confrontation and, by the sparkle in her eye, it would seem she was reveling in it. But Aim? He would have given anything for her just to keep talking. Her voice was like pure honey—warm, a little dark, and all sugar.

"First of all, *baby sister*," Dane said, towering over her, "meet Aim. You two haven't crossed paths yet, so be polite and shake the man's hand."

Hannah turned to him and smiled, stretching out her hand. He palmed his beer in the other hand, wiping the condensation off on the front of his jeans before accepting hers.

And the second their fingers met, he *knew* that wherever she was, that was where he belonged. Aim always thought that people who described meeting *the one* were full of nothing but piss and wind. That there was no way on earth two people who knew jack-shit about one another could have an instant connection that sucks all the air out of the room and becomes the flash point for the rest of their lives together. But this? When Hannah Mason's skin touched his and her gray eyes locked with his brown ones... He saw everything.

All the missing pieces of his life were held by this woman. He would follow her anywhere.

"Second," Dane barked, causing him to slip out of the moment. He glared down at Hannah, "get the lights off the bikes. For fuck's sake, you were raised better than that. Dad would've tanned your ass over that nonsense, and you know it."

It took all of two seconds for Aim to set his beer down and raise a hand. "I'll help."

2

OKAY, SO STRINGING CHRISTMAS LIGHTS ALMOST COMPLETELY AROUND the bikes may not have been the best idea she'd ever had. Would it have been worth it to see the looks on the faces of the men she'd called family for almost her entire life?

Hell yes, it would have. She even had a camera ready to capture the moment.

Did she know that a man's bike is almost more sacred than whatever he's slinging in his briefs?

Yes.

Did she know that at some point, she'd get a dressing down for it, even though she hadn't been home in months, and her brother would have made her clean the bikes with her own toothbrush as penance?

Maybe.

What she didn't know was that she was going to meet *him*.

Of all the men she'd come to know throughout her strange life as the once daughter and now sister of the president of a motorcycle club—that may or may not have circumvented jail on multiple occasions because the chief of police considered them family and didn't want to do the extra paperwork—she had never *felt* anyone like him. His presence was calm and quiet but still... dangerous—like there was a spring waiting to pop loose at any moment. All she'd known about him was that he was an inch or two shorter than her brother, the hue of his eyes mimicked a glass of smooth whisky, and his voice made her feel secure.

And the moment their hands had met, she'd known her life would never be the same. He was dark but comforting, like a quiet night.

Which reminded her she needed to get her secret Santa gift out from under the tree, like ten minutes ago, because there was no way she could give it to anyone else now that he was... Well, just now that he *was*.

Aim.

Another jolly pirate nickname, no doubt. Most of them had one. Only Dane and Caius went by their given names, but even those sounded weird.

"What's your real name?" she blurted out, suddenly grateful the darkness hid the unexpected heat on her face.

Doing his level best to untangle a string of lights, he stopped and looked at her. "Andrew," he replied. "Andrew Fletcher."

"Andrew," she repeated. "I like it. Can I call you that instead?"

"Honey, you can call me anything you want, whenever you want," he replied quickly. He inhaled sharply, pausing a beat before speaking again. "Probably shouldn't have said that."

"Why?"

There was another lengthy pause, and Hannah felt her heart-beat kicking into overdrive. It wasn't until that moment she realized how close they were. She was on one side of what she had just learned was his bike, and he was on the other, both working the light strands loose. Less than a foot separated them. Sucking in a deep breath, he looked toward the garage, the loud music and laughter still spilling out into the darkness between them. When they'd come out to clear the lights, the first thing Aim—no, Andrew

—had done was unplug the main extension cords. Now there was only a sliver of moonlight.

Pulling his gaze back to her, he set a wrapped cord of lights on the seat.

"Do you mind if I just shoot my shot here and speak plainly?"

Hannah tilted her head and narrowed her eyes—even though he likely couldn't see her in the dim light of the parking lot. Most of the guys tended to walk on eggshells around her even though she'd know them for years, but not this one. Oh, no. He just spit the words out there, as if he didn't have a care in the world. She liked it. A lot.

"Shoot your shot, huh? Awfully bold since we just met. But I'll allow it. Say what's on your mind."

"Okay, so... I'm not supposed to be a permanent fixture here."

"Yes," Hannah said with a smile. "I get that since we are just now meeting."

"See, but that's the thing, Hannah. Can I call you Hannah? I just kinda like it way it rolls off the tongue, you know?

"Again, petty bold there, sir."

"Yeah, well, I have this weird need to say a shit ton of words right now. But I get it, we just met. You don't know me. However, this"—he stopped and pointed towards the club house and at the lights that were still illuminated outside"—I'm not this guy. I hate Christmas. I hate being around people. Hell, typically, I hate people, period. Sport mode is my normal, and every day, I wake up and think *today is the day I'm going to throw deuces and ride*, but I haven't been able to blow myself out of here. The guys are great, don't get me wrong, but I can't go a few days without Dane, Caius, or Deacon asking me if I'm ready for a Kill Devil cut yet. And I'm not. I don't do permanent."

Hannah set her strand of lights on the ground and leaned in a bit. She said nothing, just waited.

There was a tense pause as she watched him take in another deep breath, then he pulled a beer out of his jacket pocket. After twisting off the lid, he took a deep swallow and looked back at her. He held it out to her, and when her hand grazed his, she felt electricity jolt between their fingers. It seemed to run up her spine.

"You felt that, too, didn't you?" he asked.

She nodded.

"Thought so. That's the problem."

"I don't see how having chemistry with someone is a problem," she said before bringing the bottle to her plump lips. She let them linger on the glass ring where his had just been.

"We don't have *chemistry*, Hannah," he said, stifling a soft moan before gently taking the bottle back from her. "Chemistry is... sparks. We don't have sparks. We have a nuclear warhead that feels like it's about to drop and decimate an entire city, and I don't like it because it's not natural. Hating this feeling has nothing to do with you and everything to do with whatever bomb is about to explode. It's not normal to feel this way about someone you just met and that you know hardly anything about. I mean, before tonight, the most I knew about you was your name, that you were a schoolteacher, you just moved back to town for a new position as the town's school counselor, and that you're Dane's sister—his only sister, and his fucking *baby* sister at that. But if I'd passed you on the street? I wouldn't have known who you were. I'd for damn sure have noticed you, but I wouldn't have known. I hadn't seen you."

He leaned in closer, and she realized they'd been holding the beer bottle at the same time. Andrew lifted his other hand and lightly ran his thumb over her cheekbone, the rest of his long fingers gently threading into her hair.

"But I see you now," he said. "And I don't know what to do about it because there's no world—hell, no universe—in which I am good enough to live in your light."

Hannah's breath hitched a little—just enough for her to feel it burn in her chest. She closed her eyes and let it out on a slow exhale, the tingles spreading through her shoulders and her belly from his fingers in her hair.

"If I told you I'm not afraid, what would you say?" she asked quietly, her voice shaky.

"What aren't you scared of?" he asked. The distance closed between them, and she wanted to feel his lips on hers more than she wanted her next heartbeat.

"Of living in your darkness."

3

"*I'm not afraid of living in your darkness.*"

Merciful Christ. This woman.

To feel this way about her was a shock to his entire system, but the fact she stood there, willing to walk with him through his shadows, choosing him and asking him to choose her...sent fire racing through his veins.

He'd spent enough time with Deacon and his brother, Father Gianni, to know that sometimes in life things just didn't have an explanation. Hell, Deacon and his own wife had the whole instantaneous love thing, and no one had ever questioned it. So why was it so hard for him to accept for himself?

Whatever the reason, however the planets aligned or whatever cosmic fart was allowing this moment to happen, *it was happening.* But before he threw caution to the wind—and risked a beat down of epic proportions from Dane—she needed to know some things. It was important to him—no, fuck that, imperative—that she was walking into whatever this was with her eyes wide open.

"Hannah," he whispered.

"Hmm."

"Speaking plainly, remember?"

She nodded.

He sucked in a deep breath and, for some reason, looked over at the garage again. He flicked his wrist and glanced at the illuminated face of his watch. Time had lost all meaning while talking to Hannah, and it was just now dawning on him that the two of them had been gone for over an hour...and not one person had come to check on them.

"Okay," he ran his thumb over her cheekbone again and let it drop to her bottom lip. "First, I don't have any family. None. It's just me. Second, I've killed people. A lot of people. There isn't a delicate way to ever say that, so it's best to just spit it out."

"I know you were a sniper in the Corps, Andrew. That doesn't bother me."

"No." he replied, cutting her off. "Outside of the military. My morals are pretty gray."

"Your morals would never allow you to hurt me or another innocent person. That much I know. I see you, Andrew. And if we're being honest here, it's not like I'm your average, innocent girl next door. Take a look around. This is where I grew up...who I grew up with." She smiled. "Next hurdle."

Andrew sucked in his bottom lip and stared at her, flabbergasted by her candor. Damn it all. He was going to go for it. He had to kiss her—everything else be damned. Just as he lowered his face to crush her lips to his, the door flew open, and the silence was broken by a very loud, very off-key version of "Grandma Got Run Over by a Reindeer."

"You get your Grinchy asses in this house right now so we can open presents!"

Neither one could get a read on which of the guys had said it because as quickly as it had opened, the door slammed shut again.

Reluctantly stepping back, he walked around to the front of the bike and held out an arm for her.

"It appears we have been summoned. Should we table this

conversation to be continued later when all the drunk elves have passed out?"

Looping her arm through his, she smiled up at him.

"Oh, yeah, handsome. You can bet your sweet, bubble ass we're having this conversation."

"Hey," he paused for a second, glancing over his shoulder at the aforementioned body part before holding open the door for her. "I haven't even kissed you yet, so lewd comments about my ass are inappropriate."

Hannah chuckled wickedly. "Oh, honey, if you think what I said out loud was inappropriate, you should hear what's going on up here." She tapped at her temple and gave him a wink before walking in front of him through the door.

She was either going to be the death of him or the greatest miracle to ever exist in his universe.

For once in his life, there was zero gray area.

4

SOMETHING MADE HER WAIT.

In the midst of the cacophony of what amounted to unruly, oversized, drunk children exchanging what were supposed to be secret gifts, Hannah managed to keep back the one she was given. She wanted to open it, but looking across the room at Andrew— God, she loved the way his name rattled around in her head. She held the package tightly to her chest.

She didn't know who it was from and didn't really care. What she wanted was for them to have a moment where she could watch him open the gift she'd brought.

When they'd drawn for the Dirty Santa game, her slip of paper had read *Male*. That was it. She'd wracked her brain trying to come up with the perfect thing for any one of the adopted brothers in her strange and crazy life. What she'd ended up buying had been completely on a whim. She couldn't understand why she'd listened to the strange albino man at the Farmer's Market she had visited in Asheville. It had made absolutely no sense. None, whatsoever.

Until she'd met *him*.

Everything had clicked into place the second their eyes met.

Her night. Her comfortable darkness.

For the rest of the evening, they maintained their distance, biding their time until they could be alone again. They laughed and enjoyed the company of their family and friends, and Andrew even played along when Deacon's wife Rosie wanted to see how fast they could wrap a man in tinsel.

It was...interesting.

But now that the evening was drawing to a close and, one by one (or two by two), people began to shuffle home or find a place to crash in the clubhouse, Hannah could feel her body tighten and her heart race. She busied herself with putting away food and hitting the switch on the myriad of inflatables that dotted the garage, knowing full well, at any minute, her life could change forever.

"Question."

Andrew's voice came from close behind her, low, husky, and deep enough she felt it vibrate in her back.

"Answer," she replied breathlessly.

"Why'd you girls put up all this stuff?" He nudged one of the Santa inflatables with his boot as it withered to the ground.

"A few reasons," she replied with a soft smile. "One, I'm sure you've noticed that people in town have gone a little off the rails lately. You know, all of the assaults, break-ins, and crime that's ticked up, and with Chief Bradshaw calling all the time for backup, we figured a night that was just *fun* was in order."

"Yeah, I've picked up on it. Like Mercury is in astroglide or something," he replied.

Hannah snorted a laugh. "Think it's retrograde there, pal."

"I said what I said. So, what's the other reason?"

"You."

The air hung heavy between them.

She set an empty beer box on the table and spun around just as he closed the space and placed his hands on either side of her, caging her between his arms and the table. Somehow, it felt like they'd been face-to-face like this a million times for a million years.

Just the normalcy of how their skin felt, even barely brushing, was perfect; like this is what was always meant to happen.

"That's curious because I don't like this shit. The need to blow off some steam and get stupid, I get, but unless I was giving off mixed signals as to how I feel about social gatherings, I'm a little confused," he said, his gaze never leaving her lips. "Dane put you up to it?"

"It was mostly Caius and Rosie." She licked her lips as she spoke. "Our self-proclaimed Christmas whores and all that nonsense. They figured if you had a good time, you'd..." She stopped suddenly and bit her lip, realizing she'd said too much.

"Mmm." He shifted closer, slowly bridging the gap between their bodies. "They figured I would stay." It wasn't a question, just a statement of fact, but for some reason, the word *stay* leaving his lips made her stomach damn near bottom out.

"Something like that."

God, his proximity was intoxicating. He smelled like leather and soap and something spicy and sweet that lingered in her nose and made her brain misfire. Slowly, she lifted her shaking hands, her fingers meeting the lapels of the worn leather of his jacket. Even inside the garage, he kept it on, and she was thankful for it because just gripping the sturdy material in her hands seemed to steady her nerves.

He leaned in closer, almost seeming to go for her lips before his head dipped to her neck. The warmth of his mouth so close to her skin sent sinful ripples through her. The seconds ticked by like hours as he hovered there. Because of their proximity, she felt him take in a slow, deep inhale before bringing his lips to her mouth.

"I'm aching to kiss you," he said, his words spreading through her like a smoked whisky. "Everywhere." She felt the slightest touch of his lips on the shell of her ear. "You make me question everything. What I want." His tongue dipped out, barely touching her. "What I need." He placed a whisper of a kiss below her ear. "Who I am."

Hannah could actually hear her blood pounding through her veins with every soft, punctuated word. Her breath was shaky, and her knees threatened to buckle. She was hyperaware of his hands snaking their way to her hips, his long fingers pressing into her curves ever so slightly.

"And I will if you'll let me," his breath was hot against her throat. "But first, I need to give you something and lay all my cards on the table. I'm going to get my ass kicked, I know it, but I can't find it in me anywhere to care."

It was a strange segue, but before he pulled away, she could've sworn she felt the tiniest lick along her collarbone. The man was turning her into a useless puddle of hormones. She didn't respond, just nodded acceptance when he took hold of her hand and tugged her towards the Christmas tree. Pulling up a chair, he guided her to sit before grabbing another one for himself and straddling it backwards, facing her.

Damn it, why is that such a guy power move?

Leaning over to reach under the tree, he picked up a small white box tied with a thin, silvery gray ribbon. Holding it out in front of him, he met her eyes.

"I bought this because I *had* to, but not when you might think," he started. "I'm sure you bought something for the Dirty Santa game, too, right? Well," he took in a deep breath and let it out. "I drew and didn't know what the fuck I was going to get because my slip didn't say an age or any shit on it, just *Female*, but I realized I had something that my gut told me would work. It's going to sound crazy as hell, but I picked this up almost a year ago. I was rolling through a little town in Upstate New York and stopped in at a market along the main drag. I was just poking around, and it caught my eye. I tried to walk away but I couldn't. As soon as I let myself think about the exchange, I knew this was what I was going to use. It made zero sense to me then, but if we're going by the last six hours, then it completely tracks."

He paused again before reaching for her hand and placing the small white box in her palm.

"The moment I met you—and I mean as soon as my eyes met yours and we touched—I knew that this...this thing that's between us...was why I bought *this* particular item."

She stared down at it for a moment then looked back at him, meeting his eyes. Their gazes remained locked as she carefully untied the silky gray ribbon, a ribbon that currently matched her eyes exactly. She discarded the lid and there, sitting on a cotton cushion, was a dainty silver bracelet with a thin metal band.

Hannah lifted it out and examined it, analyzing the extremely delicate engraving.

"Spes est in lumine."

Taking the bracelet from her, he undid the clasps and circled it around her wrist.

"I bought it without knowing what it meant. For all I knew, it could have been some freaky ass curse from *Evil Dead*, but I felt a pull toward it. Something *made* me get it." As he fastened the bracelet, his fingers made slow circles on her wrist. "Deacon translated for me, since he's all creepy smart and shit. You know what it says?"

She shook her head.

"It's Latin. It means *there is hope in the light.*"

Hannah sucked in a breath and closed her eyes, a lump beginning to form in her throat. She started to say something, but a finger to her lips stopped her.

"I know this is strange and sudden, and I know I am not good enough to live in your light. And God knows what the morning will look like if we give in to whatever the fuck is happening here, but I also know that sometimes, a wheel is set in motion for a reason, and wherever the destination is... Well, it's what's meant to be." He paused and sucked in his bottom lip for a moment. "I am a blank slate for you, Hannah Mason, and if you really meant it—that me being, you know...me... Fuck, what I'm trying to say is that if you choose to rewrite your story with me, to be my light, then I'll stay."

Hannah looked down at the bracelet again, running a finger over the words. A sudden slew of hot tears hit the back of her eyes and joined with the lump in her throat. From the pocket of the elf costume she still wore, she withdrew a black box, slightly larger than the one he had handed her, tied with a blood red ribbon. She grabbed his hand and gently placed it in his palm.

"How can we rewrite something when every word is already the same?"

Before this moment, she had been utterly terrified of handing over this gift. It was random yet personal on a level even she didn't comprehend. Not until she'd read the words on her bracelet had it all snapped into place.

Andrew pulled at the ribbon, holding her gaze until he was able to lift the lid and withdraw a one-inch-wide leather cuff.

"I asked Deacon what it meant, too," she said, drawing his attention to the stamped lettering within the leather.

"*Pax est in tenebris.*"

"There is peace in the darkness," she whispered. Gently taking the cuff from him, she pushed back the sleeve of his jacket and fastened it around his wrist. "How is this even possible? Divine intervention?" she asked softly.

"I don't know," he said. "I just listened to my gut when that pasty-assed, freaky dude at the market showed it to me. He told me I would give it to the person it was meant for when the time was right. Other than that, I don't care." The look of shock on her face barely registered before, suddenly pushing himself up from the chair, he kicked it out of the way and lifted her by her arms, crashing his lips down onto hers. The effect was immediate and incendiary. She'd never experienced that kind of flame—white hot and instantaneous. It wasn't sloppy or frantic, but rather intense and controlled, as if he was trying to devour her soul. He cupped the back of her head, anchoring her so he could taste every inch of her mouth. Her fingers buried in the back of his jacket like she was trying to cling to what little bit of sanity she had left.

"*Fuck*, you taste like heaven," he whispered against her mouth before his tongue made another delicious lap against hers. "Ask me to stay, Hannah. Ask me."

Between kisses, she struggled to breathe.

"Stay. Please. With me. For me."

"Forever."

She wasn't sure when it happened, but the wall met her back and his thick thigh pressed between hers. She felt the cool air between them when his mouth dropped to her jawbone, and his open-mouthed kisses sent her body spiraling. She pushed at the shoulders of his jacket, and he stripped it off without pulling away. Glancing down, she could see the black and gray ink that covered his forearms and the way his black T-shirt pulled tight across his abdomen.

"Say it again," she said, her voice a pained whisper.

"I'll stay. For you, with you. Always, Hannah. In this life and whatever the fuck comes after."

Hannah thrust her fingers into his close-cropped, sandy blonde hair. "I wish this was longer," she murmured against his lips, "long enough that I could really get a grip on it." She pulled his mouth to hers again. Whatever this fire was made of, it was designed to burn them both alive, and she didn't care if they took the whole world down with them.

Pulling back slightly, he looked into her smoky gray eyes. "Your wish is my command. You want it grown out? It's done." He pressed his forehead to hers before dipping his mouth to her throat.

Achingly aware of his thigh between hers and his big hands holding her hips, it was on the tip of her tongue to tell him where her room in the clubhouse was, but the lights suddenly flicked on.

They both froze in place, their eyes still closed, standing perfectly still, hearts pounding the same rhythm but at a mile a minute. The silence stretched on forever until a deep voice carried across the room.

"See. I told you they'd get together."

Carefully, Andrew cracked his eyes open and tilted his head until they both saw Dane, Caius, and Deacon standing in the doorway.

"Okay, fine. I owe you fifty bucks," Caius said to Deacon.

"Uh, you owe us *both* fifty, dickhead." Dane crossed his arms over his thick chest. "I said it would be before the New Year, and you said it would be Easter. So. Pay. Up."

"Dude. I still think it's twisted you're not just okay with this, but actively pushing for it," Caius grumbled, reaching into his pocket for his wallet. "Like, he's basically dry humping your sister, and you're taking my cash. What kind of masochistic, bad-guy brother are you?"

Dane snatched the money and glared at Caius. "I dunno, ask the devil. I'm sure he, or one of the minions he's had descending on us, could tell you." Shoving the cash into his pocket, he glared at Hannah and Andrew. "Now, first rule—no fucking my sister where I can hear it. Or see it. Actually, I don't even wanna know that it happens, so separate and leave some room for the Holy Ghost, you got it? She's grown, but there's a line I don't want crossed anywhere in my presence. Believe me when I say this is not only for the sake of my own mental health but also because I know you like your teeth in your head. Second"—he reached behind him and tossed a heavy bit of leather at Andrew's feet—"you put that on, and we expect to see your ass in church next week."

Andrew pulled away from Hannah and stooped to pick up the leather Kill Devil cut. On the front was a hand sewn patch that said AIM. On the opposite shoulder was a pair of embroidered guns crossed at the barrel. Flipping it around, the back had the club's logo—an open-mouthed skull with a serpent slithering out of the mouth and flanked by angel wings, the whole thing pierced from the crown by a sword that extended through the base of the jaw.

And it had both rockers.

"Fuck," he muttered.

"Merry Christmas, brother," Deacon said, giving him a sly smile before slapping Dane and Caius on the shoulder, signaling for them to leave.

"Welcome home," Caius said, giving him a wink.

When they were alone again, he held the cut in his hands. Out of nowhere, Hannah took it from him and walked to his back, nudging for him to lift his arms enough so she could slide it on for him. As she walked around to face him, she smiled.

"Suits you," she said. Staring into his eyes, she noted the slight smile on his face. "What?"

"I just had a thought. Well, two thoughts and a question."

"What was it you said earlier? Oh yeah – so, shoot your shot. I'm listening."

Wrapping his arms around her waist, he pulled her in for a kiss.

"I absolutely love Christmas now, and I'm pretty fucking sure we have a guardian angel that made sure we found each other."

Hannah chuckled, "You said the guy who sold you my bracelet was pasty. How pasty?"

"Babe, if he was a bunny, he'd be pink everywhere he wasn't white. For real. Solidly white hair and skin and the weirdest, nearly translucent blue eyes I've ever seen in my life...and I've seen some weird shit." Aim replied on a laugh that died on his lips as he looked up at Hannah again. She looked stricken. "What's wrong? Why do you look like you just saw a ghost?"

She let out the breath she had been holding on a shaky smile. "Nothing... It's just that I'm pretty sure the same guy sold me your bracelet...in Asheville. Maybe we do have a guardian angel. What-ever the reason, I'm glad it worked out." Her smile broadened. "So, what was your question?"

Aim smirked as he hooked an arm around her waist and dropped a kiss on her lips. "I just got a room here, so I figured I should give you the option. Your place...or mine?"

ABOUT THE AUTHOR

MABRY BLACKBURN is a writing duo made up of two friends who clicked after meeting on Twitter. They bonded over a shared love of dark humor, whisky, and a hard-fought, well-earned happily ever after.

A CHRISTMAS FLAME

BY JOANNA MORGAN

A CHRISTMAS FLAME

LEVI WRAPPED HIS ARMS AROUND BROOKE FROM BEHIND AS SHE HUNG up a little ball of greenery with a red bow. He breathed in deep, chin on her head. She smelled like toasted marshmallows and pomegranates with a hint of cinnamon.

"You know, I don't need that as an excuse to kiss you." To prove it, he turned her in his arms and pressed his lips to her soft, smiling ones.

"I know you don't." She laughed, wrapping her arms around his neck. "But it's our first Christmas together, and your first one, period. We need decorations."

Though he'd been in the mortal plane for decades, he'd never celebrated Christmas. None of the elemental warriors had. It was always just another day in the grinding war against chaos and the destruction of the universe. But seeing Brooke's excitement for the holiday warmed him, made him look forward to it. Her cheeks were pink with pleasure, blue eyes sparkling, and she seemed to *glow* with happiness. She was somehow even more beautiful to him than before.

"If decorations are what you want, then we'll get more." He planted another kiss on her lips, and she grinned under his mouth.

"We don't have to go crazy. Just a few things."

"Whatever you want." He'd buy any of them, all of them, for her. "Hell, I'll make our suite the North Pole if that's what you want. Why don't you come sit on my lap and tell me what else you want for Christmas?" he asked, waggling his eyebrows.

Her tinkling laugh followed them as he tugged her toward the bed and sat on the end, pulling her close then across his knees. She settled in with a little wiggle, and he had to crank down on the lid holding back his desire before he self-combusted. He could never get enough of her it seemed.

"Now, Brooke," he said, settling his arms loosely around her. "Have you been good this year?"

"*Very* good," she said, eyes lit, fingers playing in the hair at his nape.

"Very good, huh. Hmm. So what would you like from Santa for Christmas?" He needed ideas. Despite how she kept trying to play it off, he knew how important this holiday was to her. How special it should be for her. But he'd run dry of gift ideas since they'd replaced all her belongings, and then some. He spoiled her every time she let him, which wasn't often enough for his liking.

She bit the corner of her bottom lip and shrugged. "There isn't really anything I need."

"Unacceptable." He couldn't let their first Christmas go by without a gift to give her. He was no fool. "Think hard. What is something you really, really want?"

She squinted, her juicy bottom lip trapped between her teeth again. "A kiss."

A wicked fire lit within him. "One like this?" He gave her a noisy smack on her closed mouth, and she giggled.

"Nooo," she answered, dragging out the word, hand on her hip.

"I'm afraid you'll have to be more specific then. What kind of kiss?" He could tell by the darker blue of her eyes that she was enjoying this little game. So was he.

"A long, slow one."

"Like this?" He dipped his head and feathered his mouth across hers, taking his time. Lingering, tasting.

She kept trying to deepen the kiss, but he wouldn't let her.

"Levi," she said in a false whine, tugging on his black T-shirt to bring him closer. "With tongue."

He grinned, more than happy to oblige. He turned her so she was straddling him instead of sitting sideways and captured her lips again in a long, drugging kiss, using his tongue to lick the seam until she opened for him, stroking against hers in a wet glide. He fed from the sweetness of her mouth as his hands roamed her body, building the heat between them. He got so caught up that his mind momentarily blanked to anything else.

He pushed his hands up under her shirt but skirted her breasts, wrapping them around her back and then down, pulling her hips tight against him.

They both groaned at the contact.

Flames tingled under his skin, and he was sure if he wasn't steaming already, he would be in a moment.

But then she whimpered, shifting in his lap, and the sound of her passion and the feeling of her sweet heat pressing against his erection sent his heart pounding and his body temperature skyrocketing.

He pulled back an inch, and Brooke rested her forehead against his, clinging to him. They both panted. "A kiss like that? Is that what you want for Christmas?"

She nodded, eyes closed.

He waited one beat. "Where?"

She leaned back and looked at him, confused. Her face flushed, and her beautiful, swollen lips parted. He reclaimed her mouth for one hot second, then pulled away.

"Anywhere you want," Brooked panted, trying to drag him back to her mouth, but he resisted.

"No," he said with a smirk. "This is *your* Christmas present, not mine. You'll have to be specific." He held her gaze. He was sure his eyes were glowing with fire when she met his look, so he licked his lips slowly, letting her know the exact offer he was making. Letting her see the hot hunger within him.

Her chest rose and fell as her breathing increased.

"Tell me where you want me to kiss you, baby."

He could see the struggle in her, between her desire and embarrassment, but he wanted to hear her say it, his heart rate jacking up in anticipation.

She leaned forward to whisper hotly in his ear, and he grinned darkly, flames leaping to life inside him. In one move, he stood and turned around, lowering Brooke onto the bed.

He'd give her what she wanted now...and find her a gift later.

Brooke watched him from her place in the center of the bed, cheeks blushed and blue eyes several shades darker with her desire. He flung her shoes and socks off along with his own shirt and then slid up her body until he could kiss her again.

She threw her arms around his neck, welcoming his kisses, but he resisted the urge to stay at her mouth and sat up once more, pulling her T-shirt up and off along the way. Despite the creamy mounds of her breasts calling and tempting him, he instead laid his lips across Brooke's ribs as he undid the button and zipper on her jeans. Leaving her panties on, he peeled them down her sleek legs, peppering kisses on her hip, her thigh, her knee.

He left his own jeans on, too, because he wanted to please her. Brooke liked to be teased, and he liked to tease her, but that required him to keep his sanity a bit longer than her. And if it wasn't for the barrier of clothing, he might give in to the temptation to bury himself inside her sooner than intended.

He retraced his previous path with his lips once again poising over her breasts, her heavy breathing bringing them back toward his watering mouth every second. Tugging down the lacy edge of one cup, eyes on hers, he lowered to her eager nipple. He flicked the hard nub with his tongue while he sucked, watching her vision glaze. He switched to the other side and did the same, rubbing his palm over the sensitized peak he'd just left. Slipping his hand down her torso, he cupped her over the fabric of her panties, barely moving his fingers. Heat flowed from him, increasing her sensitivity and pleasure. He went back and forth on her breasts until Brooke had her hands in his hair, her hips pushing sinuously against his hand of their own accord, telling him what she wanted without a word. But Brooke had asked for a kiss, and that's what she would get.

As her arousal increased, her control of her element decreased. With each moan, her skin became slicker with moisture. Pure water condensed on her from her power, and he drank from her, taking tiny sips from the curve of her neck, the tips of her nipples, the planes of her abdomen, her hipbones.

He tangled his fingers in the waistband of her panties and tugged them down one hip and then the other, licking the sensitive place where her leg bent, scraping the thicker flesh with his teeth.

When she lifted her pelvis, he pulled the scrap of fabric off completely and let them fall somewhere at the end of the bed. Then he rose to his knees and, grabbing Brooke's shins, flexed her legs deeply, exposing everything to his hungry gaze. And hungrier mouth.

With his first lick, the sound that came from her caused him to close his eyes and groan, heat climbing up his spine in a tingling trail to his brain. He had to resist, had to delay his own pleasure, no matter how hot her noises made him. He clamped his mouth to her, and in a slower, more deliberate manner, kissed her the way she'd asked him to.

She quivered in his grasp, cries ragged, hands fisted in the sheets, until neither of them could stand anymore. If he waited any longer, he would burst into flames and incinerate another pair of jeans.

With a final suckle, he stood and shed the remainder of his clothes and then knelt between Brooke's still spread thighs. He positioned himself and leaned over her, entering her as he did. The sensation of being inside her turned his backbone to jelly, and he groaned as he sunk in further, forehead pressed to hers.

She wrapped her legs around him and arched her hips, and they started a slow and deep rhythm that picked up pace quickly.

Her body, slick with sweat and elemental moisture, steamed painlessly under his hot touch.

She was water and he was fire, but together, they were nuclear. The higher they went, the steamier the room got until condensation ran down the foggy windows like it did on her skin.

Flames blossomed across his shoulders, down his arms, and across the backs of his hands as he rocked into her, catching her cries in his mouth.

With Brooke safe from harm through their bond, they caught fire simultaneously.

Hours later, Levi woke in the dark, disquiet whispering through him.

It amazed him how easily he could fall asleep now, with Brooke in his bed. Though he needed less sleep than a human, her touch had a way of calming and relaxing him.

What had awakened him so suddenly? He listened hard for a moment, but the only sounds in the silence were their breathing. Carefully, he sniffed the air, trying to detect the barest hint of burning plastic, the smell of the enemy, but there was none, only the warm scent of the woman beside him. It must have been random.

He was drifting off again when he heard the barest of whimpers from Brooke. He rolled over on one elbow and looked at her. She lay curled away from him, brown hair, black in the dim light, partially covering her face.

He stared at her a moment, but she appeared to be sleeping peacefully. As he lowered himself back to the mattress, he heard it —a broken inhale that ended in an almost soundless cry.

He brushed the strands back from her face, revealing the crease between her brows and the downward curve of her mouth.

Brooke was having a nightmare. It had been several months since her last one.

Levi curled his hand around her waist and pulled her back against him, kissing the side of her face. "Wake up, Brooke. You're dreaming."

After a few gentle kisses, she turned her head towards him. "Levi?"

"Yeah, baby. You were having a bad dream."

He felt her nod, then she shifted, and he loosened his arms so she could turn to face him. She did, but still curled up, her face against his chest. As he placed his arms around her again, she released a shuddering breath, and he felt the fine tremor start in her body.

"What is it?" he asked, lips against the top of her head, waiting for her answer. She wasn't asleep—she still breathed harshly against his chest hair, and her body remained tense.

She gave an audible swallow. "I was back at the dam."

His heart dropped, and he tightened his hold. She'd been kidnapped, drugged, her subconscious assaulted as the Chaolt, the minions of Chaos, tried to get her to lose control of her latent elemental powers and cause a disaster.

"Charlie was there."

One Chaolt in particular.

He knew she hated to say his name, and hearing it made him clench his teeth, but he was the face of her nightmares. The man that had caused the apartment fire she'd been trapped in, who'd taken her to the dam to try to break her mind. Who'd showed her the terrible things he wanted her to do.

"I know it didn't really happen, the dam didn't really break, I didn't kill"—another ragged inhale and exhale—"all those people. But the dream was so real at the time. It's like my body doesn't know that it was a nightmare. It feels like it happened. And I can't forget. I keep remembering it, and reliving it, and—" Levi held her tightly through a few dry sobs. "I'm so afraid that someday he'll find me again, and it will become a reality."

"That will never happen," he assured her, steel in his voice. "You're safe." He willed every cell in his body to transmit that promise as he clasped her tighter, warming her with a gentle heat from within.

She nodded and whispered. "I know. I just can't help worrying about it, subconsciously."

He didn't know how to respond to that, so he rubbed her back, and she incrementally relaxed as she fell back to sleep in his embrace.

He stared into the dark, unable to doze off. She'd had nightmares about fire for months after her apartment, too, but he guessed, somehow, his own fire had helped her conquer the fear of it. His wouldn't hurt her. Couldn't, now that she was his soul mate.

But he could do nothing about her fear of water, of what was inside her. Anger and helplessness ignited within him. There was nothing anyone could do, not even Walker, their commander and water elemental who was helping her learn to control her powers. As long as that bastard who'd taken her was out there—

His rising ire cooled as quickly as burning coals splashed with water.

Suddenly, he knew what to give Brooke as a gift for Christmas.

He slowly unwound his limbs from hers and left the room, a plan taking shape.

✳

"Do you know the one who calls himself Charlie?"

The Chaolt he had pinned to the wall didn't respond, only stared at Levi, her expression confused.

He repeated the question, twisting his knife in the ribs of his prey. She grimaced and cried out but responded, "Fuck you!"

Levi felt the fire rising inside of him and took several deep breaths in a row. He didn't want to end this too quickly. He'd had no luck locating the bastard, despite asking every Chaolt he'd come across for the last two weeks. One of them *must* know something. So he needed to be patient and not fry the enemy soldier yet. He needed information more than he needed another stinking pile of ash in the alley around him.

But that didn't mean he couldn't toast her a little bit.

His powers weren't nulled by the enemy anymore, the way the rest of the other elemental warriors' were. The way they'd always been before. Until Brooke.

Slowly, Levi pushed his fire into the blade in the woman's chest, heating the metal. She cried out.

"This is the last time I'm going to ask. If you don't tell me something, you're going to be dust in three seconds."

The woman panted but stayed silent.

"One," Levi ground out.

They glared at each other, angry static eyes meeting his, awash in orange flames.

"Two." He turned up the heat even more, and the smell of burning plastic increased as she thrashed under his hands.

"Three," he said grimly. Another dead end. *Damn it.*

"Wait!"

Levi yanked back on the lava rising within him, breathing hard to keep from losing it.

"I know Charlie. I'll tell you where he is"—the Chaolt swallowed—"if you let me live."

Levi considered it for a moment. The woman was probably lying, but this was the only lead he'd had in weeks.

With a curt nod, he withdrew his fire and his blade and stepped back, primed for the enemy to run immediately. But to his shock, she didn't.

She didn't speak either, hands on her knees, gasping, staring pointedly at the knife in Levi's hand.

Teeth grinding, he made a show of sheathing his weapon. The Chaolt noted the action and spoke quickly. "He's stationed on the south side of town. With a family."

Levi grew cold. A...*family?* "His?" he asked tersely. Could Chaolt have families? Actual lives, outside of this war? He did. He had Brooke, so maybe it was possible. But if it was true, that added another layer of fuckery to this situation because he didn't want to hurt Charlie's family by killing him...

The Chaolt shook her head.

That didn't make Levi feel much better. If Charlie was put with a family as part of his mission, then either someone in that household or nearby was his target. Either way, now it was doubly important he find the bastard because he had to protect the unsuspecting people in that impostor's life. And his neighborhood. Because depending on the strength of the Sleeper Charlie found...the damage could spread for miles.

Sleepers were humans with latent elemental powers, like Brooke. Chaolt hunted them, manipulated them through their dreams, and caused them to self-destruct with as much collateral damage as possible, releasing elemental power and chaos into the world.

Brooke's powers were no longer latent, either because of their bond or because almost being destroyed by the Chaolt had brought them to the surface. None of them were sure which. They weren't sure, either, whether the Chaolt could still get to her, still use her.

And that was the base of her fears, her nightmares. And why he *must* find Charlie and finish him.

"Who's he after? What's the address?"

The enemy shook her head again, standing hunched with a

hand to her torso. "I don't know. I don't have anything other than that."

Levi stayed silent, jaw clenched, but he didn't reach for his weapon.

They stared at each other as the Chaolt backed up a couple steps before turning and running away.

For a few dark seconds, Levi considered ending her anyway. He didn't need his knife to do it—he had his fire.

She would tell Charlie he was looking for him.

Levi thumbed fingers lit with flames but then curled his fist and snuffed them in his palm. He was a man of his word, no matter how hard it was to keep.

If he left now, maybe he'd find Charlie before the Chaolt did. Before he was warned.

He was supposed to go Christmas shopping with Brooke this evening, but this was more important.

He dialed his cell as the smell of burning plastic and the clang in his brain faded, proving the Chaolt had run far and fast.

Brooke answered.

"Babe, I'm sorry, I'm not going to be able to go with you. I have an extra patrol to do."

He felt no guilt at the lie.

They'd *both* sleep better when this was done.

Topaz Ridge Nevada was a mountain town founded by miners. Population twenty-one thousand. The 'south side of town' was only a few square miles. It shouldn't take long to patrol the area and find his target, or any other Chaolt in the area. Sure, the one he'd let go had a head start, but she'd said she didn't know his address. She could have been lying, of course, but he was bargaining on the chance they didn't monitor each other's movements too closely. He and the other warriors had debriefings every day, so Levi knew their movements, but there were only four of them. A great deal more than four Chaolt existed in Topaz Ridge, even after he'd cleaned them out with holy fire a few months ago.

Like roaches, they always came back. There were always more. And because the town sat near an Elemental portal, drawing Sleepers from all over, they'd never leave Topaz Ridge alone.

The thought gave him a momentary pang of sadness. Brooke would never be totally safe, the town, never totally secure. But then he gritted his teeth, because it wouldn't matter.

None of them knew whether Brooke could still be targeted now that she was bonded to him, and they weren't in a hurry to test it for obvious reasons. But once Charlie was gone, Brooke could sleep soundly knowing that Levi would protect her from every other foe. He just couldn't protect her from her nightmares.

Except by killing the stinking meatbag who had kidnapped her.

He used to have a kind of radar sense, where if an enemy was close, he could pinpoint how far away they were and what direction they were in. Around the time he met Brooke, that sense went away for some reason. Now he had to search blindly.

Levi drove slowly through the streets, windows down to the cold December air.

Anticipating the clanging sensation in the back of his brain, sniffing for the smell of burnt plastic that meant the Chaolt were near.

After a few blocks, he found them. But the signs were weak, and he had to cover the grid of a few streets several times before he figured out where they were strongest.

He rolled to a stop in front of what appeared to be a banquet hall. The parking lot was full of cars, and inside the door that stood open, colorful lights flickered and holiday music played.

A party. Charlie was at a Christmas party. Or some Chaolt was, but Levi was betting it was him.

For several minutes, Levi struggled with uncomfortable feelings of seeing the humanity in the enemy.

When they were faceless hordes attacking Sleepers and causing disasters, it was all too easy to do his duty and end their lives.

When they begged for their lives, ran away from the fight, and went to fucking *holiday* parties, it was harder.

But they weren't human. Perhaps they had been at one time— none of the Elementals knew. Now they were just Chaos wrapped in a fleshy package. They didn't bleed when they died, they turned into a stinking pile of dust. They were a threat to all of humankind —all of the universe, really. Because if they succeeded in destroying the mortal plane, they'd move to Primordia, the homeworld of the Elementals. And from there to other worlds until there weren't any left, and the cosmos turned itself inside out and ceased to exist.

Fuck. He had to move before the other Chaolt had a chance to warn is target or join in the fray.

Levi exited the car and checked his knives. Guns drew too much attention, so he'd have to get close enough to shank him. He left his leather jacket open for easy access. The wind had become bitter and stung his face as he walked across the parking lot. It would snow tonight.

He stood in the doorway, cheery music and warm, food-scented air filtered around him. But behind it lurked the sinister smell of chaos.

Levi walked in, the clang in his brain blocking out the notes of vintage Christmas music. People stood around, laughing and drinking in small groups. No one really noticed him. It only took a few seconds to spy the man he was looking for.

The bastard he was here to kill.

He stood in the back of the room, drink in hand, talking to another man. Standing there in a stained button-up shirt and a comb-over, he looked too weak, greasy, and innocuous to be haunting his woman. Not threatening at all.

But he knew it was what was inside Charlie that haunted Brooke. His ability to make her dream horrible things, the possibility that he could make her do them.

Was the one he talked to his target? The Sleeper that he'd cause to self-destruct, possibly harming all these people? If all he cared about was collateral damage, this would be a great opportunity for it. Thirty or more people crammed into a one-room banquet hall. Maybe a fire would break out, and they'd all be trapped inside...

Levi paused and reached out with his other senses, searching with his fire for a kindred power. Like sensed like. But there wasn't one. So whatever calamity Charlie was hoping to cause, at least it wasn't fire.

But that also meant Levi couldn't drain the Sleeper, if they were here, and stop the disaster from happening.

He should call the other warriors.

Charlie's head snapped up, and he excused himself from his conversation, dark eyes searching the room. Levi could barely see the static in them when they made eye contact.

So maybe the Chaolt could sense when Elementals were near, too. *Interesting.*

Charlie smiled and lifted his drink to him, but it didn't reach his eyes.

Levi didn't bother with a fake smile as he walked towards him, but Charlie held on to his.

"What are you doing here?" the man murmured when Levi was within earshot.

"I'm here to kill you,' Levi replied, just as quietly.

Charlie looked annoyed. *Annoyed.* "This isn't the time or the place for a battle—surely you can see that. And if you think I'm going to follow you outside just so you can kill me, forget it."

Levi's internal temperature began to rise. "I could kill you right where you stand."

"In front of everyone?" he smirked, posture confident. "I'm pretty sure that's against the rules, Elemental."

He was right, of course. Levi hadn't really thought through what he would do when he got inside. He'd simply been intent on finding the guy and doing *something.*

Levi clenched his fists, anger and fire heating the center of his chest. "Maybe I don't give a fuck about the rules."

The edges of his vision turned orange, a sure sign his eyes were glowing with power. Fear and recognition lit the enemy's face.

"You're the one from the dam."

After he'd found Brooke drugged and tied to a chair, he'd carried her away from the room and into a sea of enemies. Their only way out had been for him to nuke everyone. Thankfully he'd been able to protect Brooke and his fellow warriors. Charlie hadn't been there when it happened, having escaped before Levi and his team had arrived. But it seemed that news of the attack, like fire, had spread.

"That's right." The other elementals' powers were nulled out in the presence of Chaolt. Which was another reason the warriors had to use weapons to fight them. But not Levi. Not anymore.

For a few seconds, orange and static irises clashed in tense silence.

But then Charlie smirked. "Hun," he said, summoning someone over Levi's shoulder.

A petite blond woman approached, and he pulled her close to his side, grinning. "I'd like you to meet my girlfriend."

"Hello," she said, not quite meeting his eyes. Despite her cheerful, clashing sweater and the reindeer horns on her head, her smile seemed forced. Levi studied her for a second. He didn't need his elemental senses to see the darker shade of skin under the thick makeup around her eye or the way she held herself, rigid and contained, even as Charlie pulled her closer to his side.

Levi clenched his fist against the flames burning under his palms and glared at his enemy.

"I'm betting as long as she's here, as long as we're surrounded by all these *people*," he said, stressing the word, "you're not going to do jack shit to me."

That caught the woman's attention, and Levi felt her stare on him. Was it hopeful or fearful?

It didn't matter. Charlie was right. Levi wouldn't risk a fight here, wouldn't risk anyone else getting involved or hurt.

And the way his internal flames clawed at him, he couldn't risk releasing them at Charlie, on the off chance he'd lose control like he had a few times before and harm someone else.

Motherfucker.

"Not here. Not now. But sometime." It was a promise. To him, to Brooke, and to himself.

But Charlie didn't seem worried. He lifted his glass, eyes glittering, smile cold. "Merry Christmas."

"What's all this?" Levi asked, setting down his duffel bag and hanging up his coat.

A large pile of bags sat on the floor by the door, full of boxes of every size.

Brooke peeked from around the corner, a sheepish smile on her face. "Christmas decorations…"

Levi surveyed all her purchases, hands on his hips. "Oh." It really was going to look like the North pole in here.

"I know it looks like a lot," she said as she walked toward him. "And it is. But you weren't there to stop me," she said, mock pouting.

Levi pushed his hair back with one hand, sighing. "I know, I'm sorry. I wanted to be…"

After a moment, she said, "I know. You've been busy lately with your extra shifts."

'Extra shifts' to try to find that bastard, Charlie. He looked at the floor to hide his guilt as she stood on her tiptoes to give him a kiss.

"It's okay. I took my mom with me."

He nodded, distracted, Charlie's cocky face swimming in his vision.

"You okay?" Brooke asked, head tilted, silky brown hair spilling over one shoulder.

His vision cleared and he gazed at her. She was lovely in an over-large red sweater and black leggings, sincere with concern for him on her face.

"I'm okay," he said. "Just tired." And pissed, but he wanted to hide that. He didn't wish to ruin her mood or her evening.

"Why don't you go shower and then come sit on the couch with me? We'll Netflix and chill," she said, one side of her lovely mouth tipping up.

He eyed the packages. "You don't want to put all this up?"

"Not right now. You're tired, and if I'm honest..." She blinked several times at the bags, "I think shopping sucked all the energy out of me. I'm tired, too."

"Ok," he said, nodding. "If you're sure."

"Yeah, I'm sure," she said, shrugging. "Just promise me you'll help me decorate before Christmas."

"I promise," he said, committed. He was still determined to make this a great Christmas for Brooke.

"Okay." They smiled at each other. "Go on. I'll grab some snacks."

He went for the shower, relieved. He definitely wasn't feeling festive right now. He was angry about the situation, that he'd finally found Brooke's tormentor and hadn't been able to do a damn thing. He clenched his fists. But when the water began to steam off him at a rapid pace and fog up the bathroom, he knew he had to relax before Brooke noticed. Or before he burned something unintentionally. He closed his eyes, forcing his thoughts back to Brooke. To peace, and love, and all those good emotions that helped him keep his fire in check.

He felt calmer when he was done, Brooke tucked under his arm while they watched Hallmark movies and snacked on warm brownies scattered with crushed candy cane pieces. Brooke was halfway through a second one when she set it back on the plate, one hand on her stomach.

He glanced at her. "You okay?" She looked a bit green around the edges.

"I'm fine," she said, attempting to smile. "Just had too much sugar today I think." She took a sip of ice water from her glass on the table.

"Are you sure—"

"I'm certain,' she said, hugging his arm. "And guess what?" she asked, looking up at him.

This was probably a ploy to change the subject, but he couldn't resist her excited expression. "What?"

"I got your present today," she said with a sparkling grin.

"You did?" he asked, mildly curious.

"Yes. And I think you're going to love it."

His smile slipped and his mood darkened, thinking of earlier. "I haven't gotten yours yet."

"That's okay," she said, laying her head down on his shoulder. "I just can't wait to give you yours."

He couldn't wait to give her hers, either. His jaw clenched as he stared blindly at the TV. One way or the other, he had to get Charlie.

Only now, Charlie knew he was after him. So, at the very least, he might run out of Levi's reach. And at the most, he'd set a trap for Levi when he came for him again.

Damn it. He had to make his move, and quickly. Before Charlie could escape. If he did flee, he'd have to pursue him. If he set a trap, well... Levi would have to set one of his own. But he'd need help.

"I need to speak to Walker."

"Right now?" Brooke asked, surprise and disappointment in her voice as he unwrapped his arm from her grasp and stood.

"Yeah."

"Are you serious?"

"Yes. It's important." Her expression fell and guilt pricked at him. But he'd make it up to her. Soon.

"Levi, you've barely been home the last couple of weeks. I just want to spend some time with you. Are you sure you have to do this now?"

"Yeah, I'm sorry. I'll be back in a little bit."

He left their suite, remorse warring with determination, and headed to Walker's office.

It was late, but when he buzzed the intercom, his commander answered.

"Walker, you're going to be pissed, but I have a situation. I need some help."

Walker sighed. "Come in."

When Levi entered his office, Walker sat behind his desk, a map of the county, covered in red circles and empty energy bar packages, spread beneath his elbows.

Dark blue eyes studied him from behind shaggy, sandy bangs as his commander leaned back in his chair.

"What is it, Levi?"

It had taken him days, but they'd found where Charlie was staying and the Sleeper he was looking for. He stood in the middle of the park, headphones around his neck, hands in his coat pockets, nervously glancing around from beneath a knitted cap.

Connor had been surprisingly easy to convince to help them. Apparently, younger humans were more open-minded than older ones. All it took was a brief explanation about the nightmares and the strange things that had been happening around him recently, about who they were, what their mission was, how he fit in—and Ajax demonstrating his Air powers—and he'd been all in. He probably thought it was some grand adventure, despite the situation being life or death. And maybe it would be, something that he'd fondly look back on when he was older...

Except he wouldn't remember it.

As soon as they were done here, Ajax would drain him, and he'd forget everything—what happened here, what they'd shown him, that they'd even appeared at his door. Otherwise, exposing and explaining themselves to a human would be too risky. Even an adolescent one.

But if Charlie didn't hurry, the entire plan was in jeopardy.

"Come on, you bastard, take the bait," Levi muttered under his breath, searching the streets beyond for movement despite the fact he didn't sense any sign of the Chaolt.

He'd been pretty confident he'd found the house Charlie was stationed at, given the stink that permeated the place even when he wasn't home, but now he second guessed himself. Could they have been wrong? Did they have the wrong Sleeper? Could there have been another Sleeper nearby besides this guy? Hell, maybe they'd found the location of a different Chaolt altogether and had snatched their target instead. Maybe it would be someone else that showed up, and then what? How would he find Charlie? He'd have to start over at square one.

He'd soon find out for sure. The vibration started in the back of his brain, and the unnatural smell of chaos blew in on the bitter wind.

Chaolt were coming. More than one from what he could tell. But it was only the one he was waiting for who stepped out of the tree line, making his way toward the kid.

Deep satisfaction burned in Levi's gut. No matter what, Charlie would not be walking away from here to terrorize Brooke, Connor, or anyone else.

Connor knew what to do. He had to stay where he was, and not move. To not let any Chaolt close enough to touch him, because none of them knew how close to the edge he was, how long Charlie had been working on him. One touch might set him on the path to self-destruction.

Charlie got close enough to Connor to talk to him, but his tone was too low for Levi to hear his words.

Levi waited, impatience and disquiet flickering in his gut. When Charlie made his move, he'd make his.

Charlie took a step toward the kid, and Levi strode out of his hiding spot in the deep shadows, a blade in each hand.

Charlie spotted him immediately, turning to sneer at him. "I knew you were still looking for me. You didn't think I'd come alone, did you?" He made a gesture in the air, and Chaolt stepped out from behind pine and barren trees and out of cars in the parking lot.

He knew he'd felt more than one, and here they were. Way too many for one warrior to handle on his own. He took a step back.

He clenched his fists, flames creeping along under his skin. He stared at Charlie, his eyes glowing with embers of hate.

Charlie chuckled, sensing the trap he'd set for Levi closing.

God, he couldn't wait to melt that look right off Charlie's fucking face. And soon, he hoped, because he'd set a trap of his own.

"I didn't either," Levi said with a grim smile.

Walker, Ajax, and Micah stepped out from behind a giant rock they'd hidden behind that hadn't been there yesterday. That's where they were to take shelter if his fire got out of hand.

And despite the fact their powers were nulled out by the Chaolt now, they'd still been very useful beforehand.

The subsiding snowstorm was the work of Walker and Ajax, combining their water and air to clear out any humans from the park and make the rest hunker down inside their homes.

And Levi and the other warriors stood on dry ground thanks to Micah. He'd manipulated the soil to absorb the moisture from the snow on their end, whereas the side of the park the Chaolt were on was covered in icy, slippery mud. If the warriors kept their footing and waited for the Chaolt to come to them, they would have an advantage.

As long as Connor stayed put, any Chaolt that tried to reach him first would fall in the moat they'd made and covered with a thin layer of dirt that wouldn't support weight.

And even without their powers, the other warriors were a force to be reckoned with. There was little doubt the four of them could handle all the enemy. Each of them could easily take out four or five, and with his fire, Levi could take out more.

It was satisfying to see Charlie realize that, to see his expression go from confident leer to apprehension, to fury.

Levi spread his fire from his hands up to his shoulders, to fill his eyes and dance along his scalp.

Charlie stared at him with a displeased twist to his mouth. "How are you able to do that, huh?" he asked him, surveying the rest of them. "When none of the others can."

Levi waited until his gaze returned to him. "Come closer and I'll show you."

Charlie threw back his head and laughed, the sound bitter and brittle. He must have realized he wouldn't be leaving here. Though the snake was sure to try.

And right on cue, he waved the Chaolt forward to attack, then took off in the opposite direction.

Levi looked at Walker. His commander knew this one Chaolt was his entire reason for the mission. Walker nodded his permission, and Levi sprinted after Charlie, trusting that his fellow warriors could handle the rest.

But the ranks of the other Chaolt closed around him, and he had to battle his way through. Augmenting his knives with elemental fire, he slashed his way through the enemy. Most of them were only wounded and would have to be dusted by one of the other three. Once he was free of the group, he searched the park for his target, and found him jogging for the parking lot.

Coward. Levi bared his teeth, flames flaring, and ran full tilt toward him. Charlie opened the door to a truck, moments from escaping.

With a rage-filled cry, Levi spun in a circle and launched a burning blade from his hand. Like a flaming arrow, it flew through the air and buried itself in Charlie's shoulder.

He cried out and yanked it from the bone, but his momentary pause gave Levi time to catch up to him.

He wrenched him away from the open door and threw him to the icy blacktop. But he was back on his feet quicker than Levi had expected, and Charlie rocketed a meaty fist into his jaw. He saw sparks, half from the impact and half from the fire that jumped inside him as his anger surged.

Levi threw himself at the enemy, and they both landed hard on the ground. They grappled a few minutes in the slush before Levi gained the advantage. He was down to one knife, and Charlie held tightly to his wrist, not allowing him to bring it down.

But he didn't need it. He had his fire.

With his free hand, he gripped Charlie's throat, pushing fire into him in a steady stream as he choked him.

Sometimes the fear in the eyes of the enemy got to him, but not now. Not Charlie's. Instead, he saw Brooke's terror in the middle of the night, heard her cries, felt her shudders against him, and pushed harder.

His control had been much better since his trip back to Primordia, but he felt it wavering, felt the wildfire inside him trying rise. He fought to keep it a steady stream instead of an explosion that would endanger everyone nearby.

The stench of burning plastic increased. Charlie's feet thrashed, his body bucked, but Levi held on to him and his restraint despite Charlie's fingernails clawing at his arms and face.

For Brooke.

Charlie burned from the inside, his hands falling away, and his form collapsed under Levi as he turned into a stinking pile of ash.

Levi knelt in the sloppy combination of ashes and melted snow, steaming, panting. At some point, it had started to snow again, and flakes drifted down and melted instantly on his heated skin.

He looked up into the gray sky, steadying his breathing. It was hard to put his fire away once he got started. It was more like closing off a gushing pipe than turning off a burner, and he cranked down on his control, reducing the flow of power bit by bit. Finally, it was just a trickle, and he rose to his feet to go help the others clean up the rest of the Chaolt.

But when he got there, there weren't any left, and ashes mixed in the air with the snowflakes.

Ajax was in deep conversation with Connor, who looked shaky. They'd take him back home and drain his powers before they let him out of the van, erasing any memory of them and the last hour.

Levi closed his eyes and focused on the minute sensations of cold from snow landing on his face, relief and fatigue rising in him.

"All good?" Walker asked him with a heavy hand on his shoulder, prompting him to open his eyes and meet his commander's cold blue stare.

"All good," he confirmed, nodding.

It was finally over.

It was late when Levi made it back to their suite. He opened the door silently, knowing Brooke was probably already asleep. When he stepped in, he was surprised to see white twinkling lights on a short tree casting a warm glow into the darkness. He glanced around, noticing other decorations around the room and an abandoned pile of boxes, still in the bags, in the corner.

Brooke had decorated their suite without him.

He walked over to the table the tree sat upon and picked up a small package wrapped in silver paper and red ribbon. It was for him.

That's when he realized it was Christmas Eve.

Setting the present back down, he searched the dark alcove where their bed was, seeing her form outlined by the covers.

Guilt stabbed at him. He'd been so busy and focused on finding Charlie for Brooke that the days had passed without him truly realizing. And he missed doing all the things that he'd wanted to do with Brooke for their first Christmas together.

Damn it. He pushed his hair back, sighing.

As quietly as he could, he entered the bathroom and showered, washing away the soot and stench from the fight. The water stung tiny injuries he didn't know he'd had, but thankfully, he'd be healed by tomorrow.

He dried off and crawled into bed beside Brooke, hair still damp. She faced away from him, and he inched closer, trying not to wake her, so he could wrap his arm around her. When he did, he found her stiff instead of relaxed and warm in sleep. She was awake but didn't speak to him.

He didn't know what to say, so he just lay there, staring past her shoulder at the wall.

But then he felt her move, a silent shake.

"Brooke?" he whispered, raising on one arm to look at her. But she shook her head and pressed her face into her pillow, her body still quaking occasionally between harsh breaths.

She was crying.

He grimaced, then brushed her hair back from her face. "Brooke...I'm sorry."

"It doesn't matter."

"It obviously does matter to you—" he began.

"To *you*," she said pointedly, then she pulled away and sat up, back to him.

Stunned, he was silent a moment. "It does matter to me. I've been working on your Christmas present."

She turned and looked at him. "Do you think that's what I wanted?" she asked, eyes red and swollen, suggesting she'd been crying earlier too. "I could care less about a gift. What I wanted was to *spend it with you*. Celebrate it with you." She threw her hands up. "Why do men always underestimate the value of just being there?" She looked at him, sad eyes refilling with tears. "I wanted you to be here."

"I've been working extra shifts—"

"Oh, I know. And the other day I asked Walker why he was sending you on so many extra ones lately, and he said he wasn't. That you had your own agenda. So, you just didn't want to be here? You'd rather work than spend Christmas with me?"

Shit. He sat up and pushed his hands through his hair. He'd asked Walker not to mention what he'd been doing because he had been concerned that if she'd known about it, she'd be more worried. But he hadn't considered how it would look to her.

She turned away, sniffling. "It's okay if Christmas isn't a big deal to you. Really, it is. I just wish you'd told me instead of avoiding me and making promises you had no intention of keeping. I needed you here," she whispered, the last word cracking.

He held her upper arm as she went to stand, heart pounding with something akin to panic. "Brooke, I swear it isn't that. Look at me."

He waited until she did, and he stared deep into her eyes as he let his emotions fill his with flames. "I *swear* it. I did want to spend Christmas with you, I *do*, but... Your present took a lot more time and effort than I expected. And I realize now that I let that distract me from what was really important, which was spending time with you. It won't happen again. I love you."

They stared at each other until her frown relaxed. "Okay."

He slowly pulled her into his arms, and she didn't resist. But then she leaned back and looked up at him, eyes narrowed. "It better be an amazing present, to take all this time and effort."

"Uh..." He sat back, relieved she believed him but also suddenly doubtful. Maybe he would have been better off making her a gift, or taking her on a trip, or something.

She probably wouldn't think hunting down and killing Charlie was an amazing present. God, why had he? Christmas was supposed to be a time of happiness and joy, not a reminder of the darkest time of her life.

He watched disappointment and skepticism start to fill her face again at his continued silence and decided to tell her now. Maybe he could still buy her jewelry tomorrow to make up for it.

He took a deep breath. "I killed Charlie."

"What?" she asked, but he knew she heard him. He held his breath wordlessly as emotions flitted over her features.

He felt compelled to explain himself. "You've been having a lot more nightmares lately. You've been tense and worried in the daytime. Something has stirred all that up again for you, and I thought...if I could eliminate him, it would help. You wouldn't have to worry about him ever coming after you again and you could feel safe. Whether awake or asleep."

"That's my Christmas present?" Her face crumpled and she pushed her face into his chest, sobbing, gripping him with both hands by his T-shirt.

Stunned, he slowly wrapped his arms around her and closed his eyes, jaw clenching as regret and shame filled him. He was one stupid son-of-a-bitch.

"I'm sorry," he said, miserable. "I know that's a shitty gift. I'll get you something else too. I'm sorry," he said again. But she simply shook her head against him, breath hitching.

He stroked her head. As soon as he could, he'd go buy her a trip to Costa Rica. Without him, if she wanted. Somewhere she could go for a week to have fun and relax and forget about what an idiot her mate was.

She leaned back and scrubbed her eyes and nose with her wrist. "Thank you."

"For?" he asked, confused.

She palmed his cheek, staring at him, glossy eyes reflecting the lights from the tree, making them sparkle.

"For this. For noticing. For caring so much."

He blinked. "You're—happy?" She didn't look or sound happy.

She gave him a watery smile and sniffed. "Happy isn't really the right word. But relieved, for sure. Thankful." She closed her eyes momentarily and opened them again. "So freaking in love with you."

He sat up straighter, a grin starting. It *had* been a good present.

"Because you're right. I have been worried lately. Scared about the future. Concerned he might try to come back after me or—" She shook her head and looked down at her hands twisting in her lap. "I'm sorry I gave you grief. I've been hormonal, and anxious, and not sleeping well, and it's made me a little crazy."

"It's ok," he said, kissing the top of her head and pulling her close. He felt the heavy sigh that went through her, leaving her body more relaxed as it exited. He snuggled her and kissed her cheek.

"Ready to go back to sleep?"

She nodded, and they lay down together, face-to-face. They stared at each other and then kissed, and she settled her head on his shoulder. She must have been exhausted, because she fell into a deep sleep in minutes.

He however, stayed awake, staring at the lights on the little tree. His gaze shifted to the boxes in the corner.

Tomorrow was Christmas. There was one more gift he could give Brooke, something to put some joy on her face.

He extracted himself from Brooke's embrace, careful not to wake her, and got to work.

Levi quietly worked for several hours while Brooke slept to get everything ready for her. Thank goodness elementals didn't need as much sleep as humans. Just as the sun came up, he surveyed the suite and nodded. It was perfect.

He went to wake her up, gently and slowly. When she opened

her eyes, she smiled at him, and he felt like everything was right with the world again.

"Good morning," he said with a grin as he stroked her face with the back of his knuckles.

"Good morning," she replied.

"I have something for you," he said, pulling her hand to tug her to a sitting position.

"You do?" But as soon as she sat up, she saw it and gasped.

He'd put up every decoration, every strand of lights she'd bought, plus a few he'd made himself, like paper snowflakes. Candles stood on every flat surface, adding a cheery glow to the room since it was overcast and snowy outside.

"Merry Christmas, Brooke."

She threw the covers back and hopped out of bed to throw her arms around him. "It's beautiful. Thank you."

She kissed his cheek several times and then turned to gaze at the room from the crook of his arm.

"Later, we're going to have hot cocoa and cookies while we watch holiday movies. And we'll listen to Christmas music while we eat dinner. And next year, we'll decorate together. I promise."

"Ok, I'm going to hold you to that." She nodded and smiled. "Are you ready for your present now?" she asked, stepping from foot to foot like an excited child.

"Do you want to get dressed and have breakfast first?" She was still in her nightshirt, the collar falling down one smooth shoulder, her hair unraveling from a messy bun.

But she shook her head, eyes bright. "No. I've been dying to give you your present for weeks. I don't want to wait another minute."

"Okay," he said, grinning, and she took his hand and tugged him to the couch, where he sat. She handed him the small silver-and-red package.

He slowly undid the ribbon and paper, noticing the nervous wringing of her hands. He had no idea what she'd gotten him, but this was important to her.

Inside was a plain cardboard box, and he took the lid off. Nestled inside was an ornament. A tiny pair of shoes made of spun glass.

He pulled them out and held them in his palm. "They're beautiful." And they were. He loved glass art, all forms of it, but he didn't understand the significance of the shoes.

"I just wanted you to have something to open on your first Christmas, but your real gift isn't inside the box."

He looked up at her, confused.

Brooke had her hands layered over each other, pressed to her lower abdomen. "It's inside me."

The eternity it took for his brain to kick into gear was probably only two seconds, but when it did, what she was saying registered like a firework going off. "You're—"

She bit her lip, smiling, eyes filling with moisture.

"But I'm supposed to be sterile!"

"Yes, well, apparently, you're not," she said, shrugging one shoulder with a half-smile, half wince.

He carefully laid the shoes back in the box and sat it on the couch. Then he jumped to his feet and snatched her into a tight hug, instantly releasing the pressure before hugging her more gently. He pulled back, searching her face for confirmation. "We're going to have a baby?" he asked, emotions mixing inside him in a way that made his fire bubble like hot lava within him.

She nodded and gave a watery laugh, patting out tiny smoldering holes that had appeared and begun to spread on his T-shirt.

He shook his head, stunned. All elemental warriors were supposed to be sterile. But then again, their powers were supposed to be nulled by the Chaolt, and they weren't supposed to have relationships with humans. Looks like those weren't the only things that had changed by Brooke coming into his life.

Would their baby have elemental powers? More than likely. That was going to be interesting to deal with.

They had to tell Walker and hope he wouldn't make him go

back to Primordia and face the Premiers. The thought made his blood cool to ice in his veins.

But they would worry about all that later. Right now, he wanted it to be him and Brooke and their child—no outside worries or concerns, just joy and celebration.

He put his hand to her lower belly, and she laid hers over his. He closed his eyes and reached out with his powers, similar to how he did when he looked for Sleepers. He felt Brooke's small amount of fire energy, and then...

The tiniest, weakest ember on the edge of his senses.

His eyes flashed open and cast orange light over Brooke's face as he stared at her in awe.

"Can you feel it?"

He nodded, unable to speak through the block that suddenly filled his throat.

Her smile was as lovely and bright as a winter sunrise over a snowy field. Tears filled her eyes. "Merry Christmas, Levi."

He palmed her cheek. "Merry Christmas, Brooke." He kissed her with every bit of joy, amazement, and excitement inside him.

Despite him almost screwing it up, their first Christmas together would forever be a special memory.

ALSO BY JOANNA MORGAN

Elemental Warriors Series:

Burn

Rise (coming April 2023)

ABOUT THE AUTHOR

JOANNA MORGAN writes paranormal and fantasy romance. She lives in Michigan with her husband and two kids. A Romance addict, nature lover, and chronic daydreamer, she often finds herself absorbed in romantic visions of different worlds and characters. Sometimes, she even writes them down.

FIT FOR A GODDESS

BY S.C. GRAYSON

FIT FOR A GODDESS

XANDER

XANDER'S SANDALED FEET POUNDED UP REDDISH DUST AS HE BOBBED and weaved through the crowded marketplace. He darted around a burly man surrounded by red and black pottery, narrowly avoiding running headlong into a woman shouting about the best olive oil in the region.

Even on normal days, the stall-lined streets were a hub of activity, but with the Panathenaic Games beginning today, it seemed as if everybody from a one-hundred-mile radius stood between Xander and his goal. The crowds gawked at the marketplace selling everything from textiles to weaponry, instead of paying attention to where they were walking.

He should have known better than to look for a gift for Aediene today, but his jittering nerves had driven him out of the Sanctuary and into the heart of the city. Second-guessing his plans for the festivities with Aediene, the thought had struck him that flattering her with a gift might set the right tone. After all, the Games were the largest celebration of the year, and Aediene deserved to enjoy all the festivities had to offer, including a gift. Still, as he pushed through the crowds at the marketplace, nothing seemed to hit the exact note he was searching for.

Perusing, he'd run his hands over fine red textiles, woven with gold. Even as he had reached for the coin purse at his belt, something told him it wouldn't be the right thing. Fine cloth was the traditional gift for a woman at the holidays, but Aediene deserved something all her own. Something that showed her Xander had given this thought beyond a traditional courting gesture. He had briefly considered a golden arm band woven in the pattern of a Herculean knot, but the symbol of everlasting commitment might seem too forward when they had never even... Well it didn't matter. He planned to remedy the issue soon enough. That was the point of the gift after all.

It occurred to him at some point during his browsing that a weapon would be the most fitting gift for a Warrior like Aediene, but no weapons found in the city would be superior to those crafted by the Smiths at the Eteria. Maybe at some point he would ask Antony to forge her something using the Light, perhaps a spear worthy of her prowess. A grand gesture for an even grander occasion. That didn't help him now though.

He had lost track of time trying to find the perfect gift, thoughtful but not overly grandiose, and ended up empty-handed. Hopefully, he could still make it to the arena in time to watch the opening of the Panathenaic Games. *Pankration* would be the first event, and he didn't want to miss Aediene's performance. She was always at her most beautiful when she was dumping an unsuspecting wrestler in the dirt. While Xander had grown used to watching her fight by channeling blasts of Light through a spear, there was something spectacular about witnessing her take down an enemy with her bare hands.

Finally, Xander found himself in the milling crowd on the edges of the arena. He searched for Aediene's proud posture and chestnut braid and smiled at the sight of so many Eteria tunics studded throughout both the spectators and the competitors— bright reds and deep blues, green and purples scattered among the grays and tans. It warmed his heart to see his companions in the Light celebrating.

Normally, the Eteria kept to themselves, living in the Sanctuary to focus on dedicating their lives to the Light, only venturing out for confrontations with the Shadow—interfacing with the rest of the world as anonymous protectors and nothing more. Every few years, though, the Eteria showed up in force to the Panathenaic Games, a reminder that celebration and camaraderie were a way of honoring their duty as well. After all, the power of the Light came from all that was good and beautiful in the world. The Games might draw the most spectators, but they were part of a larger winter celebration of the Goddess Athena. After all, glory in combat was only one of her aspects, and the Games were just a single way of honoring the Goddess. When the competitions concluded, there would be a week of feasting and dancing and music—a holiday worthy of the city's patron Goddess and a time of joy for all.

Of course, Warriors like Aediene often joined in the athletic competitions, showing their skills in wrestling, boxing, and *pankration*. A few Defenders from Xander's order threw themselves in the mix as well, mostly in the foot or boat races. Some Smiths and Healers even broke out lutes and lyres for the musical contests, but everybody participated in the feasting and the revelry. The city overflowed with life, strung with colorful streamers and flowers. A whole week of music and dancing, feasting and frolicking dedicated to Athena.

That's what made these days so special to Xander. Aediene could have been the Goddess herself with her intelligent smile and unparalleled skill with a spear. In his mind, this festival was a chance to celebrate *her*. Finally, a holiday from battle and training where he could give her the attention she deserved, the way she deserved it.

Now if he could just *find* her.

※

Aediene

Using her hand to shield her eyes from the sun, bright and warm despite it being winter, Aediene scoured the crowd for Xander's lanky figure. She had hoped he would make it to the stadium in time to see her compete. After all, the color that rose high on his sharp cheekbones told her he liked what he saw whenever they trained and fought together. Aediene hadn't missed the way he glanced at her thighs when her tunic rode up during a high kick, or how stilted and awkward he had been after she knocked him on his back and held the butt of her spear to his neck in the practice ring last week. They had even shared their first kiss after a particularly intense mock battle, both still coated in dust, adrenaline pounding in their veins.

Still, in the weeks since then, things hadn't moved much farther than those furtive kisses, sweet as they were. Aediene, never one to sit back and wait for things to happen, had entered herself in the *pankration* competition at this year's Games. If watching her kick an overconfident soldier or two in the face didn't put some fire in Xander's blood, she didn't know what would.

Of course, none of this would come to pass if he didn't get to the stadium in time. At least if her plan failed, she could drink away her sorrows with Thad at tonight's feast where wine would not be in short supply.

"Let the games begin!" the announcer shouted.

Aediene had been drowning out his words until this point, too lost in thought, but this caught her attention. The crowd roared and the *pankration* competitors filed out into the packed dirt center of the stadium. Aediene fell into step, and even as her heart clenched with disappointment that Xander was going to miss her first fight, her soul lifted with the cheers of the spectators. Even if she didn't get to seduce Xander, she would revel in the thrill of competition. She looked forward to actually enjoying the way her body sang in combat, and not worrying about where the Shadow would strike next or if it was gaining the upper hand.

As Aediene lined up across from a man built like a bull, she grinned. In answer to her obvious pleasure, her opponent's frown only deepened, pulling thick, dark brows together. Despite her considerable height, the fighter before her was twice her width, built like a minotaur. The muscley ones were always the most fun to take down.

Clang!

The ring of the bell marked the beginning of the fights, and as it echoed across the stadium, all the pairs of opponents began circling each other. Once the field was narrowed down, the matches would happen one at a time, to give the spectators a better view. For now, though, the masses fought for the privilege of being crowned one of Athena's champions.

Luckily for Aediene, the Goddess of wisdom and war seemed to have a soft spot for her.

As her opponent lunged, Aediene crouched low, sidestepping at the last possible moment. The man nearly tumbled to the dirt, carried by his momentum, but kept his footing narrowly. Aediene kicked out at his chest, planning on pressing the advantage, but he was faster than she anticipated.

Using the excess momentum, the bull of a man whirled around, striking out with an open hand. Already off balance from her kick, Aediene couldn't dodge completely out of the way. The heel of his hand hit her shoulder instead of the center of her chest where it had been aimed.

The blow was strong enough to knock the wind out of Aediene if it had hit its mark. As it was, she stumbled back, feet scuffing on the dirt.

Her opponent charged forward, keeping on the pressure. With her equilibrium askew, she couldn't dodge out of the way in time to avoid his meaty arm. He grabbed her across the shoulders, forcing her into a grapple and trying to bear her down to the ground with his superior mass. Luckily, he wasn't thinking about Aediene's feet.

She swept one leg out and around his calves, catching him behind the ankles. His base knocked out from under him, he fell to the dirt on his back with a thud. Aediene worked with the momentum of his fall, coming down on top of him, elbow pressed to the hollow of his throat.

The cheers of the crowd, blocked out before by Aediene's concentration, filtered back in as her opponent signaled his surrender. She removed her elbow from his neck and pushed to her feet with a grin wide enough to make her cheeks hurt. As she reached down to help her opponent up, he batted her hand away with a scowl. Aediene just shrugged as he struggled to his feet and stormed off towards the edge of the stadium in a whirlwind of frustration. She wouldn't revel in losing in the first round of the Panathenaic Games either.

Glancing around her, it appeared she and her opponent were among the first to finish their fight, although more hands raised in surrender as she watched. The temporary reprieve gave her an opportunity to return to scanning the crowd. Her heart stuttered harder than it had during the fight as she finally caught sight of dark curls, messy on top of a lanky silhouette. Xander was here. Even if he had missed the opening round, the coming fights were sure to be more interesting anyway.

She raised her arm to wave her victory to him, only to pause. The darkness in the crowd behind him moved in a way that was at odds with the sparkling sun from above. She squinted, trying to get a better view, and prayed she had just been imagining things. The darkness twisted again, the unnatural movement putting ice in her veins.

Aediene didn't know why the Shadow would be at the games, but it couldn't be good.

❄

Xander

The grin that split his face was so wide it was nearly painful when he finally caught sight of Aediene, just as she bore a man twice her size into the dirt. She had been stumbling away from him, and anybody who knew Aediene less well than Xander might have thought she was about to lose. Capable as she was, she had turned it around.

Xander threw his arms into the air in victory with a loud whoop of celebration. People around him glanced at his sudden antics, but he only had eyes for the woman on the field as she brushed the curls that had escaped her braid from her eyes. She surveyed the arena, gaze finding Xander almost immediately, as if some sixth sense told her exactly where he would be standing.

Xander answered her wave with one of his own, but his heart stuttered as she frowned at him. He had been counting on the joy of victory for tonight's festivity, but Aediene's expression was not one of pleasure. Were his plans for the celebration ruined before it even began? What had he done to earn Aediene's ire? He had stood witness to her impressive temper before but rarely been on the receiving end of her anger.

As he worried, Aediene began trotting towards the edge of the arena. He wasn't going to have to wait long to hear what bothered her, as she was never one to avoid speaking her mind. Still, as Aediene placed her hands on the barrier bordering the crowd and vaulted smoothly over it, Xander saw she was not looking at him but focused on a point somewhere over his left shoulder.

Xander twisted to follow her gaze, brows furrowed. At first, he saw nothing but cheering spectators, roaring at another victory on the field. Maybe Cyril was behind him making rude gestures at Aediene, as he tended to do since she had spurned his attentions.

Just before he turned back towards Aediene to ask what was wrong, he saw it. A Shadowed limb slipped out of sight, a stark stripe of darkness around a fluted white column. Before he could even wonder why a Shadow was at the Games, he was off, pushing through the crowd. People grumbled as he edged past them, forcing them to move aside, but Xander paid them no mind. He felt more than heard Aediene at his back, a sense as familiar in a fight as his own breath.

They picked up speed as they reached the outskirts of the crowd, having more room to maneuver. By the time they passed the pillars at the edge of the spectator area, they were sprinting, feet synchronized in their pounding on the cobbled walkway.

The pair skidded around the corner into an alley, empty of people as everybody piled into the arena to watch the competition. The Shadow reached the dead end of the street, stopping to look over its shoulder. The dark silhouette was foreign and familiar at the same time, bipedal with two arms like a human but disproportioned in a way that set Xander's teeth on edge no matter how many times he fought them. This one twisted the tear in its Stygian flesh that served as a mouth into a smile, as if taunting them. Then it dashed up the wall in front of it, too long arms acting like tentacles as it flung itself off window frames and uneven stones.

Xander slid to a halt even as Aediene hurtled past him. He only paused for a moment as Aediene charged towards the wall, launching herself upwards at the last second to catch hold of a windowsill on the second story. She followed the Shadow's path, albeit slightly slower due to the limitations of human hands and feet.

Tearing his gaze away from Aediene, he doubled back to a street branching off the alley, planning to cut them off. Running around the corner and along the side of the building Aediene and the Shadow were scaling, he caught a brief glimpse of Aediene's crimson tunic as she hauled herself onto the roof and sprinted along the edge. The Shadow reached the end of the structure and launched itself over the gap between buildings, body billowing more like smoke than flesh. Aediene jumped after him, crouched landing only slowing her down infinitesimally before she was on her feet giving chase again.

Xander kept pace on the streets below, running through the layout of this part of the city in his mind, searching for places they could pin down the creature. The Shadow seemed to have other ideas, though, leading them towards the outskirts of town instead of towards denser areas where there were more nooks and crannies in which to corner an enemy.

Realizing that the Shadow was most likely leading them to the hills separating Athens from the Sanctuary, Xander made a split-second decision. He turned away from the chase on the rooftops, taking a more direct route to the edge of the city. As he lost sight of Aediene's chestnut braid snapping behind her, Xander sent up a brief prayer to Athena that his battle strategy would work. After all, she should be watching over the festival being held in her honor.

Dashing down the wider main road, it was only a matter of moments before Xander broke free from the shelter of buildings and onto open grass. He turned and dashed towards where he guessed Aediene and the Shadow would be emerging. If he hadn't been panting from the exertion, he would have sighed in relief as her red tunic came into view, right behind the dark figure, charging across the rooftops but slowed by the periodic jumps and changes in elevation.

Xander moved to intercept them. As the Shadow reached the edge of the roof, it took a flying leap. Its long arms extended to slow it's fall, looking almost like twisted wings, before it hit the ground with a thud that would have left it with broken bones if it were made of flesh and blood.

Aediene didn't hesitate as she hurtled towards the edge of the roof as well, and Xander was stuck somewhere between frustration at her recklessness and pride in her implicit trust in him. As she leaped and one leg extended into thin air, Xander threw out his arms. The familiar warmth of the Light coalesced in his belly and shot forth from his fingertips, creating a step just under Aediene's outstretched foot. A series of glowing golden stepping-stones materialized in the air in front of Aediene, even as the Light exiting

Xander's body tugged at the base of his stomach. He fought the urge to be sick. It was so much harder to use the Light without a weapon of some sort to channel it with.

He didn't have time to worry about that now. The Shadow was charging straight towards Xander. Bracing himself once more, he raised his hands, an iridescent shield springing up before him, spanning out in a shimmering, golden half-moon shape. He breathed in through his nose as a wave a nausea crashed over him once more.

Seeming to see that it was being corralled, the Shadow tried to turn away, darting to the side to avoid the barrier of Light. The change in direction slowed it just enough for Aediene to make her move. A javelin of Light appeared in her hand, and she launched it forward without breaking her stride. It shot cleanly through the Shadow's chest, who gave one ear-piercing shriek before exploding into a cloud of smoke.

Aediene

Swallowing thickly, Aediene pushed down the sudden wave of nausea that hit her at the use of the Light without a weapon. She had become so used to channeling her weaponized blasts through her bronze spear that she had forgotten how difficult it was to do so without a medium. Still, the feeling dissipated quickly enough. It wasn't hard to push away the unpleasant sensation as she basked in the triumph of her teamwork with Xander.

They might not be in sync in the way she hoped to be yet, but they could still practically read each other's minds in the heat of battle.

Thinking of Xander, she trotted towards where he still stood to see him frowning. Running her gaze up and down his lanky figure, she found him to be unharmed. She rested a hand on his tanned shoulder to draw him out of his reverie.

"Are you all right?" she asked, her voice seeming quiet to her ears compared to the blood that roared in them during the chase.

"Oh, of course," Xander responded, placing a hand over her own. "Just worried about a Shadow showing up at the Games."

Aediene nodded. The same thoughts echoed in her head. Still, the Shadow had picked an inopportune time to attack when the crowd had been full of Eteria members capable of destroying it.

"We kept it from hurting anybody, and that's what matters," Aediene reassured. "You'll feel better once we've cleaned up and cooled off. We'll have to alert the Commander to the Shadow's presence as well."

Xander nodded and followed her as she set off across the field towards the Sanctuary. The large white building where the Eteria members lived, dedicating their lives to the protection of the Light, wasn't a far walk. It stood imposing and beautiful, all tall, fluted columns and shining marble, just on the other side of some grassy hills.

They walked in companionable silence for a while, and Aediene let Xander's magnificent mind work, knowing he would speak when he was ready. After all, it had taken him years of training together for him to befriend her, even though she had caught him staring at her often. It had taken even longer than that to express his romantic interest.

For now, Aediene just enjoyed the soft swish of the knee-height grasses they waded through and the warmth of the afternoon sun on her shoulders, more pleasant now in winter than it was in the baking heat of summer. It would add to the myriad of freckles springing up on her skin from long days of training outdoors, and not for the first time, she envied Xander his bronze skin that tanned deeply without blistering or peeling.

"Why would a lone Shadow attack the Panathenaic Games? Do you think they are getting bolder?" Xander broke the silence.

"Possibly." Aediene shrugged, even as she thought on Xander's words. It seemed like the Warriors were being dragged from the

Sanctuary more and more often to drive back the Shadows from this estate or that village. "Maybe it was just a fluke."

"But the Games of all places... They are supposed to be full of camaraderie and celebration. All things that are the antithesis of the Shadow's existence. How could one be there?"

Xander was right. The Shadow was fear and despair and hatred —all the negative emotions of humanity given form. It didn't seem right for one to show itself at the most joyous celebration of the year.

"Maybe that is exactly why the Shadow was there," Aediene mused. "It wanted to ruin a celebration that was supposed to be a reminder of all the good in the world. A tribute to the Light. It wanted to steal from us an occasion that would have rejuvenated the Eteria and strengthened our resolve."

"Well maybe it worked then," Xander said glumly.

Aediene glanced over at him to find him looking far older than he was, his shoulders slumped. Granted, both Xander and Aediene were nearly fifty, but neither of them had aged beyond looking like they were in their twenties, and they never would, thanks to their connection with the Light. Despite the magical properties of the Light keeping them youthful, the weight of the growing Shadow seemed to burden them physically.

"It didn't ruin anything," Aediene argued, determined to not let the Shadow take this day from them. "We are going to report the Shadow's presence to the Commander and then go enjoy the feasting. Thad has been bragging about an amphora of rare wine he bought, and I am *not* missing that."

By now, they had reached the Sanctuary, passing under the broad marble arch emblazoned with time-honored words. *Every Light casts a Shadow.* But tonight was a night for looking towards the Light.

Still Xander sighed heavily as they made their way through the hall.

"You missed the rest of the tournament because of the Shadow attack," Xander pointed out, leading them into a courtyard with a fountain they could use to rinse the dust from their hands.

"It's probably for the best. I mean, the competition wouldn't be very fun if I beat everybody easily," Aediene teased, trying to lighten the mood. She smiled victoriously at Xander's throaty laugh in response, although it reminded her of her other goal in the tournament.

Maybe she lost her chance to seduce Xander by dumping other warriors in the dirt, but if this afternoon's Shadow attack had reinforced anything, it was to not delay joy—to not put off celebration out of fear of the future.

Aediene glanced sidelong at Xander, currently splashing water from the fountain on his face to cool himself. Drops of liquid clung to the curls hanging in his face and trailed down his corded forearms. Xander certainly had a lot of tanned skin that Aediene wanted to celebrate, and she was tired of putting it off.

Perching on the edge of the fountain, Aediene unlaced the leather ties holding her sandals to her feet. Xander cocked his head at her in question.

"My feet are sore from all the running," she explained, trailing her fingers up her calf in a way that was probably unnecessary for getting her shoes off. She didn't miss the way Xander's gaze tracked the movement though. "I want to soak them in the water for a second."

Kicking her other sandal off, Aediene plunged her toes into the water with a contented sigh. She may have ulterior motives, but the cool liquid was bliss against her skin, overheated from the recent fight. Playfully, she swung her feet, splashing some water in Xander's direction.

"Are you going to join me?"

Xander only hesitated a moment before sitting down beside her to take his own shoes off. Once he had swung around to bathe his feet, Aediene scooted closer, their bare knees brushing against each other.

Xander glanced down at where they touched, but his expression was still pensive. That wasn't quite what Aediene was going for.

"Why does one Shadow have you so shaken up? We fight them all the time." Aediene didn't mention that battles were now almost a weekly occurrence.

A furrow formed on Xander's brow as he answered. "I just had plans for the Games. I wanted everything to be perfect, but well... things got out of hand."

"What kind of plans?" Aediene questioned, letting her fingers drift to Xander's leg, a long expanse of thigh exposed by the short tunic-style *peplos* he always wore. The contrast of the navy-blue cloth made his golden tanned skin look even more luminous.

"Plans to spend time with you," Xander admitted with a shrug.

"We are together now," Aediene pointed out.

Xander opened his mouth, but Aediene had enough of his griping. Instead, she silenced him by swinging one leg over him, kneeling on the edge of the fountain, straddling his lap. Shocked into silence, Xander gazed up at her, the sunshine on his face making his russet eyes glimmer.

Aediene leaned over and took advantage of the way his mouth hung slightly open to slot her lips against his. Kissing him felt like a sigh of relief, something she had gotten used to over the last several weeks, ever since she had finally broken through Xander's thick skull that she cared about him as more than a partner in battle. Still, kisses were all they had shared, and Aediene did not make a habit of waiting for what she wanted very often.

As Aediene licked at the seam of Xander's lips asking for entrance, he gasped, hands flying to her waist. His nimble fingers twisted in the red linen of her tunic, as if he were afraid she would disappear if he let go. Instead, she pressed herself closer to him, not having any intention of leaving his side. The front of her torso was flush against his, and when a hard length dug into her backside, Xander broke the kiss with a strangled groan. Aediene didn't relent, though, grinding down in a way subtle enough to tease while still making her intentions clear.

"Here?" he gasped.

"Why not here?" Aediene grinned down at her battle partner and best friend with a wicked grin. "Everybody else is at the games, and I like the way your skin looks in the sunlight."

*scene break

Xander

Aediene made a habit of keeping Xander on his toes, and while sometimes it was bad for his blood pressure in a fight, he was not going to complain now. Not when Aediene's fingers carded through his hair and he could feel more than hear the moan of pleasure in the back of her throat. So, he wrapped his arms around her waist and kissed her soundly and deeply.

When she pulled back to catch her breath, Xander gazed up at Aediene and concluded that not even the Goddess Athena could compare to her in this moment. Aediene's chestnut curls escaped their braid to dance around her head, as wild and free as her smile. Backlit by the sun, she appeared to be haloed in Light. Her lips parted and her eyes danced with equal parts mischief and desire.

Briefly, Xander pictured the perfect nest he had set up in his rooms for just this moment— an amphora of the finest wine chosen by Thad, a bowl of the juiciest figs, and sweet smelling flowers scattered on plush rugs. He had wanted to bring Aediene back to his rooms after the games, drunk on victory and celebrations, to have a romantic evening. Xander had waited for—painstakingly planned for—this moment, needing everything to be perfect, convinced Aediene deserved better than the rushed couplings of trainees in the Eteria barracks. It was now he realized this was already perfect, simply because they were together.

It was with this thought that Xander dove in to kiss her once more, not willing to wait a moment longer. Aediene smiled against his mouth, seemingly amused by his sudden enthusiasm. An uncharacteristic growl escaped the back of Xander's throat, and he moved his lips to her throat, succeeding in wiping the grin from her face as his teeth on her collarbone caused her to gasp.

Not one to be outdone, Aediene pushed his tunic from his shoulders, exposing his chest to the sun. Her hands on his bare skin ignited something in Xander's chest. Any shyness or apprehension he had been holding on to was incinerated in the heat of her touch. He pushed to his feet, hands cupping Aediene's thighs to lift her with him. The squeak of surprise and delight that escaped Aediene's lips was unlike any noise Xander had heard the Warrior make before, and he was determined to drink in every sound he could pull from her.

Xander took his lips from her skin momentarily to focus on stepping out of the fountain, intent on lowering Aediene to the ground where he could press himself against every inch of her body. Aediene had different ideas. As soon as her back touched the stone floor, she tightened her thighs where they wrapped around his waist, pulling him to the ground and rolling herself on top of him.

Momentarily disoriented by the sudden change in perspective, Xander blinked up at Aediene. She, on the other hand, hastily unfastened the clasps at her shoulders and the belt around her waist, tossing the length of red fabric that served as her tunic aside. Something in her urgency, even though they would likely live for thousands of years, made Xander chuckle—or it would have if he weren't entirely focused on the weight of her settled firmly across his hips. Deciding she had the right of it, Xander followed suit, ridding himself of his already halfway dismantled *peplos*.

Finally, they were bare together. Aediene leaned down to kiss him once more, sighing in relief as if her mouth had not pressed against his in ages, even though it had only been moments. Xander let his hands wander freely, tracing the valley between her breasts, the gentle curve of her stomach, all the way down to her core. The whimper that escaped her when he stroked her there was mentally filed with the squeak from earlier as a sound that Xander could get drunk on.

In a matter of moments, Aediene was squirming on top of him, nudging his hand out of the way to fully join with Xander at last. Normally the more patient of the pair, Xander found himself approving of her urgency for once.

Whatever awaited them in Elysium, it couldn't possibly compare to this. Not when Aediene moved on top of him and pleasure exploded behind his eyes. He could no longer remember why he had put this off for weeks, except to think that whatever reason he had was exceedingly stupid. How could he have denied himself the sunshine scent of Aediene's hair in his nose, heightened by the sweat and dust of battle? Or the shaky puffs of breath against his neck as she gasped in pleasure?

It wasn't long before Aediene's movements began to lose rhythm, her strong thighs quivering where they clasped around him. Xander dug his heels into the ground and thrust up against her, determined to give Aediene everything she desired and more. When their pleasure crested, it was with Aediene's teeth in his neck and her name on his lips.

Aediene

Why Xander had held out on her for so long, Aediene didn't know, but they were going to be having words about it later. For now, she melted atop him, tucking her face into his neck and letting the dying sun warm her bare back. The gentle trickling of the fountain in the background served as a reminder that they were outside in a public place. Still, she wasn't willing to chase the feeling of satiated laziness from her muscles to move just yet. Especially not when the way Xander absently untangled what remained of her braid with nimble fingers made her want to purr like a cat.

"I should have known everything with you would feel right, no matter what," Xander murmured into the top of her head, breaking the contented silence.

At that, Aediene pushed up onto her elbows to regard him.

"You were worried it wouldn't?" she asked skeptically. Ever since Xander had finally kissed her senseless after training a few weeks ago, she had felt as if everything had clicked into place, like the cogs on one of Antony's mechanical wonders. No matter how many Shadow attacks they had to defend against, she knew things were right with the world now that Xander was at her side as more than just a comrade in arms. But did he not feel the same sense of rightness? Was that why he had waited so long to move things further?

Before Aediene's thoughts could spiral out of control, Xander drew her back by stroking her cheek with his knuckles.

"Being with you is a gift I do not take lightly," Xander murmured. "I wanted to give you romance worthy of Aphrodite herself. I wanted to wait for the perfect time. A celebration free from worries of Shadows when we could drink wine and dance. I had everything set, but I was afraid it would all be for nothing when we were drawn away by the Shadow attack."

"Well, you forgot one very important thing." Aediene leaned in conspiratorially. "You may have been trying to seduce me as if I were Aphrodite, but this is a celebration of Athena. And as a follower of the Goddess of war, nothing is a truer expression of my feelings than fighting at your side."

Xander chuckled, the rumbling in his chest vibrating pleasantly through their connected bodies. "I should have known. It's a shame all my preparations have gone to waste."

"I didn't say we couldn't *also* enjoy whatever you had planned," Aediene pointed out.

"Then enjoy it we shall," Xander declared, punctuating the statement with a kiss on the tip of her nose that made her feel uncharacteristically girlish. "But first, we really should go tell the Commander about the Shadow."

After the time shared in the sun-soaked courtyard, the earlier fight with the Shadow felt more like a distant memory than something that had happened merely an hour ago. Still, it was their duty as members of the Eteria to remain vigilant in their protection of the Light.

The pair helped each other redress, gathering scattered sandals and sorting out their red and navy *peplos*. Despite their best efforts and a quick rinse with the water from the fountain, they both ended up looking rumpled. Their clothes were wrinkled, and their hair was mussed beyond hope. As they set off through the Sanctuary towards the Commander's room, Aediene snorted at the blooming purple bruise forming at the base of Xander's neck, visible even against his olive complexion. There was no way the eagle-eyed Commander would miss that.

As they rounded the corner to the hallway containing the Commander's chamber, they almost ran headlong into the person in question. Coming to a halt, the towering woman eyed them imperiously, one brow arched in question.

"Xander, Aediene. What are you doing here? I expected you to be competing in the Games," she asked, tone as authoritative as ever.

"I was, but a Shadow attacked, and we were forced to pursue," Aediene reported, coming to attention, spine straight as her spear. "We defeated it on the outskirts of the city and did not encounter any further Shadows."

"Just the one Shadow?" The Commander clarified. "Shadows rarely attack in isolation, but it probably had no choice, given how weak it would be at such a grand celebration. No doubt this Shadow was just doing what it could to interrupt the festivities that would give so much power to the Light."

Aediene nodded once, surprised the Commander would be so dismissive of the attack, especially in a time when the Shadow seemed to grow more powerful with every turn of the moon. Still, she was probably right that drawing the Eteria away from the Panatheniac Games would be playing directly into the Shadow's hands.

"The best way we can protect the Light today is by celebrating all that it stands for," the Commander continued, echoing Aediene's thoughts. "Although from the looks of it, you two have already been celebrating the Light's gifts of love."

Xander stiffened next to Aediene, making a strangled sound in his throat and gazing intently at the floor. She managed not to break eye contact with the Commander, although she nearly choked on her own saliva in shock. Aediene might have burst into flames from mortification if not for the twitch of amusement at the corner of the Commander's mouth, at odds with her usually stoic expression. Maybe it was the joyous occasion, but a sparkle lit the Commander's eyes that Aediene didn't see while the woman was detailing battle plans.

"Now if you'll excuse me, I have a feast to attend as well," the Commander said when neither Xander nor Aediene formulated a coherent response. "I hope to see you at the festivities."

With that, the statuesque woman swept past them down the hall, robes so white they appeared incandescent, swirling behind her before disappearing around the corner.

"Well, I guess when the Commander herself tells you to party, there's really no excuse not to," Xander mused, seemingly recovered from his embarrassment, although a blush still lingered on his sharp cheekbones.

"We may have missed the end of the *pankration* tournament, but I'm sure Thad is saving us a seat at the feasting tables," Aediene agreed.

With that, they made their way out of the Sanctuary and back to the plains separating the Eteria's home from the city of Athens. In contrast to their earlier journey, now they teased and joked, stopping to steal the occasional kiss. With as much as the Shadow was weakened by joy and celebration, no creature would be able to stand coming within one hundred yards of them.

Aediene had been right, and Thad waved to them enthusiastically as they entered the city square, the movement making the golden beads decorating his braided hair shimmer in the light of the setting sun. As soon as Aediene and Xander slid onto the low bench next to the Healer, he launched into a full recount of today's tournaments. Their friend moved on to comments about which competitors had the best figures and what exactly he would do to those physiques if he had the chance. As they listened, Aediene and Xander snuck smiling glances at each other out of the corners of their eyes.

Antony, the quiet Smith dressed in purple, passed Aediene a cup of wine with a knowing smile. Nothing escaped the magical craftsman's eye, but Aediene couldn't even bring herself to blush at his raised eyebrows. Instead, she laughed, a sound of pure joy emanating from her.

Xander

As Xander enjoyed the feast with his friends, he couldn't keep his gaze from drifting to Aediene beside him. When she laughed, despite nobody having told a joke, she shrugged at his questioning look.

"Just happy," she leaned in close to be heard over the increasing noises of revelry. Her breath tickled the shell of his ear, and Xander was reminded that he still had his rooms set up for the perfect night of romance.

For now, people were producing lutes and drums, striking up a song that would last all night, until the competitions started again the next day. A few partygoers made their way to their feet, dancing to the music in the orange light of the setting sun. The drums pounded in time with Xander's heart, lifting his spirits in a way that only music and revelry could. He felt drunk on the feelings of happiness and companionship surrounding him, despite not even having finished his first cup of wine. It had been too long since the Eteria had been together like this, and he planned to make the most of it.

Xander put his hand in Aediene's and pulled her to her feet, overtaken with the need to dance with her. Aediene went willingly, letting the momentum move her close to Xander. So close that he could smell the lingering sweat not quite masking her honeyed scent. Thad whistled loudly, but the couple ignored him, instead beaming at each other.

After all, if Xander had learned anything from today, it was to celebrate the beautiful things in life, even if everything wasn't exactly how he had envisioned it. And with how beautiful Aediene looked grinning at him and leading him to the open dancefloor, he had enough worth celebrating to carry him through millennia.

ALSO BY S. C. GRAYSON

Defenders of the Light Series:

Spears and Shadows

Chaos and Crowns (coming June 2023)

The Talented Series:

Beauty and the Blade (coming January 2023)

ABOUT THE AUTHOR

S.C. GRAYSON has been reading fantasy novels since she was a little girl, and that has developed into a love of writing and story-telling. She is currently focused on fantasy romance and magical realism.

When she is not sitting in a local coffee shop writing and consuming an iced americano, Grayson is a nurse working towards a PhD in nursing with a focus on breast cancer genetics. She lives in Pittsburgh with her loving husband and their two cats, who enjoy contributing to her work by walking across her keyboard at inopportune moments (the cats, not the husband).

LONG LOST

BY LILY RILEY

1

CHARLOTTE

"It's your turn, Mina, darling."

"I hate this game. I don't want to play," Doctor Van Helsing grumbled. She shifted from foot to foot, tugging at the front of her bodice and anxiously running her hands over the tops of her wide *panniers*.

"You look absolutely gorgeous, *chérie*," Daphne assured. "That powder blue silk brings out your eyes so well."

"I feel like an over-iced pastry," she huffed. "I should never have let you talk me into coming to this dreadful ball. What are we even celebrating? Christmas was a month ago and we had our New Year's *réveillon* already."

I looked around at the luxurious decorations—boughs of blue spruce wove around a pale blue silk-covered table, which practically groaned beneath the elaborate spread of decadent dishes.

Spiced, wine-drenched roast meats, delicate seafood bisques, beef and pork pies, an embarrassment of fine cheeses, tropical fruits from distant lands—*think of the expense!*—and pastries topped with edible sugar snowflakes glistened beneath glittering silver candelabras. Blue and silver draperies hung at the windows, putting me in mind of a snow-covered bluebird morning.

"The winter solstice?" I asked.

"That's in December, *chérie*," Daphne replied absently. "Perhaps His Majesty is simply feeling festive and wishes to celebrate the beauty of winter."

I shrugged. "What does it matter? As long as we have an opportunity for the work at hand..."

"I'd much rather be back in my clinic," Van Helsing complained. "I have so much work to do!"

I handed the petulant Dutch physician a glass of champagne.

"Take your medicine," I said with a wry smile. "You'll feel much better."

She wrinkled her nose at the glass. "Champagne gives me a sour stomach and a sore head the following morning."

"It's practically a requirement for socializing with the aristocracy," Daphne chuckled, candlelight glinting off her needle-sharp fangs. Despite being a wealthy and powerful duchess, her engagement to the king's vampire emissary and her turning had left her on the outskirts of the *tonne*—though it was a consequence she heartily embraced. With the blood plague sweeping through France and the hungry peasants and *bourgeois* deliberately infecting themselves to avoid miserable starving deaths, the few humans of the aristocracy were becoming increasingly anxious. As recently turned supernatural beings, Daphne and I were working hard to try and force the king and court to see reason—to make peace and lend aid to those in need—but we were starting to lose hope. It seemed the more dire the need, the more ferociously the aristocrats clung to their power and wealth.

"The odious *Vicomte de Malin* has been eyeing you all evening,"

I teased. "That's fortuitous. If he asks you for a dance, you'll want the fortification. Besides, perhaps the effervescence will improve your mood."

Van Helsing cut her eyes to the vulgar aristocrat, who winked at her. She blanched and downed the glass of golden courage in one abundant swig.

"Don't worry, we'll protect you. If he's foolish enough to try anything untoward, I will take him out into the gardens and eat him," I giggled. My stomach growled, proving my willingness to shift into my werewolf form and dispatch anyone who laid a finger on my dear friend.

Daphne stifled a groan. "You'd have to save some for me, Charlotte. I haven't fed in two days. If I don't get some blood soon, it may affect my cheerful disposition."

Van Helsing and I looked at Daphne incredulously, then let out an unladylike eruption of laughter. Daphne was kind and loyal but known for her at-times *tenacious* disposition. She pretended to scowl, but her violet eyes glittered with mirth.

"Go on, then, Mina," I wheedled. "It's your turn."

"Pass. Daphne may go in my stead." Van Helsing plucked another glass of champagne from a passing tray. She hiccoughed and frowned at the leering *vicomte*.

Daphne sighed. "Very well. If I were not engaged to my handsome, charming Étienne—"

I rolled my eyes. "Yes, yes. We know. This is just a game, Daphne!"

"I would seduce *Comtesse de Renarde*, stab Monsieur Honoré, and sup on Malin," she finished.

"You wouldn't!" I cried, scandalized. "How could you stomach him?"

Her pupils dilated and her nostrils flared—I could sense her hunger. "Very fat. Lots of blood," she murmured, almost trance-like. I cleared my throat and she collected herself, opening her fan to disguise her embarrassment.

"That man is *awash* with garlic," I pointed out. "His blood would reek of it."

"That is a silly superstition, Charlotte. I quite enjoy garlic. The Italians are onto something, you know."

"Still, don't you think you'd want to bite someone else? He still believes bathing is ill for his health."

"Surely, but you dictated the rules of this game, and you said they had to be in this ballroom. I challenge you to find a courtier who *does* bathe regularly."

"Fair point," I replied. "Honestly, I don't think I could sleep with *or* eat someone who believed such nonsense." I wrinkled my nose in disgust.

"Well, it's your turn, anyway, if you're so high and mighty about it," Daphne sniffed.

"Right. If I were not engaged to my precious, perfect pastry, Antoine—"

"Urp." Van Helsing covered a burp, mortified. "Sincerest apologies, *mes amies.*"

"I would seduce that lovely lady-in-waiting—what's her name, Danielle? I would certainly stab Malin—though I don't think I'd stab him; I'd probably throttle him because I wouldn't want his poisonous blood all over my lovely gown. And I would sup on Monsieur Honoré."

"He beats his servants, you know," Van Helsing said quietly.

"Yes, we know," I replied, narrowing my eyes at the wealthy landowner. "It would be slow and rather painful for him, I'm afraid."

Daphne nodded sagely. Van Helsing began to look a tad green about the gills.

"Are you well, Mina? You do realize champagne is meant for sipping, not gulping, don't you?"

The doctor nodded, opening her fan with an unsteady hand. "Might we play a different game?"

I arched a brow. "It's not like you to be ill at the discussion of viscera. Do you need some air, *chérie*?"

She nodded vigorously. "It must be the champagne."

I reached for the jewel-studded *chatelaine* at my waist—an heirloom handed down from my mother. The delicate silver chains used to bear all the keys to the rooms of my family estate, but since my mother died, I'd taken to wearing the elaborate pin as a piece of sentimental, yet functional jewelry. Now, instead of the keys, at the end of each chain hung a tiny compartment disguised as a gemstone. The compartments held a set of small lock picks, a tightly coiled *pianoforte* wire I used as a garrote, and I still had enough space for secret messages, occasional poisons, and in this instance, smelling salts. I tugged at the ruby-covered box and offered it up to Van Helsing, who looked at me with the same disgust she would have displayed if I'd tried to hand her a beheaded snake—or an *English* pastry.

"Don't be ridiculous," she hissed, but her lips were pale and her complexion took on a waxy sheen.

Daphne and I led her through the sparkling gilt room, stuffed with over-important people all trying to catch the eye of His Majesty, King Louis XV. As soon as we made our way to the snow-covered courtyard, I breathed a sigh of relief. Van Helsing gripped the edge of the icy balcony and stared out into the torch-lit gardens.

"It was rather stifling in there," Daphne said, unsuccessfully hiding her concern. "Mina?"

"I'm fine," she said, closing her eyes. "I just detest these things."

"I've seen you face down supernatural terrors, amputate limbs, and stitch your own flesh wounds," I said. "Don't tell me you're overcome by a silly little party with a bunch of pompous wastrels?"

"Give me broken bones and septic wounds over an *allemande* any day," she mumbled. "Though...I don't attend to as many of those wounds as I once did. Lately, it all seems to be about helping new vampires through their transitions. I worry France will run out of blood before we see the end of the grain blight, and then who knows what will happen. We already know the blood plague has the power to mutate"—she looked at me pointedly—"and I don't want to know what happens when vampires start to feed on each other. My research hasn't been as promising as I'd hoped." She wiped her damp brow with the back of her hand and frowned. "If only the king would do more to help feed his people. I truly fear what comes next."

"He will not," came a velvet voice through the snow-soft silence of the garden. Daphne's fiancé, Étienne, *duc de Noailles* and vampire emissary to His Majesty, materialized from the darkness and strode forward, sliding a possessive arm around his soon-to-be duchess's waist and pulling her in for a ravishing kiss. Snowflakes dusted his raven-dark hair but wouldn't melt without the body heat of humanity. A small, unruly lock had escaped his queue, which—aside from his devilish beauty and rakish charm—was yet another thing that made him stand out at court. He never wore the powdered wigs or pastel colors that were fashionable, but was usually clad in rich, jewel-toned velvets and dark-as-sin silk brocades. His lean, muscular form and sharply angled face did nothing to discourage the notion that he was anything other than what he was—a predator, a *former* libertine, and ever hungry for the love of his eternal life, Daphne.

"Forgive me, *ma cher*, for taking so long. Antoine and I were trying to convince him to import more grain, but he won't hear of it. The prices of food will continue to rise, and so will the numbers of blood plague sufferers," his golden eyes flashed, matching the bite of his bitter tone. "He believes those that choose to turn are abandoning God and deserve to be punished. Not that he would say such things to us, of course. We only hear the rumors of what he says when he is alone with the other nobles."

"Choosing to survive on blood to avoid death by starvation isn't any kind of choice," came a second voice from the darkness. The low rumble of my beloved's tone raised goose bumps along my skin and sent my heart fluttering. Unlike Étienne, Antoine didn't appear to materialize from the gathered night—softly, he stepped forward like a cautious wild creature approaching from some dangerous, otherworldly woodland. Even dressed in his sharp captain's uniform, there was a touch of the primal about his tall, muscular form, his broad shoulders, and the moon-shaped scar that ran along his cheek. His chestnut hair was pulled back tightly, and his strong jaw sported a whisper of stubble that never seemed to leave his cheeks, no matter how often he shaved.

"Antoine!" I breathed, flinging myself at him and burying my face in his chest. He smelled as he always did—even before I turned him and saved his now-immortal life. Earth, leather, mint, apples, and horseflesh—he'd been out riding his favorite black Andalusian, Tartuffe, before coming here tonight. I stood on my toes to nip at his neck, a strange sort of *bon soir* between mates and a promise of lustful adventures ahead.

He blushed and dropped a soft kiss on my cheek. Unlike Daphne and Étienne, Antoine was still shy about public displays of intimacy and affection, which naturally propelled my ardor to white-hot intensity.

"Are you particularly fond of those breeches?" I said brazenly, sliding my hands over his firm ass. "Or will you give me leave to rip them to shreds when we get to the carriage?"

His blush spread from his cheeks to his ears and throat—my reward for being so bold. His moss green eyes darkened like night falling in a forest, and he leaned forward, brushing his stubble across my cheek.

"If you keep teasing me in public," he murmured in my ear. "I will be forced to punish you when we return home."

A satisfied growl emanated from my chest. "Tell me how," I breathed.

"Oh, do save it for the ride home," Daphne begged. "Those of us with supernatural senses can still hear you."

"Spoilsport," I pouted. Antoine winked at me, making me seriously consider leaving the ball early.

"Please," Van Helsing interjected. "Give me leave to return to my clinic. Or to go home. I'm too weary to be polite to the men whose servants I treat for various forms of abuse."

"But we only just arrived!" I complained. "And it's incredibly lucky that the *vicomte de Malin* has been lusting after you—we're so close to finalizing a course of action for him and we could use your help in learning his whereabouts over the next few weeks."

"I do not work for the Order," Van Helsing replied. "I do not want to be involved in your organization's brand of punishing justice. I only care to heal people and to find a cure for the blood plague."

"Of course, *chérie*. We know how you feel about the Order, and we'd never ask you to betray your conscience. We only wish to know when he'll be leaving for his country estate. We just want to have a little...*exploratory adventure* in his private study. There are some questions about some rather indelicate and potentially treasonous activities. We've asked his servants but they're too afraid of him to tell us anything," I explained, approaching to link arms with her.

"What will the Order do with the information?" she asked hesitantly.

The Order—a long-shadowed organization of the powerful and elite—often performed their own investigations into potential threats to king and country. They delivered justice that was, at times, beyond His Majesty's reach. Daphne and I had been working from within to curb their penchant for violence against impoverished vampire-kind, but it was getting harder to convince them to do what was necessary to support the middle and lower classes. Under the guise of establishing a group of women agents to serve the Order, we'd formed *les Dames Dangereuses* and were keeping a close eye on our male contemporaries. I didn't fault Van Helsing for being distrustful of them—I often felt that way myself. Still, I did what I could to help provide balance and ensure that the people being *punished* truly deserved what came their way. The *vicomte de Malin* deserved more than most.

"Truly, *chérie*, I cannot say. But if we find the proof that we're looking for—that we are almost certain is there—I suspect he will meet an untimely end." I shrugged. "Given the number of servants from his household alone that you've patched up, I would think you'd consider that a fitting end."

"I can't have another man's death on my conscience," she said quietly. The phrasing struck me as odd, but I didn't press. It was likely she had seen death come too often in her line of work. I understood and respected her decision, but I couldn't hide my disappointment.

I nodded. "As you wish, *chérie*. I'll not press you again. Daphne, it looks like we're on with our original plan."

Suddenly Antoine, who stood furthest back from our little cabal and closest to the ballroom, hissed at us.

"Hush!" he whispered. He tipped his nose up to catch the scent of something on the wind. "He's coming, *mes amies*."

He and Étienne melted back into the darkness, leaving Daphne, Van Helsing, and I alone on the terrace. As predicted, Malin strode toward us with the equally distasteful Monsieur Honoré in tow.

Van Helsing flashed a pleading look at Daphne, undoubtedly hoping she would not address the men. As the highest ranking among us, Daphne could control the entire situation. If she did not acknowledge either man, they wouldn't speak to us. Unfortunately for Van Helsing, our plan dictated otherwise.

"*Bon soir, Monsieur le Vicomte.* Monsieur Honoré," she nodded briefly, her predatory smile looking polite and frightening all at once.

Both men bowed low. "Your Grace," they said in unison. Malin eyed Van Helsing with the same hunger as Daphne eyeing his pulsing neck vein. I didn't bother to hide my grin.

"Are you enjoying the wintry festivities, Monsieur Honoré?" I offered, reaching deep for my aristocratic charm.

"Indeed, *Comtesse de Brionne*, though I could enjoy it a bit more if you'd save a dance for me. Something vigorous, perhaps, to match your fertile temper." He smiled lasciviously at me, eyeing my breasts pressing against the low neckline of my bodice. *Disgusting. Perhaps I would simply eat him, after all.*

"Of course, Monsieur," I tittered. "I'd be delighted."

A disembodied growl punctuated the night air. The sound sent a thrill through me. *Ah, sweet Antoine seems a tad jealous. Poor thing. I'd much rather dance with him, but I must suffer through this to distract Honoré enough to let Daphne extract the information we need from Malin.*

Malin extended his hand to Van Helsing. Daphne attempted to redirect his gesture by ushering us back toward the ballroom again, but he remained unmoved.

"And you, Mademoiselle? I don't believe I've had the pleasure." The way he said *pleasure* made all three of us try not to grimace. Still—this was *the plan.*

"I'm afraid Doctor Van Helsing was just leaving, Malin," Daphne replied. "Perhaps you'd favor me with a turn about the room instead."

Something like shock lit in the *vicomte's* piggy eyes. "A physician! But she is a woman! How utterly absurd."

"I say, *Doctor,* I fear some of my humors may be out of balance. Perhaps we may find a quiet room where you might *examine* me," Honoré oozed, earning a mule-like guffaw from Malin.

"What a ridiculous, liberal notion," Malin continued. "A *woman* in the sciences. If your spinsterhood has forced you into a profession, pet, perhaps we could come to some sort of arrangement? I've only just cut ties with my former mistress—an opera singer of some note. There's a ready vacancy to be filled. Or perhaps you'll allow me to fill *your* vacancy."

Fury rolled off Van Helsing like waves heralding a storm at sea. Another uproarious bout of drunken laughter came from the pair. My lip curled in disgust before I could school my expression in aristocratic blandness, and unfortunately, Honoré noticed. His hand was on my wrist in a movement much quicker than I would have expected.

"Have you something to add, *Comtesse de Brionne*?" He glared at me, cruel eyes assessing my response through the sour fog of spirits. I felt my canine teeth lengthening.

Daphne kicked me from beneath her skirts—a clear direction to *stay the course. Remember the plan.*

I swallowed my rage and hunger, turning an absurd pout on the man.

"But *Monsieur Honoré*, you promised *me* a dance. Surely you haven't forgotten already?"

His grip relaxed—I almost mourned the opportunity to break his hand and rip his arm from its socket—and his oily grin returned.

"Certainly, Madame," he replied, tugging me forward. Though I was much stronger than he, I allowed him the luxury of believing he held the upper hand. Precious few aristocrats knew of Antoine's and my supernatural state, and we aimed to keep it that way.

Daphne stepped forward, as well, poised to offer Malin her hand for the dance no one wanted. Van Helsing cut her off, offering the *vicomte* a frosty smile to match the cold blue of her eyes. Even I shivered, and I'd long since stopped feeling the cold. Had the man an ounce of sense in him, he would have recognized the danger in her expression.

"*Monsieur,*" she said, glacial eyes glittering. "I do have a vacancy on my dance card." She extended her arm to him and the delighted, disgusting ass led her inside. She glanced at Daphne and I with a look that said, *Leave him to me.*

I only hoped there would be enough of him left over when she was through with him.

2

CHARLOTTE

Snow drifted down in soft, sleepy clumps, blanketing the frozen mud that crunched beneath the carriage wheels. If I were human, I would have been extremely put out by the frosty conditions, but they barely registered. The only temperature I felt anymore was usually in relation to Antoine, and it was only ever feverish.

Irritatingly, he sulked in the carriage as we ventured home, making it exceedingly difficult for me to peel his clothing from his brooding form. I made a noise of frustration as I attempted to yank the coat of his lovely blue and white formal uniform down over his impressively broad shoulders and expansive chest. He did not lift his arms to aid me, but held me firmly in his lap, jade eyes boring into mine.

"You are not listening to me, *mon amour*," he said in a low voice as I fiddled with the buttons on his breeches.

"Of course, I am! It's simply that I can hear you better when you are naked."

He didn't smile outright, but I could tell he wanted to by the way the edges of his lips twitched. He stayed my fervent touch with one hand and brought his other up to my cheek.

"I know your work is important, Charlotte, but you must understand how much I hate seeing other men paw at you."

"Jealous, Antoine? Or worried?" I teased.

"Neither. I trust you, and I know you are more than capable of taking care of yourself. I just dislike how these titled men think they can press their advantage simply because you are a woman," he said softly, running his thumb across my lips. "Like you are a mere *plaything* to the likes of them."

I leaned forward to press a gentle kiss to his forehead. "It's charades, *chéri*. That's all. When I flirt with them, it's never for pleasure. It's to give them the illusion of control. It's enough to be taken for granted, so that when I strike, they don't see it coming."

He harrumphed and frowned, flexing the moon-shaped scar across his brow.

"Besides, you are the only man for whom I would ever consent to be a *plaything*. I love you, Antoine—enough to spend eternity with you. But my work with *les Dames Dangereuses* is for all the women in France who are at the mercy of powerful men. Not all of them are as lucky as I am."

My words unlocked him, and he finally smiled, flashing dazzling white teeth in the darkness of the carriage. Hastily, he shucked his coat and slid one hand beneath the gold silk of my skirts.

"How much longer until we arrive home?" he murmured. "I want to hear more about your willingness to be my plaything."

I kissed him then, long and lush, sucking on his full bottom lip. Twining my fingers in his dark, chestnut hair, I chuckled. "Darling, if you so wish it, I'll be your *anything.*"

Predator's eyes glowing, his hot gaze shot to mine. "You are my *everything.*"

The carriage slowed, indicating that we'd approached the tree-lined drive of my family estate, where Antoine now resided with me. It was improper and scandalous, but we were engaged, and since I was already a widow, I was allowed some latitude from the censure of the *tonne.*

"*Merde,*" I swore. "Shall we send the carriage around again? We can be quick!"

His low laughter filled the space just as his clever fingers found the slick seam of my sex, already aching for him. Gently circling one fingertip at the apex of my pleasure, he growled in my ear. I bit back a moan.

"I do not *want* to be quick."

With that, he picked me up, kicked open the carriage door, and carried me up the icy steps to our home, still decorated for Christmas and New Year's *Réveillon* celebrations. Evergreen branches and holly boughs made the whole *château* smell like a wintry forest. Candles guttered in the chill wind, their light flickering on shining gold and red decorations. The scents of spices lingered in the air—ginger, cinnamon, and cloves—making my mouth water almost as much as Antoine did. When we reached the main bedroom on the second floor, he tossed me on the bed and dove down after me.

"I must make an early start tomorrow, *mon amour,*" he huffed, tugging at the ties on my skirts. "I'm off to oversee the training of my new regiment." Before the heavy silk fell to the floor, he was already unpinning my bodice and nearly ripping the ribbon from my stays.

"I thought you said you didn't want to be quick," I teased. "I think this is the fastest you've ever undressed me."

He grinned and tugged his shirt over his head. I sucked in a breath. Even though we had eternity together, I didn't think I would ever get used to the raw beauty of him. Muscles like iron flexed beneath golden skin, and dark hair sprayed across his chest and trailed below his bellybutton. The scars from a lifetime of battles decorated his too-perfect body, sharply contrasting his peaceful nature. He acknowledged my appraisal with a saucy wink, and I giggled and slipped out of my chemise.

"I can't help it," he retorted. "I've been thinking about you all evening." He pulled his breeches off and crawled up my body on the bed, dropping feather-light kisses up my legs and hips. "But I promise to take my time with your pleasure."

He nipped at my hipbone and spread my sex with his thumbs, baring my intimate secrets to him. He sighed in satisfaction, then drew one long, slow lick up my center, making me squirm and swear on an out breath. He pulled one of my legs over his shoulder and nibbled at the inside of my thigh before returning his attentions to my desperate sex. Heat flared inside me like a bonfire of old tinder, and I knew it wouldn't take long for me to find my bliss. Again and again he licked, driving me toward some distant utopian galaxy that lay just beyond reach.

"Slow down, my love—I want you too badly," I pleaded. Chuckling at my torment, he found the peak of my need and sucked at it, then slid one long finger—then two—inside me. *Perfection.* "Please, Antoine, share with me *la petite mort.* I do not want it without you."

"As you wish, *chérie,*" he growled, lowering my leg from his shoulder and moving up my body. Impatiently, I wrapped my legs around his waist and reached down to find him—glorious, hot, and hard. Gritting his teeth, he hissed a breath.

"I was going to take my time," he muttered, somewhat forlorn. "But I fear this will be quicker than I wish."

I slid him inside me on a gratifying moan from us both. He struggled valiantly to move slowly, trying to be noble and prolong my pleasure, but my love for Antoine would put Aphrodite to shame, and I could bear his slow romance no longer.

"Antoine," I huffed, slick with sweat and desire. "This is only the first bout. Fuck me like you mean it, damn it."

That heart-stopping, lop-sided grin again and he drove into me with enough force to crack the heavy oak bed. *Yes. Yes!* Harder and faster he moved, reaching the place inside me that I believed would let me see the face of God—or perhaps Lucifer. My back arched and he took my nipple into his mouth, but soon abandoned it with an uttered string of delicious obscenities. Stars danced around the edges of my vision, and that distant world spun into view, dancing closer and closer until we crashed into it together, orbiting as one perfect heavenly body. Waves of pleasure rocked through me, and Antoine held me as we came down, vibrating with exhausted joy.

"*Je t'aime, Charlotte,*" he whispered. "Now and forever."

"I love you, too, Antoine," I replied, nuzzling into his neck. "I'm going to miss you while you're away. What am I to do without you?"

His large hand swept over my stomach to rest gently on the swell of my hip, and I could hear the smile in his voice when he answered.

"You'll just have to think of all the things we can do upon my return."

"Oh, I have a few things in mind already," I sighed, tilting my head up to nip at his earlobe. "But it would be best if we tested a few of them out—just in case. What if you don't enjoy them?"

"Well, then," he conceded, pulling me on top of him. "I suppose we should try them out. *Just in case.*"

I was delighted to learn that Antoine enjoyed every single one.

The following evening, I awoke in a disappointingly empty bed, save for the rose on the pillow next to me. From any other man, I would have scoffed at the saccharine gesture, but from Antoine, it was wonderful.

I'd hardly had time to throw on my dressing gown and call for some supper when Daphne whirled in, determined to yank me from my rest and relaxation.

"The sun has barely set, Daphne," I groaned. "What has you so vexed?"

"Have you spoken with her?"

"With whom, dearest?" I replied, stifling a yawn.

"Van Helsing!" she cried in exasperation.

"Not after last night, and not in detail. I lost track of her and Malin on the dance floor, and then after the dance ended, she handed me a note with some dates on it—presumably dates that he would be at his country estate—and left for the night. I assumed she simply danced with him, found out when he would be gone, and then went home for the evening," I shrugged. "Why? Has something happened?"

Daphne closed her eyes and pinched the bridge of her nose. "Malin never returned home last night."

Shock froze me in place. "You don't think..."

Daphne looked at me helplessly. "I don't know! I don't think she would do anything, but I certainly do not doubt her capacity to do so. She'd had a great deal of champagne and was absolutely furious about his advances."

"No," I stated firmly. "Certainly not. Van Helsing wouldn't have done anything to him. She has been so adamant about staying away from the Order and anything violent or nefarious. The bastard is probably with a mistress or sleeping off his drunkenness back at Versailles. I'm sure he'll turn up."

Daphne frowned. "Show me the note."

Unnerved by her manner, I went to my hastily discarded gown to get the note from its hiding place in my *chatelaine*. Antoine and I had been so distracted in our intimate attentions, I hadn't bothered to unpin the jewelry from its place on my bodice.

It was gone.

Panic edged into my chest, but I refused to let it take root. *It must be here!* Discarded in our hasty attempt to divest each other of our clothes—or perhaps it fell off in the carriage. I rang for my housekeeper, Madame Toussaint.

"Madame, have you seen my *chatelaine*? It is not here," I said, rifling through the mess of garments on the floor.

"*Non,* my lady," she replied, brows furrowing. "I have not seen it

268 | LONG LOST

since you left for the ball last night. I'll assemble the staff and ask if it's been found."

"Check the carriage, as well, please," I said.

Daphne's eyes went wide as I hurried to dress.

"Do you think it is truly lost? Could it have fallen off your gown?" she whispered. "Or is it possible that someone stole it?"

"No—I don't know how they would have! Antoine and I came straight home after the ball. I had it when we went outside onto the terrace because I thought Van Helsing was going to faint, and then..."

No. Oh no. The fear I'd been holding at bay finally overwhelmed me as I considered the damning possibility.

"You don't think Monsieur Honoré took it, do you?" I choked out, incredulous. "Could he have? He was drunk! I don't understand why he would steal from me...it's only a mere bauble to him. He wouldn't know its true purpose or of my affiliation with the Order."

Daphne's brows knitted together and she blew out a breath. "It's possible that he's smarter than he looks. I don't know. What else did you have in the compartments? And what else was on the note from Van Helsing?"

I tried to remember. "I had smelling salts, my lock picks, my garrote, and a few other blank scraps of paper. And I only remember some dates on the note from Van Helsing, but we should probably check with her. Wait...did you go to her clinic already? What brought you here this evening?"

She sighed and came over to help me cinch my stays and pin my hair up. "I went by first thing this evening, but she did not answer. There were no lamps or candles lit and the door was locked."

Worry gathered in my stomach. "She is probably sleeping off the champagne," I said, but didn't feel entirely confident.

"With Van Helsing *and* Malin missing, plus your *chatelaine*, I fear there might be something more dangerous afoot," Daphne said.

"Well, first things first," I declared, putting on my favorite pair of gloves. "We must find Van Helsing and ensure that she is well. Let's go back to her clinic."

Daphne nodded. "Agreed. Let's take my carriage—it should still be out front and your footmen might be searching yours for your *chatelaine.*"

We stepped out into the silvery night and I inhaled deeply. I'd loved the damp smell of freshly fallen snow before I was turned, but now with my supernatural abilities, I could sense a great deal more in the air. Woodsmoke from distant fireplaces, the domestic aromas of dinners being cooked, beeswax candles dripping, the earthy smell of horses and dogs, and skeletal winter trees—their bare branches bowing beneath the weight of the snow. I could even close my eyes and my nose would paint me a picture of all that lay before me—it was a wonderful boon to temper the excruciating pain that came with shifting form. I imagined Daphne and Étienne felt the same way about being vampires. The price of blood-drinking was a high one to pay for similar supernatural gifts.

Her footman ushered us into her well-appointed carriage and she settled back against the plush seats. She opened a small side panel next to her and pulled out a small champagne coupe and a crystal decanter filled with blood.

"Have you eaten, *chérie*?" she asked, filling her glass.

In answer, my stomach rumbled. Smiling, she pulled out a small basket covered with linen and handed it to me. Inside was a sizable cut of raw venison—one of my new favorites.

"Oh, thank you, darling! You're an absolute angel." I was *ravenous.* I pulled my gloves off and concentrated on extending one long claw from my fingertip. The dagger-sharp nail grew long enough for me to slice portions of the steak off and I delicately dropped them into my watering mouth.

Heaven!

"So," I began after swallowing. "What do *you* truly think happened?"

She lifted one pale shoulder in a small shrug. "I have my suspicions, but I cannot be sure. To answer your next question, *no*, I do not think Van Helsing murdered Malin. I'm sure you're right and the blackguard will turn up—eventually. As to our other problem... I do not think it is past Monsieur Honoré to steal your *chatelaine*. Whether it was because he suspected you of hiding secrets, or because he is simply a greedy thief, I cannot say."

The venison churned in my stomach. The idea that I could have been thwarted by the evil man was disturbing at best and life-altering at worst. I'd only been bested by one man before, and I'd just spent the night in his arms. *Antoine.* I wondered where he was at this moment.

Sometime later, we arrived at Van Helsing's clinic on the *Rue Ordener*. She lived in a small apartment above the clinic, and despite her success as a physician and notable scientist, she preferred to live a somewhat spartan lifestyle. I'd long ago offered to find her a larger estate, to help expand her clinic, to secure more funding for her research from the aristocracy, and *at the very least* gift her with a sizable wardrobe so that she might accompany Daphne and I to more parties. She'd laughed at several of the offers and scoffed at the rest, thanking me for my generosity but stalwartly refusing to live a life that didn't suit her. Daphne and I loved her for that.

I was heartened to see lamps lit upstairs and scent her familiar fragrance—wool, soap, herbs, almonds, lime blossom. I saw the relief in Daphne's face, as well.

Rather than enter through the clinic door, which was locked and bolted, we approached through a back stairwell off the side alley. When we knocked, she answered immediately, looking none the worse for wear.

"Bon soir!" she said, wiping her hands on an apron and ushering

us inside a small study. "How are you, *mes amies?* You both look well."

"Where have you been? I was here only an hour ago," Daphne sighed in exasperation.

"I was out visiting patients," she replied, obviously perplexed by Daphne's manner. "Is everything all right?"

"Yes."

"No!"

Daphne and I spoke at the same time. Van Helsing's eyebrows shot up.

"Shall I make us some tea? I've got a lovely new herbal blend that will help settle your nerves," she said, busying herself around a shelf of small porcelain jars.

"Mina," I began, cutting Daphne off. "What exactly happened last night?"

"What do you mean? We were all there together the whole evening. What's going on?" she regarded the two of us suspiciously.

"No, *chérie,* I mean during that last dance and then afterward. I lost track of you while I was dancing with the vile Monsieur Honoré. Did something happen with *Vicomte de Malin?*" Daphne queried.

Her blue eyes turned frosty. "Such as?"

"We aren't accusing you of anything, Mina, but Malin happens to be missing. We simply want to know what you remember of him after the dance ended."

"Missing? When? How? *Mon dieu...*" She sat down on a wooden stool and took a moment to compose herself.

"The gossip today was that he hasn't been seen since the end of the ball last night, and no one has come forward with any information. Not even Honoré has offered an explanation, and those two are thick as thieves," Daphne replied. "It's as if the man vanished into thin air after...after..."

"After we danced," Van Helsing finished. Her gaze snapped to ours. "I didn't kill him! We danced—that was all. I flattered him enough to merit an *unwelcome* invitation to his country estate, which he said he'd be leaving for in a fortnight. I scribbled the dates down and passed them to you as I left. I came home immediately after. I'm afraid I didn't see where he went after our dance. He was vile and certainly drunk, but I swear nothing else happened after that. Despite my distaste for the man, I would never have harmed him. I prefer he face justice in a lawful way."

I nodded. "Of course we believe you, darling. Did he say anything else to you that might indicate his current whereabouts?"

Van Helsing's face scrunched charmingly as she thought back. "I don't know. I don't think so, but I'm not a spy, so I wouldn't know what to listen for. He droned on about his former mistress—the opera singer—as if to convince me that he was fully done with her and that I would be a welcome addition to his nauseating, adulterous club."

Curiosity seized me. "What was her name?"

"She's Italian, I believe. Nadia something."

"Russo," Daphne and I replied in unison. We knew of the soprano—as famous for her violent temper as her vibrato. I couldn't believe that she'd let the awful *vicomte* even touch the hem of her skirts, let alone her person, but to each their own. It was a thin lead, but certainly a starting place.

"Well," I said with a smile. "You know what they say about a woman scorned."

Daphne grinned. "*Mes dames,* I believe we're headed to the opera."

3

CHARLOTTE

THE *THÉÂTRE DES TUILERIES* WAS A SHORT DISTANCE FROM VAN Helsing's clinic, so we piled back into Daphne's carriage and made haste. Despite the hour and the bitter weather, the streets bustled with sounds of vampire peasants adjusting to their new supernatural life. Raucous laughter poured out of a handful of vampire-friendly taverns and the wind carried scents of sizzling *boudin noir* and spiced wine fortified with blood.

The winter chill had started to seep in despite the carriage's plush interior, and since Daphne and I were no longer bothered by the cold, we bundled Van Helsing in every available blanket.

"By the way, Mina, I don't suppose you recall seeing my *chatelaine* after the last dance at the ball, do you? It seems to have disappeared," I asked, now that her teeth had stopped chattering.

"*Non,* I'm sorry," she replied. "I only remember seeing it when you offered me your smelling salts. Truthfully, I was still too put out by the *vicomte* to pay much mind to anything other than returning home. Is it important?"

It had been a long shot, but I was still disappointed.

"It was my mother's," I replied. "My father had it made for her when they married. She gave it to me when she..." I trailed off, emotion catching in my throat. Reaching for a light tone, I continued. "I would very much like to have it."

She frowned. "I wish I could be more help. Perhaps it will turn up."

I opened my mouth to reply again, but the carriage slowed, signaling our arrival at the opera house.

"Are you certain you don't want to wait in the carriage?" Daphne asked. "Charlotte and I can handle this. We just want to talk to Signora Russo and...you know. *Sniff around.*"

I chuckled at the jest, but Van Helsing's expression was grave. "It was my choice to get involved last night, and it will be on my conscience if something has happened to the man. If he's hurt or injured, I may be able to help." Her eyes darkened and she muttered, "*Not that he deserves it.*"

"Very well," Daphne replied, then looked at me. "Do we have a plan?"

I lifted a shoulder in a shrug. "Not really. Go in, gain access to her dressing room, ask her enough questions to ascertain if she murdered her former lover, and take it from there."

Daphne sighed. "Normally, I have more time to plan these things, but I don't think we can afford to wait."

"I'm sure it will be fine," I said, though I felt a little less confident without my *chatelaine* at my side.

There didn't appear to be a performance tonight, but there was a lot of activity at the theater as the company cleaned, dressed the set, and rehearsed for *Orfeo ed Euridice*. Van Helsing was somewhat anxious as we entered the grand hall, but I whispered to her to keep to the shadowy edges of the room and act as if we belonged there. I was prepared for someone to stop us, but as everyone seemed rather busy, no one paid much attention to us.

When we found the candlelit corridor behind the main stage, I breathed a small sigh of relief. We could hear the impressive trill of a high *c* coming from a room toward the end of the hall, which had to be Signora Russo.

Daphne knocked on the door, and we heard a litany of profane Italian followed by frantic shuffling.

"I said I didn't want to be disturbed until we're ready to rehearse!" she bellowed, pulling the door open with great force. Her beautiful brown eyes widened when she saw the three of us standing in the hallway, and before she had the chance to recover, I pushed forward into her dressing room.

"Madame Russo!" I cried, embracing her. "It is such an honor—truly! Please forgive my companions and I, but we are such great admirers of you that we were desperate to come meet you. We knew that you would be engaged on the night of a performance and decided to venture forth on an off night to make your acquaintance."

"Ah, *grazie,*" she replied, still quite stunned and confused. Not wanting to give her the chance to recover and shunt us to the door, I continued.

"*Duchesse de Duras*, may I present the esteemed Signora Nadia Russo. I am *Comtesse de Brionne,* and our companion is Doctor Van Helsing—another ardent lover of the opera."

The singer curtsied deeply to us and opened her mouth to speak, but I cut her off again.

"You are playing the lead in *Orfeo ed Euridice,* are you not? That is *so* thrilling. I simply adore a tragic love story. Actually, I adore *any* love story, but the tragic ones always have the better music, don't you find?" I whirled around her room, inhaling deeply, trying to scent the *vicomte* or anything else suspicious, but the dressing room was a riot of overpowering fragrances. Perfume, stage makeup, dust, wine, stale sweat from old costumes, and the heady aroma of a rose bouquet on top of her dressing table.

"Such lovely flowers," Daphne commented, seeing where my attention fell. "And so hard to find exceptional roses in the middle of winter. You *must* tell me who your florist is."

Signora Russo's eyes widened a fraction and I could hear the hitch in her pulse. Seizing the opportunity, I went to the table and plucked the card from the center of the bouquet before she could stop me.

Forgive me, mon petit chou, the card read. I brought it up to my nose and sniffed—it reeked of the *vicomte.*

"My, my," I drawled. "It seems you have quite the devotee."

Anger colored the singer's face, darkening her chocolate eyes and turning her cheeks as red as the roses on her table. She crossed her arms in front of her ample bosom and nodded at the door.

"I think perhaps you ladies have overstayed your welcome," she said haughtily. "It's rather uncouth of you to pry into my personal affairs—admirers or no."

At that moment, a soft thump sounded from somewhere in the room. No one moved. Daphne, Van Helsing, and I looked at each other.

"Go!" Signora Russo shouted. "Get out!"

Again, the dull sounds arose, a muted shuffling and light scraping. This time, I pinpointed it to a large armoire in the back of the room, which I'd assumed was filled with elaborate opera costumery and the singer's personal clothing.

Daphne must have heard it at the same time, for she crossed the room in swift strides and threw open the door. Out tumbled the villainous *vicomte*—blindfolded, bound, gagged, and apparently beginning to regain consciousness.

We all turned to stare at Signora Russo, whose fury remained frozen on her visage. After several moments of stunned silence, she arched a supercilious eyebrow and shrugged.

"I'll have you know, *he* started it," she snapped.

We continued to stare in astonishment. Finally, Daphne recovered enough to entreat, "Do explain."

"He came to my room late last night—or perhaps it was early in the morning, I don't know. It was dark out, and he was stinking drunk. He brought me flowers and told me that he'd made a mistake ending our arrangement. I refused him. *No one* humiliates la Signora Russo! He did not take kindly to my rejection," she said, venom in her voice.

Van Helsing went over to the man and removed the blindfold and gag but kept him bound. She looked him over and nodded to me.

"He's had a terrible knock on the head and has been given opium, I'd wager, but he's otherwise unharmed," she said.

"Laudanum," Signora Russo offered, matter-of-factly. "When he made certain advances, I hit him over the head with a candlestick, which dazed him enough for me to drug him. I planned to have the doorman take him back to his home after our rehearsal ended and leave him in the care of his good lady wife."

"You...you mean, you weren't bitter about being scorned and sought to end your torment by kidnapping him? Or killing him?" I asked, somewhat disappointed.

Signora Russo tipped her head back and laughed until tears gathered in the corners of her eyes.

"Goodness no," she replied. "When our arrangement ended, I was able to find a much more agreeable patron. I was perfectly happy until he showed up again."

The *vicomte* moaned and slumped back down on the floor. No one approached him to help.

"She knocked out the *vicomte* and drugged him," Daphne whispered to me. "I'm a bit unsure about how we should proceed. What are we going to do with her?"

I grinned. "Recruit her."

Two hours later, we'd returned the insensate *vicomte* to his townhouse with a hasty explanation, but the *vicomtesse de Malin* didn't seem overly concerned. She didn't even bother to inquire about the name of the woman he'd been with, leaving me to wonder if anyone actually cared for the bastard. His wife had simply wrinkled her nose at the bedraggled man and instructed the footmen to bathe him and lock him in his room.

As the carriage trundled back toward *Rue Ordener,* Daphne and I bickered about Signora Russo, who we agreed should be well compensated for her silence about the incident with the *vicomte.* I wanted to recruit her into *les Dames Dangereuses* immediately, but Daphne insisted we spend more time looking into her background and her politics before inviting her to join our covert agency. It made sense, I supposed.

As was her custom, Van Helsing grumbled the whole way back to her clinic, declaring that she never should have consented to help us in the first place. She swore roundly that she was done befriending vampires and werewolves, as we constantly made trouble for her. Naturally, I agreed, but reminded her that her life would likely be deadly dull without us, which she grudgingly acknowledged. Momentarily assuaged, she kissed us goodbye, and I promised to bring her a peace offering of her favorite almond cakes the following evening.

Daphne and I rested in companionable silence on our way back to my *château.*

"What are you going to tell the Order?" I asked.

"Most of the truth, I think," she replied. "Malin had a lover's quarrel and is now at home with his wife, safe and mostly sound... though I don't envy the recovery from a head wound and an ill-advised amount of laudanum. We'll still go ahead with the rest of our plans, assuming tonight's events don't impact his scheduled departure to the country."

"Of course," I agreed. "But running investigations into Malin and Monsieur Honoré's affairs will need to wait. I'm exhausted and starving. I long for justice, certainly, but first I wish to have a hot bath, a large meal, and a long sleep."

Daphne covered a yawn, which I took as tacit agreement. I noticed through the carriage's blacked-out windows that the sun was rising and the dark sky was fading to a lovely periwinkle. When the carriage trundled up my drive, I gave her a brief embrace and dragged myself out and up the stairs to my front door.

I still found it difficult at times to keep to the nighttime schedule that the country increasingly favored, but I knew it would get easier with time.

"Madame Toussaint, please send up a hot bath and some dinner. Beef, if we have it, and some roasted carrots, bread and butter, cheese, and wine, please."

"Of course, my lady," she said. "Regretfully, no one was able to fine your *chatelaine*. We checked the house, your wardrobe, the carriage—one of the footmen even went so far as to retrace the coachman's route to Versailles. It appears to be lost."

My heart sank, but I forced a smile. "Thank you, Madame. I appreciate everyone's efforts, nonetheless. I shall just have to have a new one, I suppose."

The disappointing news weighed me down with melancholy. I felt so careless, losing the one heirloom I truly cherished. A tear slipped down my cheek as I undressed, and with the fatigue, stress of the day, and hunger gnawing at me, I embraced the sadness and melancholy. By the time the large copper tub was filled with piping hot water, I was sobbing like a baby. I poured myself a large glass of wine, intent on drinking through my despair.

I was so wrapped up in my glorious wallow that I barely noticed Antoine until he rushed in, worry etched on his handsome face.

"Charlotte! What is it? Are you injured? What's happened?" He leaned forward to cradle my face between his hands.

"Darling!" I sniffed, surprised. "I thought you were away for training."

"I was—I am. But I missed you... I wanted to be with you. When the troops turned in after drills today, I shifted and ran here as fast as I could. Much faster than a carriage ride," he said, wiping my tears with his thumbs. "What has happened? Why are you crying?"

"It's nothing, *chéri*. I'm so glad you're home! How long do you have before you must return? How was it?"

Antoine pushed a damp lock of my hair from my face, the concern still heavy in his gaze.

"Charlotte," he murmured. "Tell me what troubles you."

Tears threatened to spill again and I swallowed.

"It will seem silly," I said quietly, swirling my hand through the water.

"If you truly do not wish to tell me, you don't need to," he said.

He pulled a chair over to the side of the tub, methodically removed his jacket and draped it over the back. He rolled the cuffs of his shirtsleeves up, slowly exposing his tanned forearms to the golden light of the candles and the crackling fire in the bedroom hearth. The corded muscles bunched and flexed, which was at once mesmerizing, soothing, and erotic. When he was through, he plucked my wine glass from my hand, refilled it, and handed it back to me.

"I promise I shall not laugh," he said.

He dropped to his knees behind me and tilted my head back, then started to pull pin after pin from my coiffure. I felt the soft weight of my hair fall around my shoulders as he worked, gently threading his fingers through my curls when he'd removed all the pins. The sensation was heavenly. I closed my eyes and relaxed into the pampering, exhaling much of my stress. He lightly massaged my scalp, then poured a bowl of the warm water over my head, careful to keep it off my face.

"I don't talk about them much," I heard myself saying. "My parents."

He picked up the lavender-scented soap and quietly worked up a lather, then spread it through my wet locks.

"They were wonderful, you know," I continued. "My father was kind and thoughtful, and my mother was warm and affectionate. They were lucky enough to have a love match. They wanted scores of children, but my mother couldn't have any more after I was born. Rather than resent me, like many aristocratic parents do without a son, my parents treasured me. I had a charmed childhood."

Antoine's large hands slowed, and he picked up the bowl to rinse the soap. He wrung out much of the water, then sprinkled a few drops of almond oil through my tresses and began to untangle the waves with my ivory comb. Comfortable in silence, he carried on his ministrations without interrupting.

"When my father first took ill, my mother would sit at his bedside for hours, reading to him, singing to him, helping him manage the estate—they were partners in love and in life. His death shook her deeply, and it wasn't long after that she..." Tears began to flow again, but I was compelled to continue. "Before she died, she gave me her *chatelaine* with all the keys to the house. Normally, the housekeeper would have it, but my mother was every inch the lady of the house. She worked to keep our servants comfortable and happy, and managed our family like a true queen. I've worn her *chatelaine* every day since she passed and now it is... gone. Lost, or stolen, I do not know. I know it's a mere bauble, but losing it feels like losing her all over again."

I breathed slowly, squeezing my eyes shut to keep the rest of my tears at bay.

"It isn't lost or stolen," Antoine said quietly.

My eyes snapped open and I whirled around to look at him, sloshing a good deal of water out of the tub.

"What?" I exclaimed.

He sighed. "Because I was ill—going through my turning over Christmas—I never got you a present. I knew the *chatelaine* was an heirloom from your mother, so I took it to a jeweler yesterday to have it cleaned, add a few more small compartments, and have some of the loose stones re-set. I was hoping to surprise you with it, but I didn't realize being without it would distress you so much. I'm sorry, Charlotte."

I blinked.

"It's not lost," I said simply, mind reeling, emotions condensing like clouds before rain.

"It is not."

"Monsieur Honoré didn't pilfer it while we were dancing, which would have made me the worst sort of spy," I confirmed.

"Spy? Or agent?" Antoine said, covering a smirk at our inside joke. "No, *mon amour,* he did not steal it from you."

"You took it—because you wanted me to have a Christmas present?"

He nodded, wincing slightly. "I'm sorry."

Relief, elation, and compassion washed over me, and I leaped from the tub, toppling Antoine onto the plush carpet. I cried even harder than before, but they were tears of joy.

"You wonderful, wicked thing," I sobbed between kisses. "How could you torment me so?"

I felt the low vibrations of his laugh through the fine lawn of his shirt. "Next time, I'll try not to be at death's door for Christmas. Perhaps I'll have more time to come up with a better gift that doesn't involve driving you mad."

"I should get that in writing," I mumbled, tugging at the falls of his breeches, desperate to undress him. "But for now, it's only fair that I return the favor."

"You're going to give me a gift?" he teased. "Or you're going to drive me mad?"

I grinned. "Oh, *chéri*—isn't that the same thing?"

THE END

ALSO BY LILY RILEY

Les Dames Dangereuses **series:**

The Assassin and the Libertine

The Agent and the Outlaw

The Doctor and the Devil (coming in Spring 2023)

ABOUT THE AUTHOR

LILY RILEY is a romance novelist currently focused on historical paranormal books that feature a little bit of cheek and a lot of steam.

When Lily isn't writing about dreamy supernatural beings in 18th century France, she enjoys sipping champagne, eating cake, and dancing naked by the light of the full moon.

A CHARLEY DALTON CHRISTMAS

BY R. LEE FRYAR

A CHARLEY DALTON CHRISTMAS

I'VE ALWAYS LIKED "GOD REST YE MERRY GENTLEMEN." LESS effervescent than "Joy to the World," less dependent on nostalgia than Bing's "White Christmas," it hit the right notes between bitter and sweet for me. And when the house belted it out on a Victrola that was the height of style in 1919, and the kitchen air thickened with the buttery aroma of baking cookies, the old carol made me hate Christmas a little less. It wasn't my favorite holiday. Too many bad memories.

"Charley," Alice called from the living room, "are you coming to help me with the tree or am I on my own here?"

"Coming, coming." I checked the cookies first. The house wouldn't let them burn, but I took a certain pride in being there to whisk each baked tray out of the oven and onto the cooling rack. The countertops were already covered with cookies—coconut macaroons, chocolate chip, gingerbread, peanut butter kisses, and now sugar cookies. I watched them cut themselves into stars and bells for a few seconds before I went to help Alice with the tree.

This year we had a Frazier Fir so large it almost brushed the ceiling. Alice, buried in the middle of the branches, hadn't even positioned it in the tree stand yet, but the lights glittered and flashed amid the ornaments fastening themselves on every bough. Our haunted house had outdone itself with holiday spirit once again. Yaupon boughs and magnolia leaves arranged themselves on the shelves, and spools of red and gold ribbon braided together slowly, garlanding the crown molding while Robert Ezekiel, the oldest man but youngest ghost, kept an eye on it.

I took hold of the tree, and together, Alice and I wrestled it into the tree stand. I tightened the screws.

"What do you suppose the house does with the trees after Christmas?" I asked, watching the ghost water glug into the container. "They're already dead. They can't die again. What happens to them when the house takes them out on the fifteenth of January?"

"I suspect it sticks them in the ground wherever they came from and they root and grow again. Even trees have ghosts." Jeff looked up from the couch where he sat cutting out snowflakes for the windows. It didn't snow in Savannah, but we always had paper snowflakes. Even December twenty-fourth , it was seventy and raining. I glanced at the pile of neatly wrapped presents assembling in the corner for us to place under the tree when we were finished decorating, feeling about as low as I'd ever felt at Christmas.

I still didn't have a present for the only living person in the house, Austin.

Now, I wasn't one of those guys who waits until the last minute to buy a Christmas present for the special man in his life. I'd been thinking about it for weeks, but I had yet to come up with anything.

Well, anything good.

I was baking him a turkey with all the trimmings, mashed potatoes, candied yams, green beans—buy frozen, you weird man, and I'll make them taste so good you won't ever eat a canned bean again —and two kinds of pie: real shoofly pie because it was his favorite, and bourbon pecan pie because it was mine. But cooking was what I did. It shouldn't be a gift.

The only other option was a blowjob .

I was really grasping at straws now, and not the cheese straws I was making for Austin because I'd gotten desperate. How was I supposed to come up with a gift for a living man when I was a ghost confined to my house and adjacent neighborhood with nowhere to shop? Ms. Edie, our neighbor, had gone to visit her son in Atlanta two weeks ago, leaving the day before it occurred to me she could buy a gift for him and I'd pay her back somehow. Piss-poor timing on my part.

"Here's your ornament, Robert," Alice said, digging into the trunk that had popped up in the middle of the living room floor. She unwrapped the little snow globe with the clock tower and handed it to him to hang on the tree.

"Levi!" Alice called.

Upstairs, the sound of marbles stopped abruptly. A second later, Levi plummeted through the ceiling, boots first, then overalls, homespun shirt, and a happy, faded and freckled face, topped by a shock of red-blonde hair. "Yay—Christmas!"

"Easy there!" Robert barely got out of the way in time to avoid a ghost through the head, which would be a calamity. We really didn't need a headless ghost in the house for Christmas.

"Me, me, me..." Levi dug through the box with the kind of glee that made me smile. The old, worn, jaded ghost seemed to be undergoing his second childhood since Austin had come. He didn't have much of a first one. It was nice to see the brightness returning to both his eyes and his transparent body after he'd been through so much unhappiness in life and death.

He emerged from the box with a hand full of train tracks and his own ornament, a pewter steam locomotive. He hung it on a branch below Robert's clock tower and took his train and tracks to assemble. Soon, his favorite Lionel reproductions would be running around the room on Christmas morning, clackity-clackity-choo-chooing until we couldn't hear ourselves think.

"Mine," Alice said, taking out a glass bell with a beautiful etching of a whiskered cat on the surface. She hung it up high, well out of the reach of the cat himself, George Washington, watching the proceedings from Austin's therapeutic, back-massaging chair. I did a better job than that chair, mind, but he liked to sit in it with the motor running while he watched television —sit-coms mostly, not ghost shows because he lived in one.

"Where's Jeff?" Alice asked.

Sure enough, he'd vanished, leaving scissors and snowflakes behind.

"Just like a man. Disappears whenever he's needed. Levi, go get him." Alice set his ornament, an ornate bookcase with an angel reading in front of it, on the chair. "Your turn, Charley."

I reached in, pushing generic red and green balls, garlands, and ribbons out of the way. My ornament was heavy. It ended up at the bottom more often than not.

When I'd first come to the house, I had no idea what I'd find in that box on Christmas Eve. The other ghosts had ornaments that reflected something about them. Levi and his train. Alice and the cat and the bell. Jeff, the philosopher, a bookcase. But what was I? Who was I? At the time, I wasn't even cooking for the house yet. I worked in the greenhouses mostly, rebuilding our past from a decaying future. I'd felt down through the soft tree skirt fabric, wondering if I'd pull a hobo clown out of the chest, something to remind me that I'd been a homeless bum without a home or a family for most of my life. It wasn't anything like that at all.

It was a ceramic gingerbread house.

I held it in the palm of my hand now, touching the cool sides, smiling at the candy shingles and butterscotch windows. I settled it on one of the upper pine branches, where a light would flicker warmly through the ornament, illuminating the tiny marzipan people inside. A family. A home. What I'd always wanted. Now I had all that and more. I had Austin.

I wished he were here decorating with us today, but he wasn't.

The local historical society was having their Christmas celebration, and naturally, he had to be there. At least it wasn't a party with the paranormal society, which would mean he'd be hanging around with his ex, my least favorite person in the world. And he wasn't working on a case, which always left me a butterball of yellow anxiety while he was away. I was always terrified some ghost would do something horrible and I wouldn't be there to save him or at least rip into the other ghost for touching him. But I wouldn't complain—even if this was the anniversary of the worst day in my life. He did it for us.

Jeff came into the living room with Levi, chewing on a gingerbread cookie. "Excellent, Charley, as always."

"Thanks." I looked up at my ornament, light flickering on the family inside. Then it hit me.

"Everyone stay right here," I said. "Don't leave!"

"Aren't you going to watch Robert hang his ornament? Charley! Tradition!"

Fuck tradition. I bolted upstairs, going right through the ceiling. I didn't need to wait around for Robert to hang up his doting Santa with the child on his knee. I'd decided what I wanted to give Austin —a photograph of all of us.

And a blowjob. Why the hell not? It was Christmas.

I found the ancient Polaroid camera where it had been left in the attic a few years ago, horribly dusty, but it looked fine to me. I hurried down the stairs with it—I could go through floors, but it couldn't.

"Smile!" I planted myself in the doorway and clicked.

"Charley!" Alice huffed. "I didn't even have my hat on." But she gathered around with the others, and we watched the photograph come out.

I held the picture up, looking carefully at it. I could see the living room, the window, the peeling wallpaper we were currently in the process of removing piece by careful piece, but no ghosts.

"Shit."

Alice raised her eyebrows. "Charley."

"I mean...shoot."

"What's this about, Charley?" Jeff asked.

"Something for Austin, you know? A picture of us for Christmas," I muttered.

"That's a great idea," Robert said. "Let me try. You get in the picture, Charley. He'll want you in it."

"But what about you?"

But Robert was already pointing the camera at us. Click. REEEEEEP.

"Well..." Robert squinted. "I can sort of see Alice."

"That's not me. That's the front porch post through the glass," Alice said. "Why isn't it working?"

"Try it again," Jeff suggested, and once more, we all froze in front of the tree, grins plastered on our faces.

Nothing. I did think that white, blocky blob in the picture was Alice. But I wasn't about to say she looked like a post. I wanted to keep my testicles.

Jeff held up the picture thoughtfully. "I think I know why the ghosthunters have such a hard time with this. It's because we didn't all die at the same time. We're in different times, even when we are in the same place. We need something faster—something that won't blur so much when we are moving."

"A phone," Robert said. "That might work."

"I wanted something he could hold," I said, staring at the image of the living room without us in it.

"It's possible to save pictures on a phone and then get them printed later," Robert said. "My wife used to do that."

"Did he leave his phone?" Jeff asked.

"I don't think so," I said. Austin rarely went anywhere without it.

"Maybe when he gets back—"

"It won't be a gift if it's not a surprise," I said. "I'll go look."

I swept upstairs again, taking that piece of junk Polaroid with me. Who knew it was so hard for ghosts to take pictures of themselves?

I ferreted around in our room, looking in all of Austin's usual spots. Bedside table. Nope. Top shelf in closet. Nope. Underwear drawer. Nope. Oh. Hello.

When I'd flipped back the crumpled boxers and socks, there it was. But this wasn't his phone. It was a different color, and it looked new. He hadn't told me he was buying a new phone. I turned it on, expecting to see his usual screen with the picture of the house on it, but instead, a picture of some lake with a mountain behind it popped up. I carried it downstairs, thumbing through his contacts and social media, but everything was suspiciously blank.

Downstairs, I handed it over to Robert. "Here. You're better with these things than me." I stood beside the tree behind Alice and Levi, beside Jeff, and forced a smile on my face. Whose damned phone is it?

"Oh," Robert said. "I've never used one like this before. Where's the camera?"

We broke formation and huddled around him while I showed him where the camera was. He got it on the second try and snapped a picture of us in front of the tree.

Still nothing.

"What's wrong?" I said. "It ought to be better than that fucking Polaroid."

This time, even Alice didn't flinch. We were all pretty frustrated.

"I've got an idea," Levi said. "Why don't we just take a picture of you, Charley?"

"I wanted the whole family," I said.

"But it's you he'd most like a picture of, I bet," Alice said. "Charley, get in front of the tree. Now smile. Not like that, it looks like you have a toothache."

Heartache, more like it. I couldn't ask him. I didn't think I could take the truth. It had to belong to someone living. I was dead, I was going to be dead forever, and maybe I did give good blowjobs, but they weren't sloppy, wet ones. I didn't even have the living heat of a body to keep him warm at night.

This time, success.

Well. Sort of.

"There's a green glow here, Charley," Alice said with an air of triumph. "That's you."

"That's the Christmas tree," I said, trying to lose the color of jealousy before it got the better of me.

"Still, it's something," Alice said with a hint of smugness.

"I wonder if it would be better in the kitchen," Jeff said. "You spend so much time there. It might make a difference."

"All right." Now I wasn't sure I wanted to give Austin a picture of me at all. He might not want it. Damn it. I knew better than to fall in love with a living man. But I followed Alice to the kitchen and posed against my kitchen counters, with a backdrop of all the cookies I'd stress-baked waiting for Austin to get home and love me.

"Better." Alice said.

I stared glumly at a white smudge in the middle of the photo. I might have been a sunspot if there had been any sun coming in the window, just a bright blast of something that might or might not be there, not a man who loved and was loved.

"What if Charley was more...substantial?" Robert said. "Could we do something that would make him look, I don't know, more—"

"Alive?" I finished glumly.

"Exactly."

"Flour." Alice said. "I've seen it on shows. Blow a cloud of fine powder and it catches on things that can't be seen easily. You have that flour Austin bought."

"Hang on—I'm baking cookies for him, too!"

"It'll only take a cup," Alice said.

In a minute I was as dusted with flour as a pie-cloth and

blinking it out of my essence angrily. "You didn't have to throw it in my face!"

"That's what you want to show up. Smile!"

I didn't.

Nothing. This time absolutely nothing.

"Damn it." I wiped the flour off with a tea towel. It was almost five now, time to cook dinner. I didn't know when Austin would be home, but five was his usual. This being a party, it might be midnight. He was probably dancing with whoever owned that phone.

"Maybe something more sparkly?" Levi suggested, grinning.

Sprinkling me with sugar didn't help either. This time I was a shimmering sunspot.

Alice sighed. "Well, I think it's the best we're going to get. It's not going to be perfect, Charley. You can't expect a picture to show you like you really are anyway. They never do."

"Yeah, I hope I don't look that much like a glitter bomb."

She handed me the phone. "We tried."

"Yeah."

On a whim, I pointed the camera at her and shot as she disappeared through the doorway. Nothing.

"One thing you might do," Robert said. "You can point the camera at yourself. They call it a selfie. It might work."

It took me about sixteen shots of Robert and Jeff, who were still interested in the project, before I figured out how to turn the camera to where it would take my picture. Nothing.

Jeff shook his head. "It may be a matter of finding the right time. When the ghosthunters do it, they set their cameras to take pictures for hours."

"Well, I know it's hard for them," I said, picking up the phone and snapping another picture of my grim face. "But I thought it would be different if a ghost did it."

Jeff smiled. "Maybe it will be. Keep trying."

I did.

I rolled snickerdoodles for Austin. Shot pictures.

Made jam thumbprints for Levi. Shot pictures.

Shaped crescent cookies for Jeff. Shot pictures.

Cut shortbread for Alice. Shot pictures.

Baked oatmeal raisin—really, Robert, oatmeal raisin? Shot pictures.

Nothing at all.

Austin didn't come home. We ate our traditional Christmas Eve clam chowder, oyster crackers, and Christmas cookies, just us ghosts. Like every Christmas Eve before.

I could have gone to bed as usual. But the idea of lying there alone in the dark, waiting for Austin to get home, made me a sour shade of blue-green misery, and so I stayed up instead, cleaning up after my baking frenzy and listening to Nat King Cole sing The Christmas Song. Asshole. What did I care about roasting chestnuts over an open fire? Or whether reindeer really knew how to fly? Fuck, it hurt to be dead when nothing could possibly change that. All I wanted for Christmas was to be the man Austin deserved, a man with a bit more substance than pecan divinity, that's all. Nat could take his Christmas magic and stuff it. I was steadily working my way from blue-green morose to a hot-red shade of pissed-off when Levi came downstairs to check on me.

"If you don't go to sleep, Santa won't come," I said, drying a cookie sheet.

"I stopped believing in Santa when I died," he said, reminding me that he was so very old. "Are you okay, Charley?"

I leaned into the kitchen counter, not wanting to face him. "I'm fine. It's just—it's a hard day for me ," I said. "I wanted him here."

"Why didn't you ask him to stay?"

I shook my head. "He had work."

"He had a party. That's not work."

"Same thing. He does it for us. It's for the house." I set the tray in the rack and soaped up the next one. "I'll handle it, Levi. I'm a grown man. What happened to me all those years ago isn't going to happen again. Austin isn't going to run out on me like my lover did. I'm not going to go home, explain myself to family who hate me, and get thrown out on my ear. That's in the past. I don't need to burden him with it."

Levi stared at me. Below the hem of his little white nightshirt, his knobby, perpetually bruised knees stuck out. The shirt was too small for him because it had been made for someone else, the boy he was missing, the boy he'd accidently killed. "He'd still want to know." He turned, passed through the wall, and disappeared.

Fuck. Tomorrow was Christmas, and for one day at least, he deserved to be a kid. I hated that I'd troubled him with my too-adult trauma. I finished the dishes and was busy drying the brined turkey for Austin's dinner when I heard the key turn in the door.

What happened next was an accident. I'd been so busy sulking, I forgot I'd set the phone next to the sink.

No, I didn't drop it in the soapy water. That couldn't have happened anyway. The standing water was from the past, and the turkey brine had long since gone down the drain. Nope. It was worse. I dropped the roasting pan on top of it. The corner hit the glass, there was a sickening, shallow, cracking sound, and the front of the phone resembled a spider's web.

"Shit." I tossed a tea towel over it and turned as Austin came into the kitchen.

"I thought you'd be in bed," Austin said. He tugged the tie loose from around his collar, but he hadn't gotten out of the tux yet and... damn, damn, damn. I wasn't a clothes-make-the-man kind of guy, but Austin in a tux was something I'd never get tired of looking at. He had this amazing hair, and it went so many ways when he let it down, but tonight he'd pulled it back, and between that, his brown skin, and the white and black tux, he looked every inch the most handsome man in the world.

"I—I wasn't tired. I made you cookies." I gestured at the counters. My words were lost somewhere between the roaring lust in my essence and my need to shriek at him for going off and leaving me alone when I needed him so much. I would always need him.

"I'll never eat all these." He raised an eyebrow.

I looked helplessly at the stacks and stacks of cookies I'd made for him—snickerdoodles, gingersnaps, pecan sandies. "Well, I thought you could give some away."

"The neighbors know I can't cook." He walked toward me, and before I could yell at him and tell him my apron was filthy, he wrapped his arms around me and pulled me into himself.

"Oh, Sparky." I pressed my face into the top of his head, drinking in the fragrance—his cologne, the pint of hair gel he'd needed to get that slick, polished look, the slight musky sweat that had managed to break through his deodorant. He was love. He was family. He was home.

"I'm sorry, Spook," he said, stroking my back. "I didn't mean to be so late. I'm not doing this next year. That was the most boring thing I've ever sat through. If I never have to hear a bunch of old white men wax lyrical about the Civil War again, it will be too soon. I'd love to have them over some night so Levi could tell them what it was really like." He sniffed me. "What'd you do, marinate in cookie dough? You smell amazing. The whole damned house smells amazing. What did I ever do to deserve you?"

"Come to bed," I said. "I'll remind you." I kissed him somewhere in the back of his head, wishing I could be everything he did deserve.

He chuckled. "Nothing subtle about you, is there, Charley?"

"Nope." Except the busted phone I wasn't telling him about tonight, or that stupid idea I had to take a picture to remind him of us when he was away.

"I saw mistletoe in the hall," he said. "Want to kiss under it for a while? I'll let you take off my cummerbund."

"Race you."

"Not fair—you can go through walls!"

We got there at about the same time because I wished it, and for a good fifteen minutes, we stood there in the darkened hallway, listening to Silent Night, kissing, hugging, groping—

Then he took my pants off.

"Uh, Sparky?" I didn't get any further, because he was kissing his way up my thighs, and when Austin did that, I pretty much lost all control of language. But the mistletoe was hung in the foyer, right next to the grand staircase, in front of the front door with all that glass. I was bright white already and getting whiter by the minute. I'd be lit up like, well, Christmas.

"You worried about someone seeing us, Spook?" he whispered, leaving my cock for a moment. He nuzzled the side of my neck, nibbling.

"What if Levi comes out here?" I hissed.

"Mmmm. I think I'll risk it. You taste so sweet."

Yeah, I'd been sugared up worse than a kid on candy, but... I kissed Austin back, pressing into him slightly. "We could take this upstairs."

He gently moved my apron aside, gripped my cock and stroked it gently. This took some doing. It was easy to go right through me when I wasn't concentrating. And hell, concentrating with him working my erection over with those skilled hands wasn't easy. "We could," he said. "That would be nice. We're supposed to be nice for Christmas, aren't we?"

"Yeah." I breathed. He folded my apron over, and I got a great look at my cock in his hand, his fingers teasing that spot below the head where magic always happens. "Damn, damn, damn..." I blinked hard as he leaned down and kissed it.

"Too bad I'm feeling naughty," he said, and went down on his knees, right on a stack of pillows he'd evidently borrowed from the living room sofa when he came in, the stinker.

"You planned this." I tipped my head back in ecstasy.

"Maybe," he mouthed around me, then he started to suck, and damn, when Austin sucked me, it was Christmas coming early,

302 | A CHARLEY DALTON CHRISTMAS

that's what it was. One hand gripped my cock, the other slipped behind me, through me, into my ass.

I dimly registered Silent Night giving way to Baby, It's Cold Outside. It might be snowing there, but it sure was getting hot in here. Aside from the soft, bubbly music, the only other sound was Austin sucking as I gave up and gave in, thrusting into his mouth. When this was over, I sure wasn't stopping with his cummerbund.

"Fuck," I whispered, setting my hands into Austin's shoulders so he could feel just how much I loved what he was doing. It was something we'd agreed on, that I wouldn't hide my feelings from him with a block, and he'd never hold back on me, but when I saw his thoughts tonight, I couldn't believe it.

I didn't want to do this in the room, Charley. Not tonight. It's that day, isn't it? They hurt you long ago, coming in the door on Christmas Eve, and he hurt you worse, leaving you. I wanted to suck you here, because if anyone comes through that door tonight, if anyone ever tries to take you from me, I won't leave. No one is ever going to hurt you like that again, Spooky. My sweet Spook. Come on, sweetheart. Come and let me know you believe this.

My tears came, almost at the same time as I did. "Austin, Austin." I buckled at the knees as the feelings rocked me, and I grabbed him around the middle, pulled him up, and hugged him into me. "Austin. Oh, I love you. I love you so much."

"Charley," he whispered, holding me in the aftermath as I shook and pressed into him, needing all his closeness. "Why didn't you tell me to stay if you were that upset? I would have stayed." He touched my cheek gently.

"I know." I sobbed, dry-eyed because ghosts don't cry, but inside, I was a flood. "I thought I could handle it, then I just couldn't stop thinking about it all day, how everything ended that night and I was alone. I couldn't bear that again, ever again."

"You'll never be alone again," he whispered in my ear. "I wanted you to know that. Now we can go to bed if you want."

I laughed. "But I still haven't taken off your cummerbund."

So, I did. And let's just say the floor in the living room saw some pretty heavy action, because if a man starts something with a horny ghost under the mistletoe, it'll end up under the Christmas tree, one way or another.

I'd forgotten all about the phone by the time we made it up to the bedroom and collapsed. Austin fell asleep the way he usually did—satiated, sweaty, and nestled right in my chest where I told him he belonged. Right where my heart used to be. But I absolutely remembered when I got up at four the next morning to start the turkey.

The house was already handling our Christmas dinner when I pulled on a fresh apron and took Austin's bird out of the refrigerator. The smell of roasting meat, thyme, bay, and sage perfumed the air. On the counter, a tray of toasted bread and cornbread shredded itself into a bowl while green onions and garlic diced themselves on a cutting board.

What I had to do was a little more challenging. Before Austin, I fancied myself quite the chef. But the house did most of the work. I'd since found out I was mostly just a good cook. Also, slicing real onions with a dull knife and washing the cutting board between every vegetable by hand was a real pain. But I had the instructions he'd printed out for me on exactly how to roast a turkey, and I planned to have his meal on the table at the same time as ours. We ghosts had a double oven with a warming drawer, six burners, and an army of knives and cutting boards. He had one balky oven, one functional burner on the stove, and a microwave. I hated that damned thing. He'd promised me a new range, an exact replica of the one I cooked on, but it was a bespoke piece. We wouldn't get it until next summer.

When I set the turkey on the counter to work the butter under the skin, I remembered the phone. I pulled it out from under the tea towel, stared at the broken glass and black screen for a moment, then turned it on. It flashed once, then blacked out again. Great. Just great.

I wrapped it up in the towel and put it far away from the sink, then started in on the bird. This would be the very best Christmas dinner he'd ever had. I was determined to make up for my mistake.

By the time the ghosts appeared, I should have had breakfast ready. But it was Christmas morning. Levi pounded down the stairs at five on the chime, yelling, "Presents!"

So, everyone else came down.

The ghosts went to the living room. I could hear Levi whining about opening one—just one—and Alice telling him to be patient, Jeff saying that Christmas comes but once a year, and Robert grumbling that he needed coffee before he was ready to do Christmas. Before I could check if the pot was ready, Austin came into the kitchen.

"I'm not done with your toast—"

He kissed my cheek. "Leave it. I'm perfectly happy with coffee." He sniffed. "Wow, that smells good, Charley."

"I ought to stay with it—"

"Come on," he said, rubbing my shoulder. "They want you there and so do I."

He fixed his own coffee while I set our cups and a cocoa for Levi on a tray. We walked into the living room together.

"Lookie, lookie!" Levi waved a pair of roller skates in my face.

"You'd better not scratch up my kitchen floor with those," I said.

"And look at what Austin got me!" He flashed the gift up under my nose.

"A pogo stick?"

Austin grinned. "He can use it in the back yard. Not like anyone is going to see it bouncing all by itself back there."

I shook my head and gave Robert his coffee.

"I guess we're doing presents now," Austin said, grinning. "I'll be right back." He trotted up the stairs, bouncy as a pogo stick himself.

Jeff tore open the corner of his present, evidently feeling that Levi's free-for-all meant he could open his gifts.

"Here, Charley," Levi said, plopping a carefully wrapped house gift in my lap.

It was squishy and wrapped in paper that went out of style forty years ago. An antique Santa laughed cheerfully up at me from his sleigh as I unwrapped it and took out a new apron, this one striped green and white. "Aww, thanks," I said, smiling at the ghosts.

Alice beamed at me. She perched a new hat on her head and tilted her chin so I could admire it. "What do you think?"

"I think you'll rip those feathers and flowers apart until you get it just the way you like it," I said.

"You know me well," she said. In a rare moment of affection, she planted a kiss on my cheek. "Merry Christmas, Charley."

Austin returned, carrying three wrapped gifts, but he didn't look as happy as he had. "Robert," he said, handing the old man a tiny box. "Alice, I'm going to have to assemble yours this afternoon, and this is for you, Jeff."

"What about me?" Levi said.

"You got your present, you poltergeist, now go out and use it," Austin said.

Levi raced by him but stopped for a hug before tearing off, scaring the cat.

"Oh, thank you!" Alice said. "A hat rack—I've never had one this nice." She tore open the box and scanned the instructions. She'd have it together before Austin broke out his screwdriver.

"Perfect. This is just perfect," Jeff said, not waiting to go to his library to crack open his new book.

"The Authoritative Calvin and Hobbes?" I raised an eyebrow.

Austin smiled. "He said he wanted to laugh more."

Robert was staring at his gift with the oddest expression on his face. It was a tie tack with a single red ruby in the center. "Thank you," he stammered, going pink with gratitude. The house had gotten him new garden gloves and boots. But Austin had remembered that, before he was gardener to a haunted house, Robert had been a businessman.

306 | A CHARLEY DALTON CHRISTMAS

"Least I could do," Austin said. "You've been a huge help with the accounts."

Robert blushed even more and fussed with the front of his striped pajamas, as if fumbling for a better reply, but he was interrupted.

"Come see me!" Levi yelled, sticking his head through the window. "I can go all the way around the house!"

There was a crash, he vanished, and so did the pogo stick, but there were no howls of pain. He was giggling fit to burst.

Alice sailed through the glass, scolding. Jeff and Robert followed, both of them laughing.

Austin turned to me. "I had something special for you. But I couldn't find it where I left it."

"I wanted to give you something special, too," I said. "But this will have to do." I kissed him, lingering on his lips until he'd half fallen over in my lap and we were moving together on the couch in a way that made me hope Levi would try to hop around the house about ten times.

Austin gasped when we broke apart. "Best Christmas present ever," he said, stroking my cheek.

"I wanted it to be more," I said. "I was so lonely for you yesterday."

"I wish you'd told me."

"I didn't want to burden you. You've done so much—"

"Charley, for fuck's sake." Austin sat up in the middle of me. "You are not a burden. I love you. I love you so much. It kills me that you were here, hurting and not saying anything. You've got to stop doing that. Talk to me once in a while, okay?"

"I know," I said, cuddling around him in unhappy folds of shamed purple. I just didn't want to lose him.

Which brought me to my next mistake. "I've got to tell you something, Austin. Yesterday, I borrowed your phone to take some pictures of us. I wanted you to always have us with you. But I couldn't do it. I tried and tried. And then I broke it."

"You broke my phone?"

"Yeah. I dropped the turkey roaster on it and cracked the glass. I'm sorry."

Austin reached into his pocket and pulled out his phone. "I had my phone with me yesterday.

Then whose phone was it? I quelled a telling shade of green. "I found it in your drawer."

"Where's it at?"

"Just a minute." I rose, sailed into the kitchen, then came back through the hall with the phone wrapped in the towel. "Here."

He took it and looked at the glass. "You just cracked the screen. I'll get it replaced first thing after the holidays. But damn, you're hard on technology." He handed it to me. "I'll get you a case for it."

"Me?"

"Yes, you. It's your phone, you crazy-ass ghost. It's your Christmas present. And don't you try to pretend with me. You thought it was someone else's phone, didn't you? I can see you're green."

"I thought—maybe..."

"I know what you thought," he said with a snort.

I glanced at him sideways. "I am kind of an ass, aren't I?"

"Yes. And I love you anyway." He pulled me down and kissed me again.

Outside, hoots of ghostly laughter resounded as Robert's bald head sprang into view for a moment and then tumbled out of sight.

"I wanted you to have a phone," Austin said. "I know you worry about me when I'm working, and to be honest, I worry about you, too. It's an old house. Sometimes I break into a cold sweat thinking about what might happen if it caught fire. You're my family. If something were to happen, God forbid, you can text me. You can text me whenever you want, Charley. I miss you as badly as you miss me."

I pulled him into myself, snuggling him into me like I was a blanket. "Damn, Austin. I wanted so much to make this day special for you, and all I did was break your present. I couldn't even take a picture of myself."

Austin chuckled. He pulled out his camera. He leaned back into my shoulder and held the camera at arm's length. "Smile."

We looked at the screen together.

And there I was. Smiling in a baffled, goofy way, my eyes half shut, and Austin, perfect as always, sitting right in the middle of me. I was transparent and the faded colors of the secondhand couch showed right through my head, but I was there. "I don't believe this! Gimme that!"

He handed me the phone. I held it out, snapped. Perfect. Austin's smile, my arm around his shoulder, sitting on a couch in a haunted house on Christmas morning.

"Why?" I asked, baffled. "We tried and tried yesterday."

"I don't know," he said. "Maybe we'd better go outside before Robert gets wound up and bounces down the street on that thing? What will the neighbors think if they see an empty pogo stick hopping around the graveyard?"

Austin was right, of course. He ran upstairs to get his coat. The rain had ended, but the air was colder than it had been, seasonally crisp, almost like real winter.

I lingered by the tree, thinking.

Jeff had said that ghosts existed in different times in the same space and that's why we couldn't get a clear picture. How had Austin's presence changed that?

I'd been dead for forty-five years and he was alive as alive could be. But maybe loving him as much as I did, him loving me as much as he did, created a moment where things like ghosts and the living collided, briefly, to be together. I was in his arms, he was in mine, and the camera recorded that, immortalizing what was already immortal. When I thought about it, maybe Nat King Cole was right after all. Christmas was magic. It's the same time, the same space, because we want it to be.

. . .

God rest ye, merry gentlemen,
   Let nothing you dismay.

"Are you coming?" Austin asked, buttoning his coat.
   "Absolutely," I said.
   We walked out the door together.

ALSO BY R. LEE FRYAR

Haunted Hearts Series:

Flipping

ABOUT THE AUTHOR

R. LEE FRYAR is a writer from the River Valley region of Arkansas. She writes paranormal romance and fantasy. Most of the time, there's kissing in it. When she isn't writing, she is a bad gardener, a slightly better watercolor artist, and a pretty decent cook.

Don't miss all the amazing books from Mystic Owl, an imprint of City Owl Press. Find them all at www.cityowlpress.com

Turn up the heat this holiday season with this sexy collection of gifts from your favorite Mystic Owl authors.

Each story has been hand-curated by award-winning, bestselling, and debut authors to please lovers of romance in the paranormal, sci-fi, and fantasy sub-genres. Place it under the tree, in someone's eReader stocking, or give yourself the gift of a few stolen hours of pleasure as you sink into each winter themed happily ever after.

From vampires to fairy tale retellings and everything in between, these scorching hot short stories are sure to hit the spot, curl your toes, and fill you with holiday cheer. So, stoke the fire, nestle under a blanket, and slip in between the pages with your next new favorite authors.

100% of the proceeds from the anthology will go to Girls Write Now, an organization dedicated to breaking down barriers of gender, race, age and poverty to mentor the next generation of writers and leaders who are impacting businesses, shaping culture and creating change.

Please sign up for the City Owl Press newsletter for chances to win special subscriber-only contests and giveaways as well as receiving information on upcoming releases and special excerpts.

All reviews are **welcome** and **appreciated**. Please consider leaving one on your favorite social media and book buying sites.

Escape Your World. Get Lost in Ours! City Owl Press at www.cityowlpress.com.

ABOUT THE PUBLISHER

City Owl Press is a cutting edge indie publishing company, bringing the world of romance and speculative fiction to discerning readers.

Escape Your World. Get Lost in Ours!

www.cityowlpress.com

 facebook.com/YourCityOwlPress

twitter.com/cityowlpress

 instagram.com/cityowlbooks

 pinterest.com/cityowlpress

Made in the USA
Middletown, DE
04 December 2022

15877523R00194